SHADES OF DARKNESS

"I didn't ask you to get involved in any of this," she reminded him.

He studied her for a long moment. "Do you want me to tell you what Kgosi meant when he asked me if you knew?" he abruptly demanded.

"Yes."

"He sensed you were my mate."

Chaaya hissed, as if she'd taken a blow to her stomach. It didn't matter that she'd sensed the emotional bonds weaving them together. Or Basq's fierce need to protect her. Or her own need to protect him.

It was still a shock to hear the word spoken out loud.

"Mate?"

He stepped toward her. "Do I truly have to explain what the word means?"

"I know what it means, but…" Her words trailed away as another shiver raced through her.

He moved until he was close enough to lightly brush his fingers down her cheek. At the same time, he deliberately leashed in his powers to allow the air to warm above freezing. She tilted back her head, becoming lost in the striking beauty of his eyes. "How can you be sure?"

He cupped her cheek in his palm, wrapping his other arm around her waist. "Like you said. Destiny…"

Books by Alexandra Ivy

Guardians of Eternity
WHEN DARKNESS COMES
EMBRACE THE DARKNESS
DARKNESS EVERLASTING
DARKNESS REVEALED
DARKNESS UNLEASHED
BEYOND THE DARKNESS
DEVOURED BY DARKNESS
BOUND BY DARKNESS
FEAR THE DARKNESS
DARKNESS AVENGED
HUNT THE DARKNESS
WHEN DARKNESS ENDS
DARKNESS RETURNS
BEWARE THE DARKNESS
CONQUER THE DARKNESS
SHADES OF DARKNESS

The Immortal Rogues
MY LORD VAMPIRE
MY LORD ETERNITY
MY LORD IMMORTALITY

The Sentinels
BORN IN BLOOD
BLOOD ASSASSIN
BLOOD LUST

ARES Security
KILL WITHOUT MERCY
KILL WITHOUT SHAME

Historical Romance
SOME LIKE IT WICKED
SOME LIKE IT SINFUL
SOME LIKE IT BRAZEN

Romantic Suspense
PRETEND YOU'RE SAFE
WHAT ARE YOU AFRAID OF?
YOU WILL SUFFER
THE INTENDED VICTIM
DON'T LOOK

And don't miss these Guardians of Eternity novellas

TAKEN BY DARKNESS in YOURS FOR ETERNITY
DARKNESS ETERNAL in SUPERNATURAL
WHERE DARKNESS LIVES in THE REAL WEREWIVES OF
VAMPIRE COUNTY
LEVET (ebook only)
A VERY LEVET CHRISTMAS (ebook only)

And don't miss these Sentinel novellas

OUT OF CONTROL
ON THE HUNT

Published by Kensington Publishing Corporation

Shades of Darkness

Alexandra Ivy

LYRICAL PRESS
Kensington Publishing Corp.
www.kensingtonbooks.com

LYRICAL PRESS BOOKS are published by

Kensington Publishing Corp.
119 West 40th Street
New York, NY 10018

All Kensington titles, imprints, and distributed lines are available at special quantity discounts for bulk purchases for sales promotion, premiums, fund-raising, educational, or institutional use.

Special book excerpts or customized printings can also be created to fit specific needs. For details, write or phone the office of the Kensington Sales Manager: Kensington Publishing Corp., 119 West 40th Street, New York, NY 10018. Attn. Sales Department. Phone: 1-800-221-2647.

Lyrical Press and Lyrical Press logo Reg. U.S. Pat. & TM Off.

First Electronic Edition: November 2020
ISBN-13: 978-1-5161-1094-0 (ebook)
ISBN-10: 1-5161-1094-3 (ebook)

First Print Edition: November 2020
ISBN-13: 978-1-5161-1097-1
ISBN-10: 1-5161-1097-8

Printed in the United States of America

Chapter 1

Troy, Prince of Imps, stifled a yawn as he strolled through the marble corridor of the mer-folk castle. It was a stunningly beautiful place that stretched for endless miles beneath the ocean. The walls were decorated with exquisite murals, and massive chandeliers hung from the vaulted ceilings. There were carved statues lining the wide corridors and delicate furnishings covered in fabrics that shimmered in pale shades of blue and green.

Even better, the beautiful mer-folk drifted through the spiderweb of rooms in gossamer gowns that left little to the imagination.

So why was he bored?

Troy halted in front of a section of wall that was a clear panel to reveal the dark waters outside the castle that were populated with dazzling reefs and fish that glowed with an effervescent light. Tilting his head to the side, he admired his reflection.

He truly was a glorious sight with his brilliant hair flowing down his back like a river of fire. His face was long and pale, with vivid green eyes that held the sort of sensual power to bring most creatures to their knees. Precisely where he liked them. He was also tall and slender, with bulging muscles that he made sure to emphasize with the one-piece spandex outfit in a vibrant shade of pink he was currently wearing.

He was an exotic butterfly among a field of lilies.

Troy stifled another yawn. He was accustomed to the bright lights of big cities and the naughty delights of his various strip joints. In contrast, the mer-folk were tedious, peace-loving fey who had tragically become even more boring after Chaaya was sent to live in Vegas with Chiron and his new mate, Lilah. The young female, sacrificed to protect the world centuries ago and then recently rescued from the dark dimension, had provided plenty of entertainment. Her name should have been chaos, not Chaaya.

But now...

Troy shook his head. Why did he linger in this place?

He answered his own inner question as he turned to walk toward the massive double doors at the end of the corridor.

Inga, Queen of the Mer-folk.

That's why he stayed.

It wasn't that he was in love with the female who was a mongrel mix of ogress and mermaid, although he took epic delight in tweaking Levet's miniature snout by pretending a romantic interest. But he was utterly committed to ensuring that Inga succeeded in her new role as the leader of the mer-folk.

She was one of the few demons who possessed a genuinely pure soul. Even after she'd been abused by slavers and manipulated by Riven, the former mer-folk king, and then shoved into a position she never expected and didn't want.

Every day she woke up determined to do the best for her people, even those who hated her for being a mongrel.

Who didn't root for an underdog?

Plus, Troy had to admit there was a glorious satisfaction in being a king maker. Or in this case, a queen maker.

He was the power behind the throne.

Lost in his thoughts, Troy was distracted by the sound of voices echoing through the air.

"You are not going to bother the queen with this, Riza," a male voice chided in surprisingly loud tones. As if he was aggravated at repeating the same words over and over.

"She needs to know, Jord," a second male stubbornly retorted.

There was the click of boots on marble, then the two males stepped out of a narrow hallway that led down to the lower chambers.

They were both tall and willowy like all mermen with long, pale hair that was tinted with blue. And they were both wearing the strange armor that looked like overlapping scales, with short tridents belted at their sides. To the untrained eye they looked like toy soldiers, but Troy knew that shimmering armor was stronger than steel and the tridents could shoot out silver threads that wrapped around their opponent to trap them in an inescapable net.

"Do you intend to make a personal report to the queen each time the prisoner sneezes?" the taller of the two demanded, his too-pretty features set in an expression of arrogant disdain. "Or if she refused to eat her dessert?"

Riza scowled. His face was rounder, with a hint of petulance in the youthful features. "There's something weird about that female talking to herself all the time."

Jord snorted. "Prisoners do weird things. They sing. They yell. They see pink elephants. It has something to do with being locked in the dungeons."

"But—"

"If the two of you wish to squabble like children, you should loiter outside the nursery, not the royal chambers," Troy chided.

The two men came to an abrupt halt, as if they'd been so intent on their argument, they hadn't noticed a six-foot imp in pink spandex standing in the middle of the corridor.

Hard to believe.

Jord sent him an impatient frown. Troy's sardonic refusal to concede that the mer-folk were superior to other fey creatures meant he wasn't a favorite among the natives. That was fine. He wasn't there to win friends. His only concern was Inga and whether or not she was being treated with the respect and loyalty she deserved.

Riza stepped forward. "I need to speak with Queen Inga."

"I'm sure she's busy," Jord snapped.

"Of course she's busy, she's the queen," Troy drawled, covertly studying the younger male. He was obviously upset. Maybe Inga should find out what was going on before Troy ran them off. "But I am certain she can make time for one of her loyal subjects."

Jord made a sound of impatience. "I assure you it's not necessary."

Troy arched a brow. Why was the male so determined to keep the younger guard away from the queen? Was he the usual arrogant ass who enjoyed bullying anyone who happened to be his underling? Or did he have another reason for trying to silence the younger male?

Only one way to find out.

Troy moved to rap his knuckles against a gilded door, waiting for Inga to call out for them to enter before pushing it open. He stepped over the threshold and entered the room that matched the rest of the castle, with lots of marble and fluted columns and sparkling chandeliers. The major difference was the large dais that held the velvet and gold throne.

A throne that was currently empty.

Troy rolled his eyes, already knowing what he was about to discover as he strolled up the crimson runner that led the way to the dais. Sure enough, there was the sound of grunting as Inga struggled to her feet, and then she abruptly appeared from behind the throne.

"Good morning, Troy."

She didn't look like the Queen of the Mer-folk. There was none of her mother's ephemeral beauty; instead she'd inherited her ogre father's sturdy body that stood well over six foot, with shoulders broad enough to make a football player proud. Beneath her drunkenly tilted crown, her reddish hair grew in tufts and her features were carved with a blunt lack of finesse. Her blue eyes were the only hint that she had mermaid blood in her veins, but they flashed an ogre-red when she was annoyed. Which was more often than not.

At the moment she wore a hideous muumuu dress that was an insult to fashion. The billowing gown was a strange shade of olive with big yellow and orange flowers splattered over it. She was also speckled with paint.

A delicate shudder raced through Troy. He'd finally convinced this female to spend at least a few hours in the throne room each day, listening to the concerns of her people, but whenever she had a moment alone, she lost herself in her love for painting. It was a harmless hobby, he acknowledged, and she was exquisitely talented. The murals on the walls of the throne room were now the finest in all the castle. Still, she looked like she'd been sucked through a whirlpool, rolled in a multicolor mud pit, and tossed out the other side.

Thankfully, she had the massive trident clutched in her hand. The Tryshu was a magical artifact that chose the leader of the mer-folk. As long as Inga was holding it, there was no question that she was the queen.

Stopping next to the dais, Troy offered an elaborate bow. "Your Majesty," he said in deep, formal tones.

Belatedly realizing that Troy wasn't alone, Inga grudgingly straightened her crown and forced a smile that revealed her pointed teeth.

"Are you here to see me?" she demanded.

Both guards offered polite bows. "I apologize for interrupting, Your Majesty," Jord said, sending his companion a foul glare. "Riza is one of our younger guards. I fear he's prone to exaggerating."

Riza folded his arms over his chest. "I'm not exaggerating."

Inga blinked in confusion. "Exaggerating about what?"

"The prisoner," Riza said.

Inga's confusion deepened. "Which one?"

"The pureblooded Were," Riza clarified.

Inga stiffened in alarm. "Brigette?"

Riza nodded. "Yes."

"What about her?"

The younger guard paled, clearly intimidated by the towering ogress holding a trident that could destroy the entire castle with one blast.

"I…" Riza stopped to clear his throat. "I heard her talking."

Inga glanced toward Troy. He shrugged and she returned her attention to the guard.

"No one is supposed to enter her cell except for me, and I haven't been down there for days."

"That's why I went to check on her."

"And?"

Riza grimaced. "She was alone."

Troy narrowed his eyes. It would be easy to overreact after Brigette had nearly managed to destroy their world.

"Perhaps she's become unhinged," he suggested. "She did spend five centuries as a handmaiden to an evil beastie-thing."

"That's what I thought," Riza said. "But she keeps doing it. And the last time I checked on her, I was sure I caught sight of a shadow in the cell with her."

Inga hissed in alarm. "A shadow?"

"It was probably just a figment of his imagination." Jord intruded into the conversation, his expression grim.

"It was not," Riza stubbornly insisted. "I know what I saw."

Troy moved toward the guard. "Tell me exactly what happened."

Riza turned his back on his glowering companion to speak directly to Troy. "I was on duty when I heard the female babbling about pledging her loyalty and promising to obey without question."

"Did you hear a name?" Troy pressed.

"Name?"

"Was Zella mentioned?"

The guard wrinkled his nose. "I suppose she might have said Zella."

Inga muttered a curse. "This can't be good."

"The understatement of the century," Troy muttered. "And well past our pay grade." He squared his shoulders. "We need Chaaya."

* * * *

Dreamscape Resort, Vegas

Chiron didn't exactly stomp across the casino floor. He was, after all, a sophisticated, flawlessly elegant vampire with an image to maintain. Only a child indulged in temper tantrums.

Still, the humans seated in front of the flashing slot machines or clustered around the roulette tables shivered with unease as he passed. They didn't realize they'd been brushed by the icy power of his seething temper, but in the most primitive parts of their mind, they realized there was danger in the area.

He ignored the lingering gazes that followed him. He knew what the humans were seeing: a slender male with devilishly handsome features. His dark hair was cut short and smoothed from his lean face. Next they would notice the designer suit that cost a fortune. From there they would decide that he couldn't be responsible for their vague sense of anxiety and return their attention to their gambling. They would never suspect he was a monster beneath his polished façade.

Chiron cast a last glance around the casino before heading toward the back of the vast space. He was in dire need of some peace and quiet, and the only place to find that was in his office at the top of the hotel.

He'd managed to make it out of the public rooms and was waiting for the doors of his private elevator to slide open when his luck ran out. For the hundredth time that night.

Or at least, that's what it felt like.

"Go away," he snapped as a large male approached from behind.

Basq ignored his command, halting next to Chiron.

The younger male was taller with a thicker build than Chiron. His features were carved with bold strokes, giving him an impressive nose and wide brow. His jaw was square, and his full lips were pressed into a stern line. His brown hair was long enough to brush his shoulders and the top layer was pulled back and tied with a leather strip. It was his eyes, however, that captured the most attention. They were rimmed with a deep brown and progressively lightened to a pure white in the center.

The male had been a member of Tarak's clan until Tarak had joined with the previous Anasso. Chiron wasn't entirely certain where Basq had gone or what he'd been doing for the past centuries, but a few years ago he'd shown up at Dreamscape Resort and asked for a job.

Chiron had taken him in without question.

The male would always be his brother.

"For a vampire who just mated the love of your life and rescued your master from the bastard that held him captive for over five hundred years, you're in a crappy mood," Basq said.

Chiron searched the male's face for any hint of mockery. There was nothing. Basq had a special talent for hiding his emotions. Or maybe he didn't have any. Hard to say for sure.

"I seriously underestimated how much I depended on Ulric. I can't leave my office without a dozen employees harassing me about their tedious problems," Chiron groused. "So far tonight the kitchen staff has threatened revolt because the chef changed the menu without telling them, a janitor fell and broke his leg, and two customers got into a drunken brawl and destroyed one of the roulette tables. It's not even midnight."

The elevator doors slid open and both males stepped inside. "It was Ulric's job to make sure you weren't bothered with the staff," Basq reminded him.

Chiron scowled. Ulric was a pureblooded Were who'd been Chiron's most trusted companion for centuries. Together they'd created the chain of resorts that catered to humans around the world. But six weeks ago, the male had left Vegas.

"Plus, he mated my most valuable employee and now she's gone with him." Chiron continued his complaint, stabbing the top button on the electronic panel.

Rainn had only been with Dreamscape for twenty years or so, but she'd earned a spot as a trusted manager. She was also a rare zephyr spite who wanted to return to her family, taking Ulric with her to some super-secret, on-a-need-to-know-basis spot deep beneath the desert.

"I thought you were pleased for him?" Basq reminded him.

"I was until I realized his happiness was going to be a pain in the ass," Chiron told his companion. "Do you know, until the past month I would have sworn that Dreamscape Resorts runs like a well-oiled machine? Now I'm wondering if it'll survive the night."

"It would be easier if you shared Ulric's duties."

Chiron glanced at his clansman. "Are you offering?"

The male arched a brow. "Do you really want me dealing with the humans?"

A shudder raced through Chiron. Basq wasn't much of a people person. Not unless they were on the menu. He was, however, an extraordinary warrior. And utterly loyal. Perfect for the head of Dreamscape security.

"No, thanks," he said in dry tones. "Ulric can be…"

"Surly? Rabid?" Basq suggested as Chiron struggled for the proper word.

"Both," Chiron agreed. "But he has a surprising skill in dealing with the staff and customers."

"The same skill Lilah possesses."

The doors slid open with a small hiss. Chiron stepped out of the elevator, his expression tightening.

Lilah…

It'd been several months since he'd mated the gloriously delectable witch, but it still felt like a miracle every time he thought of her. He couldn't believe that she was truly bound to him for the rest of eternity.

Which might explain why he wanted to treat her like a princess. She was too precious for him to risk.

"I want to pamper her, not bury her in work," he said, crossing the outer reception room.

Basq followed behind him, pausing to glance out the bank of windows that looked over the Mojave Desert on one side and the Vegas Strip on the other.

Chiron wasn't in the mood to appreciate the stunning view. Instead he marched across the room that was decorated with a silver carpet and sleek chrome with black leather furniture, then he entered his private space that had been specifically created for the needs of a vampire. There were no windows, the lighting was muted, and the furniture was built to endure the weight of an elephant although it maintained a sleek elegance.

Moving to lean against the silver and glass desk, Chiron folded his arms over his chest as Basq halted directly in front of him.

"Have you asked Lilah what she wants?" the younger male demanded.

Chiron flashed his fangs. Everyone knew what Lilah wanted. She was quite…vocal when she thought that Chiron wasn't giving her enough responsibility.

If it was up to his ambitious witch, she'd be in charge of the entire Dreamscape empire. Hell, she'd be in charge of the world.

"Stop being sensible," Chiron growled. "It's annoying."

Basq grimaced. "I'm about to become even more annoying."

"What now?"

"The human girl."

"Chaaya?" Chiron asked, even though there was only one creature who could inspire the frustration that was smoldering in Basq's eyes.

Chaaya wasn't exactly a girl, considering she was older than both Chiron and Basq. And she wasn't exactly a human, since she'd been sacrificed centuries ago to battle against the evil beast that Ulric had recently encountered.

The truth was that no one knew exactly what she *was*.

Well, they knew she was a cyclone of endless trouble.

She drank, she cheated his guests at cards, she drove his staff to the brink of homicide and went out of her way to piss him off. Not a night passed that he didn't want to toss her into some dark, dreary dungeon. Unfortunately, he didn't happen to have one of those handy here in Vegas. And even if he did, he was fairly confident it wouldn't hold the girl.

As if to confirm his dark thoughts, Basq clenched his hands. "She's gone."

"Again?" Chiron made a sound of annoyance. After Chaaya had been caught using her strange, unpredictable powers to screw with the slot machines, Chiron had insisted that she have an escort when she left her private rooms. A *vampire* escort.

"I thought you had a guard watching her?"

Basq managed to look more grim than usual. An astonishing accomplishment.

"*I* was watching her."

"She got past you?" Chiron didn't hide his surprise. "I know you're getting old, but damn. That's just embarrassing."

Basq wasn't amused. "She went into her rooms. I waited outside the door, but she didn't come back out. I finally went in to check on her..." He shrugged. "And she was gone."

Chiron studied his companion in confusion. "Are you claiming she created a portal?"

Basq hesitated. Almost as if he didn't want to share his suspicion. "My guess is that she walked through the wall," he at last admitted.

Chiron's lips parted to argue, then he shook his head. Chaaya was still discovering her powers. And since she was technically a ghost, it was quite plausible that she could walk through walls.

Just what he needed.

"That's it," he rasped. "I'm done with that damned creature. I don't care if she saved Ulric's life or not."

Basq snorted. "I wish I believed you."

Chiron cursed. Basq was right. He could huff and puff and threaten all he wanted. For now they had no idea what Chaaya was or how she'd been connected to the evil spirit. Someone had to keep an eye on her. And for now, he was stuck with the aggravating task.

Lucky him.

"Did you track her down?" he demanded.

Basq nodded. "She's at the Viper's Nest."

The Viper's Nest was an elegant demon club that catered to vampires. It was also an "invitation only" sort of place. And Chiron was willing to bet his last dollar that Chaaya would be the last person on the invitation list.

"You're sure?"

"I followed her there myself."

Chiron frowned. "Why the hell would she go there? She usually prefers the filthy bars on the edge of town."

Basq shrugged. "Why does she do anything? To piss us off."

"True." The girl made it her life's ambition to be as aggravating as possible. Chiron eyed his companion. "I don't suppose you—"

"No," Basq interrupted. "You're her babysitter, not me. Thank the goddess."

Chiron sent his companion a sour frown. "Yet another job that should be on Ulric's to-do list. I swear, I'm going to hunt down that dog and personally haul his furry ass back to Vegas."

An almost smile touched Basq's lips. "I'll volunteer for that."

"No. I need you here," Chiron said.

It was true, he did depend on Basq. Especially now. He might grouse about Ulric's absence, but he was determined to allow the male time to become acquainted with his new mate and her family. Ulric might be a Were, but he was as much a brother as any of the vampires in Chiron's clan. Maybe more. He wanted the male to be happy.

"What about the girl?" Basq demanded.

"I have two options," Chiron admitted. "Go and get her, or ignore her and hope she doesn't cause a mass riot."

"Are you a betting man?"

"Not anymore." The two males exchanged a rueful gaze. "Shit." Chiron pushed away from the desk and headed for the door.

So much for peace and quiet.

* * * *

"A hundred bucks you can't finish it in one drink," the vampire drawled.

Chaaya flicked a dismissive glance over the potent demon liquor that burned with a blue fire. It wasn't the first time she'd been challenged since she'd strolled into the elegant casino.

It was easy to underestimate her. She looked mortal with her delicate features, her large, dark eyes and soft pink lips. Her skin was bronzed, and her dark hair was buzzed close to her skull to reveal the Celtic tattoos that started behind her ears and ran down the sides of her neck.

She wore a black leather jacket and matching pants that couldn't disguise just how tiny she was compared to the other demons in the place. And while she had a copper spear with a short ebony handle belted to her side, she looked like easy prey.

Which was why she was constantly being tested.

"Two hundred," she demanded.

The vampire grinned, revealing his snowy white fangs. He was a tall, red-haired male with the perfect features that were shared by all vampires. He also had the usual arrogance.

"Done."

Chaaya tapped a slender finger on the table, waiting for the demon to show his money. The vampire hissed, but he reached into the front pocket of his slacks and pulled out a stack of crisp one hundred dollar bills. He peeled off two and dropped them on the table.

"There."

Chaaya reached for the grog, and with one flick of her wrist she tossed the flaming liquid down her throat. She swallowed, bracing herself as the grog hit her stomach with the force of an exploding volcano. Once she was certain she wasn't going to pass out, she wiped her lips with the back of her hand and reached for the money.

"Done."

The smirk on the vampire's overly pretty face changed to disbelief. "What are you?"

She shrugged. "Just a girl who can't say no," she murmured, rising to her feet. She tossed a couple dollars on the table. "Here, have a drink on me."

She strolled away from the puzzled creature, heading toward the roulette table across the crowded room. She'd borrowed a few thousand dollars from Basq's private stash he kept hidden in his bedroom. Before the night was over, she intended to double her ill-gotten fortune. Or lose it all.

Either way, it was all good.

Basq would be pissed. Chiron would have heartburn. And she would have enjoyed a night of entertainment that was different from her usual drunken escapades at the tawdrier demon clubs.

Win. Win. Win.

She was passing by a brightly lit stage where a pair of frost fairies performed a sensual dance that included a lot of fluttering wings and sparkles when a hand reached out to grab her upper arm.

Chaaya halted, slowly swiveling her head to glare at the male who'd dared to touch her without permission.

He wasn't old in vampire terms. Maybe a couple hundred years. Chaaya wasn't sure how she knew, but she could sense a demon's age in the lack of power that surrounded them. This one was slender with blue eyes and skin as pale as snow. His dark hair was slicked back to emphasize the arrogance of his finely chiseled features.

Chaaya deliberately lowered her gaze to the fingers digging into her flesh.

"Are you tired of that hand being attached to your arm?" she asked in sweet tones.

"I just want to talk to you," the male retorted, stupidly maintaining his tight grip. "I haven't seen you around here before."

Chaaya covertly reached for the copper spear. Since her return to this world she'd discovered that she attracted a lot of attention, from both males and females. But she wasn't at the Viper's Nest to make friends. Or even enemies, which was a lot more fun.

She was there to release some pent-up steam. Period.

"And that gives you the right to maul me?"

The male leaned forward, a leer curving his lips. "I haven't started mauling. Yet." His gaze skimmed down her slender body. "I always negotiate the price first. How much?"

"More than you could ever afford."

"Try me."

Chaaya visibly shuddered. "Not for all the money in the world."

The male's expression tightened. "Don't be that way." His smile remained, but a cruel edge entered his voice.

"I'm not telling you again," Chaaya warned. "Let me go."

"All I want is a small taste…argh!"

The vampire's words ended on a shriek of pain as Chaaya lifted her spear and swung it down in a smooth motion. It sliced through the male's wrist with remarkable ease.

Chaaya watched with satisfaction as the severed hand fell to the expensive carpet with a dull thud.

"Next time you'll listen to a woman who tells you no," she assured him.

The male held up his bloody stump, his fangs fully extended.

"You bitch!"

Chaaya grimaced at his shrill tone, stepping back to avoid the blood that continued to spurt out of his stump.

"Don't be such a baby. It'll grow back."

Her words failed to appease the leech. Hell, they seemed to make him even madder.

"I'm going to kill you," he screeched.

Chaaya rolled her eyes. "Been there, done that," she drawled. "You're starting to bore me."

She turned as if she was about to walk away. She already knew what the vampire would do. Leeches could be so depressingly predictable. On cue, there was a low growl behind her, then the vampire was leaping through the air.

With a speed and strength that she'd never possessed when she was a mere human, Chaaya crouched low, allowing the male to fly over her head. He landed in an awkward position and she moved before he could regain his balance, kicking him in the center of the back. The blow was enough to send the male stumbling forward, right into the crowd gathered around the roulette table.

There was a roar of fury from a Were who turned to grab the vampire by the throat and tossed him across the room. A mistake. Instantly the dog was swarmed by a mob of angry leeches.

Chaaya grinned. She enjoyed gambling, but this was much more fun.

With a war cry she'd spent centuries perfecting, she held up her spear and dashed straight into the fray.

Chapter 2

The Viper's Nest was several blocks away from the glittering Vegas Strip. At one time it'd been a solidly middle-class neighborhood with picket fences and station wagons parked in the driveways. Now calling it a dump would be a compliment.

In fact, most of the block was nothing more than empty lots where the houses had been burned to the ground, leaving behind charred foundations. Or at least that's what was visible to the human eye. Behind the illusion was a five-story brick building with heavily tinted windows to protect the sun-challenged demons who visited.

Inside, the club was as posh as any Vegas hotel. There was lots of marble, lots of fluted columns that soared toward painted ceilings, and cozy, private rooms that allowed demons to indulge their deepest fantasies.

Javad strolled across the front lobby. He was a tall, slender vampire with chiseled muscles beneath his black slacks and gold silk tunic that fell to his knees. His curly hair was as dark as a raven's wing and brushed his shoulders. His face was lean, and his features were hawkish, like a bird of prey. And unlike many vampires, his skin held a rich color. He'd spent too many years in the brutal desert sun before being turned to entirely lose the glorious sheen.

His eyes were black, and he was told that they smoldered with enough power to make grown trolls run in terror. On the side of his neck was a stylized tattoo that revealed he'd been an assassin during his life as a human.

He couldn't remember that time. A vampire awoke without any memories or even a knowledge of who or what he was. Still, he'd maintained his lethal fighting skills. And added several more over the centuries.

He was a well-honed weapon who was used to fighting without mercy.

Until Viper.

The clan chief of Chicago had found Javad after he'd escaped from the brutal vampire who'd sired Javad and taken him into his clan. Eventually, he'd sent him to Vegas to manage this demon club.

He owed the male...everything.

Moving through the lobby that was scattered with a few leather sofas, Javad's bare feet barely made a sound against the cool marble floor. He glanced toward the center of the room that was dominated by a fountain. He chuckled at the sight of the golden statue of a male holding a massive sword over his head that spouted water. It was supposed to represent Styx, the current Anasso, King of the Vampires. Viper had a twisted sense of humor.

His amusement disappeared as he was distracted by the vampire who had just entered the club. He'd sensed the powerful male as soon as he forced his way through the illusion. Chiron was one of the few demons in this city who could potentially match him in sheer strength.

Which meant that the male's arrival had his full attention.

"Chiron." He ran an assessing gaze over the male. Not to admire the expensive suit—he was looking for weapons. When he found nothing, he lifted his gaze to study the intruder's impatient expression. "This is an unexpected surprise."

The male moved forward. "Not now," he growled.

Javad smoothly stepped to block the male's path. The Anasso might have declared that the Rebels were once again apart of the vampire nation, but this was an invitation-only club. And he was in charge.

"I'm afraid I'm going to have to insist." His smile revealed his massive fangs. "Professional courtesy, you understand."

Ice coated the nearby fountain as Chiron narrowed his gaze. Javad braced for a strike. Clearly, the male wasn't used to being told no.

Then, with a visible effort, Chiron leashed his temper. "A female in my care was seen coming into your club."

Javad wasn't sure what he'd been expecting. Certainly not a social visit. The two vampires had lived in the same city for decades without crossing paths, something that they'd both made efforts to achieve.

Now he arched his brows. "A female in your care? Does your mate know?"

Chiron wasn't amused. "I need to find her."

"Tough. My guests pay an enormous fee to protect their privacy. You can do whatever you want to her once she leaves the club. Until then..." Javad shrugged.

"She's not a guest. She snuck in."

"That's impossible. I have security in place to make sure no one passes through the illusion without alerting me."

"This one can."

Okay. That was enough. Javad might not have a chain of fancy-ass resorts spread across the world, but he knew how to protect the one that he managed.

"I'm trying to be nice," he growled. The floor trembled beneath his feet. He could create earthquakes that were capable of destroying entire cities. "You won't like me when I'm pissed off."

Chiron took a step forward. "And you're not going to like me if I have to go through you to get to Chaaya."

Javad was distracted by the odd name. "The human?" he demanded in surprise.

Chiron jerked. Did the male think the strange creature was a secret? Javad didn't know all the details, but he'd discovered that Ulric had traveled to England to battle against some mysterious beast and that he'd returned with a young woman named Chaaya.

For a minute it looked like Chiron was going to refuse to answer, then his hands clenched and he forced himself to speak.

"She was born human, but she was sacrificed centuries ago. We have no idea what she is now. A ghost, maybe a spirit." Chiron's voice was edged with frustration, as if the mere thought of Chaaya was enough to make his fangs clench. "She can walk through a solid wall, so she certainly has the ability to get through your magical barriers without tripping any alarms."

Javad considered Chiron's words. The security at the Viper's Nest was specifically designed. There was an outer illusion to convince humans that this area was nothing more than an abandoned lot, and a separate spell to warn him of any demons entering the club who hadn't been issued an invitation.

It wasn't created to reveal the presence of ghosts.

"Come with me," he snapped.

He was just turning to lead Chiron across the lobby when the sound of a loud crash was followed closely by the howl of a werewolf.

"Shit." Chiron's expression was grim. "We're too late."

Javad parted his lips to demand an explanation, but he was suddenly staring at empty air. Chiron had turned to disappear from the club with blinding speed. At the same time there was more crashing and the sound of primal screams as the demons gave into their most primitive urges.

Great. The strange female was clearly in the midst of causing some sort of disturbance in the main casino, and Chiron was bailing on him.

He was going to have a long chat with that vampire.

Just as soon as he finished cleaning up the mess.

* * * *

It was a fine riot. Lots of blood, swearing, and excessive violence. Or at least it was fine until Chaaya was rudely interrupted.

She was standing on the bar, bashing a drunken sprite on the head with the butt of her spear when she caught the familiar scent.

Shit.

Chiron.

The aggravating leech wasn't in the casino, but he most certainly was somewhere in the building.

Leaping off the bar, she crouched low and weaved her way through the tangle of battling demons. She wasn't headed toward the exit. That was where she would be expected to run. Instead she entered the narrow hallway at the back of the room. There weren't many creatures in the bar that needed a bathroom, which meant she was alone as she stepped into the cramped cubicle.

Perfect.

Chaaya locked the heavy wooden door, then she rubbed her fingers down the hilt of her spear. The Celtic runes etched into the ebony sent a tingle of magic through her skin. It helped her to focus her powers.

She closed her eyes, allowing the strange sensation of…melting to flow through her body. It was the only way to explain what she experienced when she went into her ghost mode. It wasn't like she turned to mist, which is what Rainn claimed had happened to her. She didn't float on the wind.

And she didn't just become invisible.

It was closer to becoming a part of her surroundings so she could move through them. It was an amazing trick she'd discovered since returning to this world. But it did have its drawbacks, including the fact that her sense of smell remained as sharp as ever.

Which made pressing through the wall of the bathroom a less-than-pleasant experience. Someone needed to speak with Javad about his housekeeping skills.

Once she could catch the sweet night air, Chaaya returned to her solid form.

"Gotcha."

Chaaya nearly jumped out of her skin as she whirled to confront the vampire who was leaning against the wall.

"What the hell are you doing here?"

"Looking for you."

"How did you know I was here…" Her words trailed away. She suddenly knew exactly how Chiron how managed to figure out she was at the Viper's Nest. "Basq." She breathed the name as if it was a curse. "He followed me, didn't he? That jerk. Does he know it's creepy to spy on young, vulnerable women?"

Chiron's jaw tightened, as if he was gritting his fangs. "He wasn't spying. He was following my orders to keep an eye on you."

"Spying."

"And you are neither young nor helpless."

Chaaya considered his words before shrugging. "Fair enough," she agreed.

She was probably older than Basq by a couple centuries. And anyone who thought she was helpless hadn't seen her in battle.

Chiron waved his hand in an impatient motion. "Let's go."

Chaaya frowned. It wasn't that she wanted to stick around the club. She was already tired of the place. But she wasn't about to let Chiron order her around. It set a bad precedent.

She folded her arms over her chest. "You're not the boss of me."

"I am until Ulric returns."

"He's not the boss of me either," she retorted.

Chiron narrowed his gaze. "He saved your ass."

"So what? I saved his first. We're even as far as I'm concerned."

Chiron looked ready to strangle her, a familiar expression, but before he could say a word, a tall, dark-haired vampire in a long tunic rounded the corner of the building.

"You." The male pointed a finger toward Chaaya, the ground trembling beneath her feet. "Don't move a muscle."

She didn't recognize the leech, but she was betting that he was Javad, the manager of the Viper's Nest. And that he was about to blame her for the riot she could still hear raging inside.

"Yeah, maybe it's time to go," she muttered, holstering her spear and running down the dark street at top speed.

"Get back here," the male roared, but thankfully he made no effort to chase her. She was fairly certain she couldn't outrun a vampire.

As if to prove her theory, Chiron easily kept pace beside her as they threaded their way through the sleeping human neighborhoods.

"Making friends wherever you go," he taunted.

She flashed a mocking smile. "It's my gift."

Chiron rolled his eyes, but he remained blissfully silent as they swiftly moved toward the bright lights of the Vegas Strip. Together they approached Dreamscape Resorts from the back and entered through the kitchen door. They'd just reached the hallway that led to the private elevators when a door opened to reveal a large vampire.

Chaaya came to an abrupt halt, glaring at the male. He was big and strong with muscles that rippled beneath his black cashmere sweater and black slacks. Around his neck was a thin gold chain with a small amulet she'd never seen him without. He was also annoyingly gorgeous, if you liked them with perfectly carved features and the strangest, most fascinating eyes that had ever been created.

"Oh, great. Just who I didn't want to see."

Basq didn't bother glancing in her direction. He had an annoying habit of pretending she didn't exist. At least when he wasn't spying on her. Jerk.

"You have a visitor," he told Chiron.

Chiron waved a hand toward Chaaya. "Return to your rooms."

"He wants to see both of you," Basq said before Chaaya could tell Chiron to shove his command up his ass.

Chiron frowned, his expression suddenly wary. "Who is it?"

With a flutter of large, glittery wings, a three-foot gargoyle stepped through the open door.

"It is *moi*." Levet spread his arms in a grand gesture. "The knight in shining armor who women adore and vampires despair to contain—"

"Shut up," Chiron interrupted.

Levet smirked, batting his lashes. "Did you miss me?"

"No."

Chaaya smiled. Unlike the surly vampires, she thoroughly appreciated the tiny demon. Levet was funny and unpredictable, and best of all, he infuriated other males to the point of insanity. What wasn't to like? She hadn't seen him since she'd been kicked out of the mer-folk castle weeks ago.

"*I* missed you," she assured him.

The lumpy gargoyle face melted with pleasure. "Ah, *ma belle*. I have missed you as well. The mer-folk castle is a much duller place without you." There was a soft snort from Basq that Chaaya ignored. Levet ignored him as well. "How are things here?"

"Same ol', same ol'." She abruptly grinned. "I caused an epic riot at the Viper's Nest."

"And I missed it?" Levet pouted. "That's not fair."

"We can—"

"Enough." Chiron stepped forward, his features tight with annoyance. "What are you doing here?"

"No need to twist your panties," Levet protested.

Chiron flashed his fangs. Chaaya had to admit they were an impressive sight. Long and sharp and glistening with deadly intent.

"Start talking."

Levet wrinkled his snout. ""Very well. Brigette is evil again."

Chiron slowly blinked. "What?"

"Brigette. Is. Evil. Again." Levet pronounced each word with a slow emphasis.

"I heard you, idiot," Chiron snapped. "I want to know what it means."

"She was locked in the mer-folk dungeons looking like any normal Were." Levet paused, as if considering a sudden thought. "Although, when I happened to see her a couple of weeks ago, she was foaming at the mouth. I think she might have rabies. I should have warned Inga to have her vaccinated."

The air dropped to a subarctic temperature. A sure sigh the vamps were in a mood.

"Levet," Chaaya warned.

The gargoyle fluttered his wings in a mocking gesture, but he was smart enough to answer the question. No need to provoke the angry leeches into gargoyle-cide.

"I was spending the day with Darcy, the mate of Styx." Levet paused, as if waiting for someone to be impressed with his intimate friendship with the King of Vampires. Then he heaved a resigned sigh. "While I was there, I received a message from Inga, who you know is the Queen of the Mer-folk. We can speak telepathically. It is one of my many talents." He waited again for the proper appreciation. Nothing.

"And?" Chiron snapped.

Levet clicked his tongue, his wings fluttering with annoyance. "And they have word from one of the dungeons guards that Brigette has been overheard speaking to some invisible visitor."

They all stared at the gargoyle in confusion.

"How do they know she has an invisible visitor?" Chiron demanded. "Couldn't she be talking to herself?"

Levet shrugged. "The guard also noticed a shadow in the cell with Brigette. Inga feared that Zella might be trying to get in contact with the Were."

"Is that possible?" Chiron frowned, glancing toward Chaaya. "The beast is trapped, isn't it?"

"Don't look at me," Chaaya complained. "I don't know what's going on."

"You're the only one who has any experience with the evil spirit."

Chaaya resisted the urge to stomp her foot. Just because she'd been sacrificed to keep the beast out of this world, and then spent centuries trapped in a hellish dimension with the creature, didn't mean that she knew anything about it. Just the opposite. She'd devoted her afterlife to avoiding the fiery spirit.

"I'm not the beast whisperer," she groused, folding her arms over her chest.

Chiron's jaw tightened, but he didn't explode. Instead he waved a hand toward Basq.

"Give us a minute."

The large vampire nodded, reaching out to grab Levet by his horn so he could drag him toward the door.

"Come with me."

"Hey," Levet protested, flailing his arms as he was hauled out of the hallway and into a storage room. The door was slammed behind them.

Chaaya warily eyeballed Chiron. "Now what?"

Chiron hesitated, as if searching for the perfect words. Never a good sign.

"I know it's not fair to ask you to return to the mer-folk castle."

"You're right. It's not fair. I was kicked out, remember?"

"You're the only one who can determine if the darkness surrounding Brigette is connected to the beast."

She couldn't argue with his words, so instead she deflected.

"I warned you that Brigette needed to be destroyed, but did you listen? No. As usual you did what you wanted, and now I'm expected to clean up the mess."

Chiron grimaced. "That was Ulric's decision. He hoped that his cousin could be salvaged. She's his only family."

"Then he should go investigate."

"Chaaya."

She stuck out her lower lip. She was being petulant, but she didn't care. She was supposed to be done with Zella the Fire Beast from the Hell Dimension. This was her time to actually enjoy her life. Someone else could be the sacrifice, right?

But even as she parted her lips to tell the vampire to choose some other sucker to check on Brigette, she swallowed a sigh. Dammit. Who else could sense Zella? No one, that was who.

"Fine," she conceded with a resentful scowl. "I'll go."

"And you'll take Basq with you," Chiron added smoothly.

"No. Absolutely not."

"He'll be there to watch your back."

She grabbed the hilt of her spear. "I don't need a babysitter."

"He's not a babysitter." Chiron's expression hardened. "He's a fierce warrior who is utterly loyal. He'll protect you with his life."

Chaaya believed him. Basq might annoy the hell out of her, but she never doubted he would destroy anything that might try to harm her. Not because he cared whether she lived or died, but because she was his current "duty."

"I don't need protection," she sulked.

Chiron leaned forward, eying her with a strange intensity. "Are you so sure?"

"What are you talking about?"

"You're the only one who has an intimate knowledge of the beast," he reminded her. "If it's trying to seep back into this world, then the first thing it's going to try to do is get rid of the one creature that might be capable of preventing its return."

He forced her to confront the truth she'd been happily trying to ignore. She didn't want to think about the beast or evil or encroaching darkness. She just wanted to leap from one mindless pleasure to another.

Was that too much to ask?

Obviously, it was.

She heaved a sigh of frustration. "If the darkness comes after me, then your precious Basq is going to be toast. Is that what you want?"

"Can you just once do what I ask without an argument?"

Chaaya started to remind him once again that he wasn't her boss, only to have the words die on her lips as she noticed the lines of strain on his handsome face.

"You look tired," she told him.

Chiron grimaced. "I'm worried. We thought the threat was over. If the beast is truly returning to this world, then we need to be prepared."

Oh. Chaaya nodded. "Yeah, I'm worried too."

Chiron rose to his feet, holding her gaze. "Then go to the mer-folk castle and check on Brigette. Make sure she's not spreading her poison."

"I'll go, but I don't want Basq," Chaaya countered. "He's a pain in the ass."

Chiron's lips twisted. "Strange, he just said the same thing about you."

"Because he's a humorless bore."

"He's one of the most honorable males I know. Then again, if your preference is for the scum you meet at the Diablo Club, I can understand your lack of appreciation for his finer qualities," he muttered, referring to the seedy demon bar she frequented on the edge of town.

She tilted her chin. "Those scum are like me."

Chiron paused, as if caught off guard by her claim. "What do you mean?"

She glanced away, feeling oddly vulnerable. "Disposable," she whispered.

"Chaaya—"

Whatever Chiron was about to say was interrupted when Levet shoved the door open and returned to the hallway. Basq was a step behind him, his expression tight with annoyance.

Chiron made a sound of impatience. "Do you understand the meaning of a private conversation?"

Levet flapped his wings. "Inga has opened a portal for us to travel to the mer-folk castle. We need to leave now."

"Fine. Go, but keep me in the loop." Chiron glanced toward Basq, who gave a small nod.

"What loop?" Levet blinked in confusion. "We have a loop? Like Snapchat? Oh, oh. Mine is MustLoveGargoyles79—"

"Argh. I can't bear any more." Chiron stormed down the hallway toward the main casino, the walls icing over as he passed.

"He's in a poopy mood," Levet groused.

Chaaya bit back her mocking comment. A part of her appreciated Chiron's concern. If the beast had found a way to manipulate Brigette, or worse, to enter this dimension, then they were all in danger. Extreme, end-of-the-world danger.

"He's afraid," she said in a soft voice.

"I am as well," Levet confessed, his smile fading. "If the darkness is leaking from Brigette, then the mermaids are in danger. Inga is in danger."

Chaaya squared her shoulders, squashing her reluctance to spend more time in Basq's company. This was too important to let her childish reaction to the vampire interfere with what needed to be done.

"Then we'll go and protect them, right?" she demanded.

"*Oui*. It is what knights in shining armor do," Levet agreed.

Chaaya snorted. "I'm about as far from a knight in shining armor as you can get."

Without warning, Levet moved forward to grasp her fingers in a firm grip.

"*Ma belle*, you are the only true hero I have ever known."

Chapter 3

Brigette clenched her teeth as she paced her cell, waiting for the door to open.

A part of her knew she was crazy. How could she trust another mystery voice whispering in her ear? The last time she'd allowed herself to be swayed by an anonymous stranger, she'd become a pawn to an evil beast who'd used her to destroy her own pack. But this voice hadn't promised her infinite power. Or to become alpha. Or even vast riches.

No, there'd been only one thing it had offered.

Something Brigette longed to acquire with the force of a thousand suns.

First, however, she had to get out of this damned dungeon. It didn't matter that she'd only been locked away a few months. Right now it felt like centuries. And each minute she remained captive felt like acid pouring against her raw nerves.

"Hello?" she called out. "You told me to be ready. I'm ready."

Her voice bounced around the empty dungeon. No response. Brigette clenched her hands, for the millionth time wishing she could touch her wolf. During her centuries with Zella, her animal had retreated deeper and deeper inside her, until she could barely feel its presence. And even after the evil creature had been trapped in another dimension, the wolf refused to reappear. As if it was determined to punish Brigette for her betrayal of her pack.

The loss was profound.

Turning on her heel, she was at the far end of the cell when the faint click of a lock had her spinning around to watch the heavy iron door swing open.

"Who's there?" she growled, adrenaline surging through her body. She might not be capable of shifting into her wolf, but she was still a dangerous predator.

"Follow me."

The voice wasn't the same as the one who'd been whispering in her mind. This one was male and physically in the dungeons. Brigette sniffed the air. merman. She could tell by the tang of salt.

Cautiously inching forward, Brigette glanced into the dark space between the rows of cells. There was a slender shape hurrying toward the stairs.

"Who are you?" she called out.

"I was sent by Greta." There was a tense edge in the voice. "Let's go."

Greta. That was the name the whispering voice had offered her. She didn't know if it was real or made up, and she didn't care. Her previous mistress had gone by Zella, the Beast, and the evil spirit. As long as the unknown creature gave Brigette what she desired, she could call herself Santa Claus.

Accepting that she had no choice but to trust the stranger, she exited the cell and hurried through a hidden door. The merman stayed just out of sight as he led her through the maze of stairs and long hallways, but Brigette didn't mind. She wanted distance between them. It meant she would have ample warning if he was trying to lure her into an ambush.

She climbed another flight of stairs, her eyes narrowing as she realized they had not only left behind the stark, barren walls of the dungeon, but they were now in the main section of the castle.

Where the hell was the stranger leading her?

* * * *

Basq followed Chaaya and the gargoyle out of the portal. Stepping to one side, he faded into the shadow that wrapped around him. He didn't have a lot of flashy talents. He couldn't cause earthquakes or take out the power grid. But he did have the ability to create a darkness to shroud himself, or he could spread it to fill this entire castle. He liked to go unnoticed. An unseen attacker was far more lethal.

Quickly, he glanced around, taking in the long room that was decorated with elaborate murals on the walls and a high ceiling with massive chandeliers. Beneath his heavy boots was a smooth marble floor, and at the far end was a dais with a massive throne.

Once assured there was nothing hidden in the shallow alcoves, Basq turned to study the Queen of Mer-folk, who was standing just a few feet away.

She didn't look like a queen. Or even a mermaid. She was as tall as Basq with a broad blocky body that was squashed into a hideous gown with a too-small crown perched on her large, square head.

Basq had heard Chiron mention Inga, so her appearance didn't interest him. Instead he silently admired the skillful ease with which she held the mighty trident. This was a female who he wanted standing beside him in a battle. And that was the finest compliment he could offer.

Basq's gaze moved to land on Chaaya.

She was another warrior.

It didn't matter that she was barely five foot and weighed less than a hundred pounds. Or that she'd once been human. He'd witnessed her take down a drunken goblin after he'd grabbed her ass at one of the filthy demon clubs she liked to visit. Basq had been trailing behind her, but before he could react, she'd grabbed the goblin and launched him across the bar to hit the wall with a sickening thud. Chaaya had strolled on as if nothing had happened.

That was the night his annoyed resignation at being her babysitter had transformed into a dangerous fascination.

Inga stepped forward, the trident lowering as if in a gesture of peace. "Thank you for coming," she said, speaking directly to Chaaya.

Predictably the woman folded her arms over her chest, looking peevish. She might be a warrior, but her people skills sucked. They were even worse than his, something he never believed possible.

"I shouldn't have," Chaaya complained. "You kicked me out of here."

Inga blushed, but she held her ground. "I did it for your own good. My people had become convinced that you not only cheated at cards but that you were stealing from our treasury. They wanted you thrown in the dungeons."

Chaaya sniffed. "I borrowed one stupid tiara and suddenly I'm a thief?"

Inga arched a brow. "Borrowed?"

"I gave it back."

"You stuck it on top of a statue of Neptune."

"He looked like he needed a crown." Chaaya shrugged. "I gave him one."

"What about the crystal globes that were a formal gift from the Queen of the Dew Fairies?"

"One of your guards dared me to juggle them." Chaaya shrugged. "I forgot I couldn't juggle."

Inga clenched her pointed teeth. Basq didn't blame the female. Chaaya was an acquired taste.

Taste... Basq's fangs suddenly lengthened, eager for a sip of the mysterious woman. Damn. His awareness of her was becoming increasingly difficult to ignore.

"My job is tough enough without you creating chaos," Inga said, her tone grim.

"I hear you," Basq murmured, releasing his shadow. They were wasting time with this bickering. Ignoring Chaaya's glare, Basq concentrated on the Queen of the Mer-folk. "Perhaps you should tell us why we're here."

Inga visibly gathered her rattled composure. "A few hours ago, a guard came to me to say that he'd heard Brigette talking to herself. He also swears that he could see a shadow next to her."

"What security do you have in place?" he asked.

Inga arched a brow. "You mean beyond being a mile beneath the water and isolated from the world?"

He held her gaze. "Yeah, beyond that."

The ogress blew out a weary sigh. "I have guards, of course, and no one is allowed in Brigette's cell but me."

"How is she fed?" Chaaya abruptly demanded.

"A slot in the door," Inga responded.

Chaaya absently stroked the hilt of her spear. Basq noticed that it was a habit she had when she was deep in thought.

"Could she have talked to whoever delivered the food?"

Inga shrugged. "I suppose it's possible, but the guard would surely have noticed if there was a servant there?"

Chaaya blinked, realizing everyone was gazing at her in confusion. "I'm just trying to imagine how she could be in contact with anyone. Who knows that she's locked in the dungeon? And how could they have created a connection to Brigette?"

Basq nodded in silent approval at the questions. It would be dangerous to leap to the conclusion that Brigette was communicating with the evil beast named Zella. It could easily be that the Were was crazed from her time in the dungeons and that the guard had mistaken a common shadow for something more sinister. Or perhaps another creature was attempting to release the Were for its own mysterious reasons.

They had to approach this with a logical investigation, not panic at the thought of Zella returning to this world.

"What about magic?" he asked.

Inga decisively shook her head. "The dungeons are created to dampen magic. It keeps anyone from creating a portal or using a cloaking spell to escape."

"Is she still in the dungeons?"

Inga nodded. "Yes."

"How many prisoners are you holding in the dungeons?" he asked.

"Just Brigette."

That was exactly what Basq wanted to hear. The fewer factors contaminating the area, the easier it would be to pinpoint what was happening with the Were.

"How many guards?"

"One in the actual dungeons, plus two more at the outer door."

"Have you made sure that they haven't been infected?" Basq pressed, sensing Chaaya's startled glance. Did she assume he hadn't been paying attention when Chiron questioned her about the endless centuries she'd spent trapped with the beast?

Inga considered his question before giving a shake of her head. "I didn't notice anything."

Chaaya determinedly gained control of the encounter. She might pretend to be a feckless teenager, but she was a natural leader.

"You shouldn't take any chances," she warned Inga. "Until we know if this has anything to do with Zella, you should have the guards put into quarantine."

"What about Brigette?" Inga asked. "Should I—"

The queen's words were cut short at the sound of shouting from the outer corridor. Instantly they all turned to watch as one of the doors to the throne room was shoved open to reveal a guard in scaled armor.

"What's happening, Jord?" the queen demanded.

"The prisoner has escaped," the male rasped.

"Brigette?" Inga demanded, although they all knew who it was.

The guard nodded, his narrow face flushed, as if he'd been running to deliver his warning.

Inga made a strangled sound of disbelief. "Call for Rimm to have the castle searched from top to bottom."

"Stay here," Chaaya commanded. "I'll go."

Basq grabbed her arm, preventing her from heading toward the door. "Wait."

She deliberately glanced at his fingers wrapped around her upper arm. "Hey, Mr. Grabby, let go."

He held on tight, even knowing she could…what was the word? Fade? Evaporate? Become incorporeal? Whatever.

"No." Basq and Inga spoke in unison.

The queen scowled. "It's my duty."

"I'm the only one that can't be infected by the evil," Chaaya reminded them.

"We don't know what the darkness is yet," Basq stubbornly insisted. "There are a lot of evil things that can crawl out of the darkness."

"The bloodsucker isn't wrong," Levet said, reaching up to touch Inga's large hand. "You cannot expose yourself, *ma belle*."

Inga scowled, but she didn't pull away from the gargoyle. Basq rolled his eyes. What was it with Levet and females? He must have some mystical ability to blind them to his annoying personality.

There was no other explanation.

"It's my duty," the queen muttered again.

"No. As I've been repeatedly told, this is *my* duty," Chaaya said, glancing toward Basq. "Just mine. You're not going with me." Basq shrugged. There was no point in arguing. She wasn't going to leave this room without him. Period. Chaaya made a sound of disgust as she glanced back at Inga. "Can you shoot him with your big fork?"

It was Levet who answered. "Is it not a magnificent fork? It does the most amazing things. I floated at the bottom of the ocean."

"It's not a fork, it's the Tryshu," Inga snapped. "And this is my castle."

Levet's wings fluttered. "And these are your people. They can't be protected if the beast manages to destroy you."

Inga looked like she'd swallowed a bag of lemons, but it appeared the gargoyle managed to convince her to remain out of danger.

"I hate sitting around twiddling my thumbs," the ogress groused.

"Contact your guards that were in the dungeons and have them isolated away from the public areas," Chaaya told the queen, heading toward the door. "And make sure no one enters Brigette's cell."

"Be careful, *chérie*," Levet called out.

Basq silently followed Chaaya toward the open door where they could hear the sound of shouts in the distance. Obviously, the search for the Were was on. Abruptly the female halted, turning to glare at him.

"I know you enjoy being a pain in the ass, but—"

"No."

"Basq."

"Chaaya."

Chaaya grabbed the hilt of her spear. "Someday I'm going to stab you through the heart, and no one would blame me."

"You're welcome to try," Basq assured her.

"Ass."

"Brat."

"Argh."

They were still glaring at one another when there was a whooshing sound from behind the throne, and they turned to watch one of the murals slide open to reveal a hidden tunnel.

Basq frowned, expecting a guard to appear. Instead a slender female with long red hair and a desperate expression came skidding into the room.

"Brigette," Chaaya snarled.

Chapter 4

Chaaya jerked the spear from the holster at her side, her gaze locked on the redheaded Were.

"Everyone stay back," she warned, using her evil radar to try and detect any hint of the beast.

Brigette's eyes widened in horrified surprise as she caught Chaaya's scent, obviously not expecting to find her in the throne room. The two females had never met face-to-face until Brigette had been locked in mer-folk dungeons, but they'd been involved in an epic struggle over the past five hundred years. Chaaya had sacrificed everything to keep the beast locked in the hell dimension, while the Were had sold her soul to try and release the tide of evil.

"You," the Were rasped, skidding to a halt. "What the hell are you doing here?"

Chaaya blew a kiss toward the younger female. "Aren't you happy to see me?"

Brigette peeled back her lips, releasing a growl. "Like the plague."

"That's not nice," Chaaya chided, taking a cautious step toward the female.

The Were reached beneath her drab gray robe to reveal a small trident. The same type of weapon used by the mer-folk guards.

"You were killed once," Brigette sneered. "Are you eager for another taste of death?"

Chaaya snorted, taking another step forward. "I'm not afraid of you, dog."

"You should be. I'm even stronger than before."

"How?" Chaaya demanded.

"Zella returned my powers."

"Impossible. The beast is locked out of this world."

Brigette smirked. "Are you so sure?"

Was she? Reaching out with her senses, Chaaya felt...something. A strange hum of energy that wasn't Were. Then again, it wasn't the same black energy that she associated with the beast.

"Why can't I sense Zella's magic?"

"It was..." Brigette hesitated, her eyes darting from side to side. "Modified. It was the only way to reach me through the barrier."

Chaaya's brows snapped together. "You're lying."

Brigette waved the trident in a mocking gesture. "Come and find out."

"Chaaya," Basq called out, as if she needed his warning that the pureblooded Were was dangerous.

Idiotic leech.

"I got this," she snapped, not allowing her gaze to stray from the female.

Without warning, Brigette darted to the side, twirling the trident. "You so don't got this."

Chaaya scowled. Why was the female heading deeper into the throne room instead of trying to get back into the tunnel? She had to know she couldn't overpower all of them.

Chaaya pointed toward Basq. "Guard the door."

With a nod, Basq angled toward the double doors, passing close to the Were.

"Careful, leech." Brigette aimed her trident and shot out the silvery strands.

With a curse, Basq leaped back, but instead of pressing her advantage, Brigette moved to the side. She was going to end up in the corner. Was she expecting Zella to arrive and save her? Or was she just crazy?

Inga moved to stand next to Chaaya, her oversized weapon clenched in her large hand as she glared at the Were.

"How did you get out of your cell?"

Brigette shrugged. "I told you. I have the power."

Her words made Chaaya pause. In the hell dimension the beast had been a swirling tower of fire. When it'd managed to leak into this world it'd taken the shape of a human and called itself Zella. But whatever its form, it had never been capable of manipulating physical objects with its mind.

"The power to unlock a cell door?" Chaaya challenged.

"I busted through."

"You physically smashed open the door?"

"Exactly."

Chaaya remained unconvinced. There was something off about this encounter. Not only the fact that she couldn't detect the evil pulse of the beast, but Brigette's bizarre behavior.

"And then you came to the throne room instead of escaping?" she demanded, inching her way forward.

"I deserve revenge for being caged like an animal." She glared toward Inga. This time there was no mistaking the sincerity of her words. A bleak expression twisted her pale features into a tight mask of hate.

With a flap of his wings, Levet scurried to stand directly in front of Inga. "*Non*, you will not hurt her."

They all gaped at the odd sight of the three-foot gargoyle standing guard in front of the hulking mongrel ogress. Then, clearing her throat and blinking her eyes, Inga pointed the Tryshu at Brigette.

"Enough," she snapped. "I promised Ulric that I'd keep you alive as long as you weren't a danger to my people. Now it's obvious you can't be trusted."

"Ulric." Brigette made a sound of disgust, but there was something in her eyes. Yearning? No, that couldn't be right. It was probably a trick of the light. The entire castled shimmered like the Las Vegas strip. "He's a fool."

"A fool for believing you could ever change," Chaaya muttered. Whatever her opinion of the male Were who'd hauled her out of the hell dimension, this female wasn't fit to kiss his hairy ass. Chaaya glanced toward Inga. "Kill her."

"No." Brigette lifted her trident and they all braced themselves for the attack. Chaaya wasn't entirely sure what all the weapon could do, and she didn't want any unpleasant surprises.

But even as she clenched her muscles and held her spear ready, Chaaya was caught off guard when Brigette didn't make a mad dash toward the nearby doors, or even back to the secret tunnel. Instead she leaped forward and grabbed Levet by one stunted horn.

Inga cursed, making a mad grab for the gargoyle, but Brigette was too quick. With a liquid speed, the female Were was standing several feet away, the gargoyle dangling from her fingers.

"Hey," Levet protested, his large fairy wings flapping in annoyance. "Let me go. You have pooties."

Brigette frowned down at her captive. "What?"

Levet swung back and forth, trying to break free from the Were's grip. "Evil beastie germs."

"Cooties?" Brigette asked.

"*Oui*, cooties."

Brigette lifted Levet higher, studying him in confusion. "Have you taken a blow to the head?"

"A question we've all asked," Basq murmured.

Levet stuck out his tongue. "You are not a part of this conversation, leech."

Basq growled, flowing forward. His expression was hard with anger, but Chaaya wasn't fooled. This vampire never lost control of his emotions. Never. She assumed that he was hoping to catch Brigette off guard by pretending to be focused on Levet.

There was a momentary bafflement on Brigette's face, then she pressed the trident against Levet's neck.

"Stop."

"Everyone stay back," Inga commanded.

Chaaya sent the queen a warning glance. "We can't let her escape, Inga. If she has been in contact with Zella, then she'll spread the darkness like an infection. The mer-folk will be destroyed."

She saw the wrenching fear that flared through Inga's blue eyes. The female was clearly distressed by the thought of choosing between Levet and her people. Before she could answer, however, Brigette called out.

"Do anything stupid and I'll kill him."

Chaaya turned her head to watch the female back toward the corner. She swung Levet back and forth like a pendulum, her trident still pressed against his throat.

"Don't be an idiot," Chaaya snapped. "You can't kill a gargoyle with that tiny weapon."

"That is true," Levet agreed, his tail dragging against the marble floor. "I have had many demons attempt to be rid of me, including my own mother. I am really quite difficult to destroy."

Brigette took two more steps back. "Not after I feed you to the beast."

Inga stiffened, clearly intending to attack. "Don't you dare hurt him."

"Stay back, Inga," Chaaya warned. "We have her trapped."

"Never!" Brigette released a shrill laugh. "I'll never be caged again."

Chaaya started to roll her eyes at the female's hysterical proclamation. There was nothing worse than a drama queen. But even as she was about to mock the female's fierce assertion, a shimmer of darkness captured her attention.

What the hell?

It was Inga who was first to recognize the danger. "A portal."

Chaaya cursed, realizing that they they'd been manipulated by the female Were.

Brigette had obviously known the portal was about to form there. Or maybe it'd been there all along and hadn't opened until Brigette was close enough to trigger it.

Whatever the case, they'd been idiots. And now the world was about to pay the price for their inability to stop the Were.

"Levet!" Inga cried out, charging toward the portal as Brigette stepped through the opening and disappeared with the gargoyle.

The ogress moved with surprising speed, but Chaaya easily passed her as she headed into the portal. She had to get in before it closed, or they'd never manage to follow Brigette. She was diving into the darkness when she felt icy fingers wrap around her upper arm.

Turning her head, she sent Basq a glare of disbelief. How had he managed to catch up to her? And why?

"Seriously?" she hissed between clenched teeth, the world dropping away as they were sucked through the swirling tunnel.

His gorgeous face was set in lines of grim determination. "You're not going anywhere without me."

* * * *

Brigette tried to shake off the stupid gargoyle that clung to her like an oversized leech. She hadn't intended to take him into the portal, but even as she'd let loose of his horn, he'd reached up to grasp her wrist. Now they were locked together as they hurtled through the strange portal.

Dammit. Nothing was going right.

After leaving her cell she'd been led on a merry goose chase through the castle, heading ever upward. The unknown merman had at least left a weapon for her before he urged her into the secret tunnel. She'd paused, searching the shadows to make out who was helping her, but it'd been impossible to catch more than long hair and the delicate features of all mer-folk. At last she'd grabbed the weapon and scurried through the narrow tunnel.

The last thing she'd expected was to burst into the throne room, which was filled with her most hated enemies. Chaaya, the bane of her existence. Inga, Queen of the Mer-folk. The strange gargoyle named Levet. And a leech who vibrated with a power she could feel from across the long room.

She'd instantly known she was a dead dog. Literally.

Then she'd caught the shimmer of power in the far corner. That was her exit. It had to be. She just had to stay alive long enough to get to it.

Something easier said than done.

Knowing the only thing that might keep the demons at bay was the fear that she still possessed the power of the beast, she'd babbled about Zella as she'd covertly circled toward the corner. Next she'd grabbed the tiny gargoyle. By then she'd been close enough to make a dash for the portal.

She'd intended to toss the creature aside as she entered the darkness, using him as a distraction to keep anyone from following her.

A mistake she was paying for as Levet weighed her down, making them sluggishly zigzag from side to side.

"Let go of me, you fool," she growled.

The large fairy wings flapped, glittering even in the darkness. "Not until you return us to the mer-folk castle."

She shook her arm in the rhythm of her words. "Not. Going. To. Happen."

Levet raised his free hand. "Return us or I will blast you with my awesome fireball."

Brigette growled in frustration. They continued to move through the darkness, but they'd slowed to a snail's pace. What was going on? Was it the portal? Or had the gargoyle done something to block their passage?

"You are ruining everything."

"*Moi?*" Levet sounded outraged. "I did not kidnap you and haul you into this very peculiar portal."

Once again Brigette tried to shake him off. "Go away."

Levet clicked his tongue. "I did warn you."

"What are you…" Brigette forgot what she was going to say as she caught sight of the flames that were forming in the palm of Levet's tiny hand. Christ. This portal was already weird enough. Who knew what would happen if the gargoyle used his magic? "No."

The word was still on her lips when the blast ripped through the darkness. Heat and pain hammered into Brigette as she cartwheeled through the air, her stomach heaving and her brain scrambled when she abruptly tumbled out of the portal and hit the ground with enough force to crack a rib.

Beside her a small form skidded over the cobblestone street, his wings spread wide.

"Ow," Levet groused.

"Dammit."

Brigette shoved herself to her feet, groaning as she struggled to stay upright. The pain from her rib combined with the disorientation of being tossed into a strange place made her knees weak. Of course, that was the least of her worries. First she had to get away from the aggravating Levet, and then…

Well, she'd worry about that very long list of worries once she'd shaken off the gargoyle.

Turning away from the creature, she took a step forward, only to feel a tug on her wrist. She growled, glaring down at her arm. She expected to find the gargoyle grabbing her, but he was still lying on the road. Instead, a glistening rope was wrapped around her wrist and flowed down to encircle the gargoyle's waist.

Like a sparkly leash.

She glared at the creature in outrage. "What have you done?"

Levet rose to his feet, tilting his head as he studied the glittering rope. "It appears we are magically bound together."

She bared her teeth. "Then unbound us."

He furrowed his brow. "I do not believe that is a word." He shrugged. "Of course, people are forever correcting me, so—"

"Do it!"

The gargoyle sniffed. "There is no need to yell," he protested, grabbing the rope around his waist and giving it a tug. "I cannot undo it."

Unease slithered down her spine. "Why not?"

"I don't know how it happened. I only intended to disrupt the portal with my fireball." The gargoyle continued to tug at the mystery cord. "This must have been a side effect. If you ask me, there is something cloudy about the magic that you used to form the portal."

Brigette scowled in confusion. "Cloudy?"

"*Non*, that is not right." Levet took a second before he snapped his fingers. "Shady. *Oui*. Shady about the magic."

Brigette prepared to grab the creature and shake him until he got rid of the leash, but there was something in his curious expression that suggested he was as surprised as she was that they were bound together.

"Perfect," she snarled. "I'm freaking tied to a yapping paperweight in the middle of…" She forgot her anger toward the gargoyle as she belatedly glanced around. "Where are we?" she demanded, her gaze moving toward the pine trees that lined the cobblestone road.

In the darkness it was impossible to see more than thick shadows and hints of movement among the branches. Brigette grimaced, turning her attention to the large town that glowed in the valley below.

She could make out large, gray stone buildings with thatched roofs and narrow streets that were lit by torches. It looked exactly like London during the Victorian era.

Had they been sucked back in time?

"How should I know where we are?" Levet intruded into her thoughts. "You were the one who brought us here."

"It wasn't me." She glared at him. "Weres can't create portals."

"Was it Zella? I don't like her." Levet wrinkled his snout. "She smells like poopy."

Brigette closed her eyes, trying to reach out to the voice that had promised her salvation. There was nothing. An empty void. Which meant that she clearly wasn't where she was supposed to be.

"Crap," she muttered. "The connection has been broken."

"The connection to who?" Levet studied her with more interest than fear. "Zella?"

"Shut up."

Levet stuck out his tongue. "Dogs are the worst."

Brigette yanked on the leash, dragging the gargoyle over the cobblestones. "One more word and I'll eat you."

"No need to be testy." Levet sniffed the air, glancing around. "I think we must be in another dimension. Or perhaps between dimensions."

Ah. That made sense. If they were between dimensions, that would explain why she lost contact with the voice.

"I have to find her," she muttered, heading down the road and dragging the gargoyle behind her.

"Wait. Stop," Levet protested. "Where are we going?"

"I don't have a damned clue."

Chapter 5

Basq was prepared as the portal shuddered and they were abruptly tossed out. He didn't have the ability to sense magic, but he did know that the explosion that'd rocked past them was bound to cause a disruption.

"Stay still," he commanded, holding tight to the struggling Chaaya, as he released his powers.

The female stiffened as a smothering darkness cloaked the area around them. Not just shadows, but a blinding night that not even demon sight could penetrate. It would keep them from being seen by potential enemies, as well as protect him in case they happened to be dumped on a sunny beach.

"What did you do?" Chaaya asked.

"Wrapped us in my powers."

"Nice trick." There was no mistaking the hint of surprise in her voice. As if she never dreamed that he might be useful.

He smiled wryly. He'd devoted centuries to hiding his innate skills, not only because he didn't want to be used as a weapon, but to maintain his independence. It wasn't until Chaaya came to Vegas that his image of a solid, boringly predictable male started to chafe at him.

Why?

A question he didn't intend to answer.

"I have my moments," he said dryly.

"If you say so." She shifted impatiently in his arms. "Do you have any idea where we are?"

Pretending he didn't feel a pang of hurt at her eagerness to get away from him, Basq allowed his senses to spread outward.

He caught the familiar scent of Were and granite. Brigette and Levet. The smell had already faded to mere wisps that would soon disappear entirely, which meant they were no longer in the area. Beyond that there was nothing but pine trees and the distant stench of smoke.

Cautiously he released his powers, allowing the darkness to drain away. They were standing in the middle of an empty field shrouded in the thankful darkness of night. Behind them was a forest of pine trees and ahead was a city that sprawled through a narrow valley.

It was a lovely bucolic sight, but even Basq knew that it wasn't real.

"We're in a bulla," he said.

Chaaya regarded him with a puzzled frown. "A what?"

He wasn't surprised that she didn't know about bullas. They weren't like the space where she'd been trapped for all those centuries. That had been a permanent foyer between two worlds. This wasn't natural. It was created by a powerful magic.

"They're small pockets between dimensions," he told her, his gaze continuing to probe for any hidden dangers.

Stepping away from him, Chaaya shoved her spear into the holster at her side. The moonlight danced over her delicate features and silhouetted her slender body encased in the leather jacket and matching pants. She appeared terrifyingly fragile. At least until one caught sight of the ancient power that smoldered in her dark eyes.

"Have you been here before?"

Basq shook his head. "Not this particular one, but I've visited several others over the centuries."

"Well, well. You're just a never-ending bundle of surprises."

He ignored her sarcasm. It was only when she wasn't being a smart-ass that he had to worry.

"What happened to the portal?"

She grimaced, reaching up to touch a small scorch mark on her cheek. "There was some sort of glitch."

"Glitch?"

She shrugged, turning in a slow circle as she tried to adjust to their new surroundings.

"I'm guessing Levet released some sort of magic that made it collapse. It dumped us here."

Basq hissed. Levet was like a plague. He would appear at Chiron's without warning, cause utter devastation, and then disappear.

"That creature is a menace."

"I assume he was trying to help." She sent him a narrow-eyed glare. "Like some other interfering pain in the ass I know."

He shrugged. Did she honestly think he was going to let her chase after the Were without him? Not a chance in hell.

"Brigette was here." He pointed toward the far side of the field. "I caught her scent when we first arrived."

Easily distracted, Chaaya whirled to study the low hedge that lined the cobblestone street.

"Can you track her?"

"No, it's already dissipating."

"So quickly?"

"Places like this are created to dampen a demon's presence."

She turned back, her expression suspicious. "Why would anyone create a place to dampen a demon's presence?"

"Because most come here to hide from their enemies or simply disappear for a while."

She continued to study him with a searching gaze, but at last accepting that she had no choice but to accept that he was telling her the truth, she heaved a harsh sigh.

"Well, that sucks," she muttered. "How am I going to find her?"

"You can't," Basq bluntly informed her. "We need to return to the mer-folk castle."

She snorted, heading for the road. "Not until I have Brigette in my hands. Dead or alive."

Basq's fangs throbbed with frustration. He'd spent endless centuries moving from one place to another, always keeping others at a distance. And even when he'd traveled to Vegas to join Chiron, he'd maintained a sense of isolation. He didn't let anyone ruffle his composure.

And then Chaaya had arrived at Dreamscape, and she'd busted through his carefully constructed barriers. Or maybe she'd used her mysterious abilities to ghost through them.

Either way, she had a unique talent for rousing the emotions he didn't even know he possessed.

Basq stood still as Chaaya crossed the field. His gaze lowered to take in her fine ass that filled out the leather pants with slender perfection before returning to the shoulders that were set to a stubborn angle. He'd known all along that she was destined to drive him crazy. That's why he'd tried to convince Chiron to find someone else to act as her babysitter.

Now he was stuck with her. At least until he could get her back to Vegas.

With long strides, he was walking at her side. "Brigette could be anywhere by now."

"You just said you could smell her."

"She was dumped here, like us. But she more than likely has already found another portal," he insisted.

She jumped over the hedge and started down the cobblestone road. "No. She's here."

In a blur of motion he was once again walking next to her. "How do you know?"

"Just a feeling."

"A feeling?"

"Yeah, feeling." She sent him a mocking smile. "Some of us have more than ice flowing through our veins, leech. We have emotions and intuitions and feelings and..."

Without warning, Basq reached out to grasp her arm. A strange sensation churned through him. Not anger—or at least, not precisely—but a potent combination of need and frustration and something he couldn't name. Coming to a halt, he turned her to meet his fierce gaze.

"Keep it up," he growled.

She met his glare without fear. "And?"

The air between them suddenly erupted with a fierce desire. It sizzled and snapped with a tangible force, as if the awareness they both kept tightly leashed had suddenly been ignited by their proximity.

"Neither of us wants to find out," he warned in a soft tone.

Her mouth parted as if she intended to make a smart-ass comment, but then their eyes clashed and she abruptly snapped her lips shut, jerking her arm free.

"She's in this dimension," she insisted, stomping down the road. "I don't know how I know. My powers are like me. Weird, unpredictable, and usually worthless. But I know."

Basq resisted the urge to try and stop her. He'd already discovered what happened when he touched her. Combustible desire. Besides, neither of them had the ability to open a portal. They were going to have to find someone in the city to help.

"You are many things, Chaaya," he muttered, walking into the valley. "But you're not worthless."

* * * *

Inga clutched the mighty Tryshu in her hand as she watched Troy saunter into the throne room. He had changed into white leather pants that molded to his long legs and a bright blue Hawaiian shirt he left open to reveal his impressive six-pack.

"Well?" she demanded.

Troy halted next to her, his long crimson hair shimmering like fire in the light of the chandeliers.

"They're still searching," he told her.

Inga made a sound of frustration. It'd been Troy who had insisted that she remain in the castle while he sent out several mer-folk to search for Brigette.

"How hard can it be to find a three-foot gargoyle?"

Troy wrinkled his nose. He had an ongoing competition with Levet. Inga didn't entirely understand it. Some male ego thing that would never make sense to her.

"Unfortunately not hard enough," he drawled. "My point is that Levet is like a bad penny. He always returns. Usually when you least want him around."

Inga narrowed her eyes. She didn't care what anyone thought about the tiny gargoyle. He was precious to her. And even if he never returned her feelings, she would sacrifice everything to rescue him.

"I'm going to search for them," she announced in grim tones.

"Where?" Troy pressed, his sardonic expression easing as he regarded her with a hint of sympathy. "They could be anywhere in the world. Or even another dimension."

"I…" Inga heaved a sigh. The imp was right, of course. Once the portal closed, there was no way to follow it.

Troy reached to grab her free hand. "We need you here, my dear."

"Why?" She shook her head in disgust. "I've already proved I'm completely incapable at this stupid queen gig. I can't even keep a prisoner locked in my dungeons."

Troy squeezed her fingers. "Because you were betrayed."

"What?"

Releasing his grip on her fingers, Troy stepped back to regard her with a somber expression.

"It's the only explanation. Think, Inga," he insisted. "The dungeons are void of magic. No visitors are allowed without your personal approval. The only way for Brigette to escape was for one of the mer-folk to release her."

Inga flinched. His words hit her like a physical punch to the gut. Betrayed by one of her own people? No. It was bad enough they could barely glance her direction without shuddering in disgust. But outright treason…

"The beast could have opened her cell." She desperately tried to find some other explanation.

"If the beast could touch this world enough to open a cell, why not create a portal in the dungeon? Why bring her to the throne room before creating her escape route?"

His reasonable questions rasped against her raw nerves.

"What are you suggesting?"

"A trap." He deliberately paused. "For you."

Inga's jaw clenched until her teeth threatened to crack. "All the more reason I need to track them down."

"That's impossible." Troy held up a slender hand to halt her mutinous refusal to accept defeat. "Unless you discover Brigette's accomplice. Whoever opened her cell must know where she was going." His smile was a grim challenge. "Find your traitor and you'll find that damned gargoyle."

Inga forced herself to consider his words. As much as the thought that she'd been betrayed might hurt, Troy was right. She couldn't follow Levet through the portal. The only way to find him was to discover how Brigette had gotten out of her cell, and where she was headed.

"We'll start in the dungeon," she abruptly announced.

Troy bowed his head. "Lead the way, Your Majesty."

Chapter 6

Chaaya entered the dingy bar on the fringe of the city. Instantly the familiar atmosphere settled around her.

She felt at home in the dark, rancid space. The open timbered ceiling was low enough to brush against the heads of the gathered demons. The air was smoky from the open fireplace and thick with the stench of unwashed bodies and sour ale. Best of all, there was a thunderous noise from the drunken demons.

Chaaya's swagger returned as she elbowed her way through the crowd. She couldn't deny she'd been feeling wonky. Being blasted out of the bizarre portal to land in a bubble between dimensions tended to do that to a girl. And then Basq had grabbed her arm and all hell had broken loose.

Heat. Hunger. Lust.

Lots and lots of gut-clenching, knee-buckling lust.

Chaaya angrily shut down the memory of his touch. It had to have something to do with this weird-ass place. As long as Basq kept his paws to himself, then everything should be fine.

Right. Right?

Glancing around the room, her jaws clenched in disappointment. There were plenty of orcs, goblins, a few vampires, and a smattering of fey creatures. No Weres. And no gargoyles, stunted or otherwise.

Still, there was always the chance that someone had seen Brigette. It only made sense to order a grog and mingle. They needed to investigate, and after the day she'd had, she deserved a drink. Another one of those win-win situations.

"Where are you going?" Basq growled, flowing behind her as she forced her way toward the back of the room.

"To talk to the bartender."

"Why?"

"We need information. Bartenders have information."

"Just don't…"

She glanced over his shoulders as his words trailed away. "Don't what?"

"Cause trouble." A fierce frown touched his dangerously handsome face. "The last thing we want is to draw attention to ourselves."

"Me cause trouble? I don't know what you're talking about." She batted her lashes. She couldn't help herself. It was like a knee-jerk reaction. She told herself it was because she enjoyed pricking his icy composure.

Now… Well, she didn't want to consider why she was so eager to stir his emotions.

His eyes narrowed, the white in the center shimmering in the dull firelight. "Chaaya."

"Relax, Basq."

"Not a chance in hell," he growled.

Chaaya snorted before turning back to shove aside a tall, dark-haired Sylvermyst so she could press against the wooden bar. Then she slammed her hand on the counter.

"Who the hell is running this joint?" she called out.

A blocky male with a bald head that was covered with intricate tattoos and wearing long linen shirt and loose pants stomped to stand in front of her. His crimson eyes and pointed teeth revealed he had ogre in his gene pool, but he was too small to be full-blooded.

"What do you want?" he snapped.

"Grog for me." She nodded toward Basq, who had moved to stand next to her. "Blood for my partner."

The bartender nodded toward a group of nymphs who stood in a miserable huddle across the room.

"Fresh?"

Basq curled his lip in disgust. "No."

"Suit yourself." The bartender turned to grab a large stein and filled it with a grog that burned with blue flames. Next he reached beneath the bar to fill a crystal glass with ruby red blood. He set the drinks in front of them. "Cash or trade?"

Chaaya puckered her lips. "How about on the house?"

The male leaned forward, his foul breath nearly sending Chaaya to her knees.

"How about I—" He brows snapped together, his broad nose flaring as if he was testing the air. "Hey. What are you?"

Chaaya grabbed her grog and took a deep gulp. It burned down her throat before hitting her stomach with an explosion of fire. She placed the empty stein on the counter.

"A mongrel." She shrugged. "Like most of your customers."

He stubbornly shook his head. "No. I've been around thousands and thousands of mongrels. You're unique."

"That's true."

"So what are you?"

Chaaya motioned the bartender closer. "If I tell you, you can't let anyone else know."

The man leaned in. "I swear."

Chaaya lowered her voice until the clamor echoing through the bar nearly drowned out her words.

"I'm a unicorn."

The male's jaw dropped in shock. "Unicorns are real?"

Chaaya waggled her brows. "Wanna see my horn?"

There was a momentary confusion, then the bartender's eyes flashed a brilliant crimson and his lips pulled back in a snarl.

"Pay up and get out."

"Here." Without warning, Basq slapped a gold coin on the counter. But even as the bartender reached out, Basq covered it with his hand. "We need information."

The bartender scowled. "What sort of information?"

"Where can we buy a portal?"

"Hey." Chaaya glared at her companion. Dammit. She should have known he'd only agreed to search for Brigette in the city so he could try and force her back to Vegas.

He held her gaze with a cool composure. "I never stay anywhere without an exit plan."

"Oh." She nodded. "That's legit."

The bartender pointed toward a table near the back door. "The imp sitting against the wall will take you anywhere you want to go. For a price."

Chaaya studied the golden-haired male with a narrow face and pale green eyes. He was twirling a long dagger between his fingers and eyeing the crowd with a cynical expression.

"Can he be trusted?" she demanded.

The bartender snorted. "No one in this place can be trusted, but I doubt he'd want to piss off a vampire." He glanced toward Chaaya with a sneer. "Or a unicorn."

Chaaya shrugged. "Now my turn for information."

The bartender folded his arms over his impressive chest. "It's going to cost another coin."

Basq hesitated, then with a grudging reluctance he added another gold coin to the counter.

Chaaya leaned forward. She wanted the crowd noise to keep anyone from overhearing her question. She had no idea if this had been Brigette's final destination or if she'd been tossed out of the portal by the explosion. But she didn't want the bitch to know they were in the city looking for her.

"Have you seen a female Were pass by?"

The bartender looked genuinely surprised by the question. "I haven't seen a Were in this place for decades. There's no animals to hunt and not much room to run."

"What about a miniature gargoyle?" she pressed.

His eyes burned with crimson fire. Shoving the coins in his pocket, the bartender pointed his beefy finger in Chaaya's face.

"I've had enough of your smart mouth."

"Slow your roll, baldy. It was a genuine question. Levet's about three feet tall with big fairy wings and—"

"Argh." The bartended tilted his tattooed head back and released a savage growl.

The entire building shook with his outrage, and more than a few demons turned to study them with bloodthirsty curiosity. The entire room was obviously ripe for a fight.

"I'll take that as a no," Chaaya muttered, quickly turning to make her way back through the crowd.

There was a teeny tiny chance she'd outstayed her welcome.

"I told you not to cause trouble," Basq chided, his expression tight with disapproval.

"It wasn't my fault."

The words had just left her mouth when a large orc moved to stand directly in her path.

He was an ugly creature with small beady eyes and a football-shaped head that was covered with small tuft of fur. He wore shabby bits of clothes that looked like they were rotting off his massive body. It was his smell, however, that made Chaaya wrinkle her nose in disgust.

It hovered somewhere between a five-day-old corpse and swamp water.

A stench that could be used as a lethal weapon if she could figure out how to bottle it.

"Pretty girlie," he stuttered, his tusks making it hard to form words. He reached out as if intending to grab her.

In one smooth motion Chaaya had her spear pointed at the lower corner of the orc's stomach. That was its only weak spot.

"Don't touch."

The hand continued to stretch out. "Me want."

"Tough," she said, prepared to give him a good poke with her spear.

Instead Basq smoothly moved to stand between them, his fangs fully extended and shimmering with a lethal warning.

The orc dropped his hand, stomping his oversized foot. "Give me pretty girlie."

"Stay away," Basq commanded.

Chaaya clicked her tongue. Typical male. Always rushing in where he was least wanted.

"I got this," she snapped, pointing her spear toward the group of goblins who were charging in their direction. "You worry about them."

With a hiss, Basq whirled to the side, his arms held out as he prepared to halt the crush of demons.

Chaaya turned and twirled her spear. They needed to get out of the bar before the crowd decided to make them the night's entertainment. She might survive being ripped limb from limb, but it wouldn't be much fun.

"We're leaving," she told the orc. "I can go around you, or I can go through you. It doesn't matter to me which one it is."

The orc smiled, revealing his yellowed, chipped teeth. Had he been gnawing on granite? Bones? The gates of hell?

"Come and play, girlie."

"My name is Chaaya." She stepped forward. "Don't forget it."

"Cha cha," he mumbled.

Chaaya made a sound of disgust. "Orcs."

The demon looked offended. "Me eat cha cha."

Chaaya held her arms wide. "Come and get it."

Provoked into a reckless attack, the orc leaped forward. Skimming her fingers down the hilt of the spear, Chaaya ignited the magic in the carved glyphs. Sparks danced over her fingers and down the blade.

The orc didn't notice. He'd already dismissed the weapon. Copper didn't affect most demons, not like silver or iron. But what he didn't know was that it was imbued with the power of the druids.

Not even bothering to avoid the weapon in his determination to grab Chaaya, the orc's eyes widened in shock as the blade sliced through his thick hide. The cut wasn't deep enough to strike a vital organ, but it was painful. The orc jerked backward, gazing down in bafflement at the blood that flowed down his stomach.

Not giving him time to be pissed at being wounded, Chaaya lunged forward, stabbing her spear at the orc as he hastily backed away. Behind her the shrill cries of the goblins assured her that Basq was holding his own, but the rest of the customers were starting to crowd around to watch the fight. Or maybe just waiting for an opportunity to jump in.

Soon they would be surrounded with no way to make their escape.

Almost as if capable of reading her mind, Basq reached back to grab her hand just as he released his powers to wrap them in his smothering darkness.

Sounds of bafflement, even fear, echoed through the bar as the demons crashed into one another, all of them making a stampede toward the door. As far as they knew, the blinding darkness was caused by a terrifying magic.

Chaaya started to follow them only to be yanked tight against Basq's body as he led them in the opposite direction. They rammed into large bodies, but Basq possessed enough brute strength to forge a path forward. At last they reached the end of the bar, and locating the back door, Basq shoved her into the narrow alley.

* * * *

Brigette couldn't believe when she caught sight of Chaaya and the powerful vampire entering the bar less than a block away from where she was standing.

She had to be cursed. What else could explain being offered her heart's desire and then having it snatched away by a lump of granite who was currently strapped to her wrist, and a strange ghostly female who refused to go away?

And worse, she was now forced to seek a means to move around undetected. Scurrying through the alleys, she at last climbed into the dank, narrow sewer that she hoped would lead her to the center of the city.

"You said this place was magical," she groused, glaring down at the gargoyle who was skipping to keep up with her long strides.

Levet's wings fluttered and he carefully held his tail out of the nasty water that flowed through the tunnel.

"It is."

"Then why does it smell like shit?"

"Perhaps because we are walking through the sewers?" Levet suggested, wrinkling his snout. "Which is baffling considering there is a perfectly good road above us that we could be using."

She sent her unwanted companion a sour glance. "I'm not prancing through the streets. Not when that bitch is nosing around looking for me."

"Chaaya is not a bitch," Levet protested. "She is a very nice ghostie girl who makes me laugh."

"She's a freak."

"Like me."

"Exactly like you."

There was a long pause as they splashed through the slimy water. Brigette ground her teeth, refusing to admit she might regret her words. The gargoyle *was* a freak. Plus he was an annoying, ceaselessly yakking pain in her ass. There was no reason to feel guilty that she might have hurt his feelings. No reason at all.

"I know why you're so mean." The gargoyle abruptly broke the silence.

Brigette snorted, halting as the tunnel came to a V. "Because I'm evil. Ask anyone."

"*Non.* Zella was evil. You were a foolish child who allowed your pride to lead you into the darkness."

Brigette clenched her hands, pretending she was trying to decide which way to go. Inside, her stomach was churning with emotions that scalded like lava.

"You know nothing about me."

Levet shrugged. "Perhaps not, but I do know what it feels like to desire to be part of a family and yet never truly belonging."

Brigette instinctively shook her arm, as if she could rid herself of the leash that kept her tied to the aggravating creature.

"I was loved by my pack," she snapped.

Levet regarded her with an unnervingly steady gaze. "But it wasn't enough, was it?"

She peeled back her lips, intending to expose her elongated canine teeth. Then she flinched as her wolf remained dormant. Each time it refused to answer her call was like another knife through her heart.

Her harsh sigh echoed through the branches of the sewers. She was tired, and dirty, and she'd never been so conscious of the unbearable weight of her sins. It felt like they were going to crush her.

"No, it wasn't enough," she muttered.

Levet tilted his head to the side. "What did you want?"

Against her will, Brigette's memories seared through her mind. She hadn't lied when she said she was loved. Her pack had been a small, tightly knit group who lived in isolation. But from the moment she was born, Brigette had been afflicted with a restless sense of dissatisfaction. It was as if there was a hole inside her and she couldn't find anything to fill it. And worse, her cousin appeared to be born beneath a lucky star, and he didn't even appreciate what he had.

"I wanted what Ulric had," she admitted, the words jerked from her lips. "A powerful father who was admired by his family, and the knowledge that someday I would be given my own pack to lead."

Levet blinked in confusion. "Why not leave? Weres are able to join other packs or even create their own, are they not?"

"Because an easier path was offered to me."

Brigette didn't add that she'd been a coward at heart. While she was in her pack, she was a spoiled, pampered princess who never had to worry about doing more than complaining she was being oppressed by her father. The thought of leaving her pack and forging her own path in the cruel, dangerous world had been too daunting.

Levet wrinkled his snout. "Zella?"

"Yeah, Zella."

"Did you know the cost?"

Her memories of her lazy, peaceful childhood were jarringly replaced with the screams of her people as she'd hidden deep in the burrow. She jammed her hands over her ears, but still the screams echoed through her.

They still echoed...

"I suppose I did," she muttered.

"She deceived you?"

Brigette had clutched onto the belief that she been manipulated by the mystery woman. She'd even told herself that her mind had been clouded with an evil magic. It was easier than accepting the truth.

But now she was done with the pretense. She'd busted out of the mer-folk dungeons for one purpose. And that didn't include lying to herself.

"No." She squared her shoulders and headed down the tunnel angling to the east. It was as good as any. "But knowing the cost and paying the price are two different things."

Levet scurried to catch up. "*Oui.* That is true."

A burst of irritation raced through Brigette. She didn't want this creature's sympathy.

"Damn," she groused. "I'm never going to be able to wash off the stench of this place."

The gargoyle skipped and pranced beside her. "Where are we going?"

Her jaws locked with frustration. "First I'm going to find a place where we can hide until Chaaya leaves."

"And after that?"

"After that I'm going to get rid of you and finish what I started."

Chapter 7

Inga paced around the empty cell, her back bent to avoid banging her head on the low ceiling. The dungeons had been created for mer-folk, not ogres—something she might consider changing once she was done with the other billion things on her to-do list.

She tried to concentrate on the stark space that had been dug out of the bedrock. It wasn't easy. Her mind was consumed with fear for Levet.

What had Brigette done with him? Had they retreated to the dark dimension? Was the tiny gargoyle being tortured? Or worse?

A pain ripped through her heart but, grinding her teeth to hold back the roar of fury, she turned to watch Troy complete his inspection. His handsome face was hard with the same frustration that thundered through her as he shook his head.

"Nothing. I hoped we would find some clue."

About to concede defeat, Inga's gaze landed on the opening to the cell. She sucked in a deep breath as she hurried to survey the heavy metal door.

"There is one."

"What are you talking about?" Troy demanded.

"Brigette claimed she'd busted down the door with her dark powers," Inga reminded him.

Troy's eyes widened as he hurried to stand beside her, eyeing the door that hung on the hinges without a scratch.

"You're right." The imp studied the thick metal. "This wasn't forced."

"Could the lock have been picked?" she asked.

Troy pressed a hand to the center of his chest, his eyes wide with a faux innocence. "You ask that as if you believe I have some practice at picking locks, my dear."

Inga arched a brow. "Troy, so far you've managed to sneak into the wine cellars, the treasure room, and my mother's private library."

His lips twitched. "In my defense, I didn't know she was your mother when I snuck in."

Brigette's mouth dropped open. Granted, her mother was a beautiful woman who had been alone for centuries, but still... She was her mother.

"Troy," she protested.

Troy shook his head. "It's not that. The door was open one day and I noticed the cabinet lined with old and very rare artifacts. I wanted to check them out."

"They belonged to Riven." Inga shuddered at the thought of the previous leader of the mer-folk. He'd used one of the nasty weapons to sneak his way onto the throne, not to mention lying and manipulating Inga for centuries. "I wanted to throw them away, but my mother insisted that they be preserved until they've been studied."

Troy sent her a horrified glance. "She's right. They need to be protected from falling into the wrong hands."

Inga pointed the Tryshu toward the empty cell. "Obviously we're not very talented at protecting things." She shook her head in disgust before returning her attention to the door. "Can you tell if the lock was forced open?"

Troy bent down, inspecting the heavy lock that she'd had made out of pure silver. It wasn't the strongest metal, but it was toxic to Weres.

"It wasn't forced." Rising to his feet, Troy eyed her with a somber expression. "Someone used a key."

Inga's jaws clenched. There was no way a stranger could have snuck into this castle and then made their way to the dungeons without being noticed. Which meant that Troy had been right.

One of the mer-folk had betrayed her.

"We need to talk to the guards who were on duty," she announced in grim tones. Only a guard would have access to the dungeon keys. "Rimm will know who they were."

Troy tapped a slender finger against his chin, his expression distracted. "You go ahead."

"What are you going to do?"

A naughty grin touched his lips. "What I do best. Sneak around and poke my nose in where it doesn't belong." He tossed back his long hair. "One way or another, we're going to get the information we need."

She reached out to lay her hand on his shoulder. "Be careful, Troy," she warned. "We don't know who's helping Brigette. If it turns out to be the beast, then the traitor might already be tainted."

"Why, Your Majesty, are you worried about me?"

"Yes," she said without hesitation.

Troy had arrived in the castle just days after she'd been thrust into the role as queen. He'd been a strange, oddly exotic creature who had sauntered through the corridors with blatant sensuality and a mocking smile.

She hadn't known what to think of him, but he swiftly proved to be her most trusted advisor. And one of her few friends.

"Never fear." He winked as he headed down the narrow path between cells. "I fully intend to survive for an eternity."

* * * *

Fury thundered through Basq as he hauled Chaaya through the spiderweb of back alleys. He'd dropped his shield of darkness as soon as they'd left the bar. The power drained him at an alarming rate. He sensed he needed to conserve his strength whenever possible.

Especially if he was forced to spend time with Chaaya.

Another wave of fury beat through him. Once upon a time he'd smugly believed that nothing could disturb his ruthless calm. He was the master over his emotions. At all times. That was the only way to survive when he was forced to live in a world ruled by violence.

Then Chaaya slammed into his life…

Turning into a narrow lane, Basq ensured that there was no one around before he halted.

"What part of *don't cause trouble* didn't you understand?"

"It wasn't my fault—" Her eyes widened with shock as he pressed her against the gray stone building behind her. "Hey!"

Basq used his superior weight to keep her in place. Not that she couldn't easily escape if she wanted. All she had to do was go into her ghost mode. But he was trying to make a point.

"Chaaya, this isn't a game."

She reached up to plant her palms against his chest, her eyes smoldering with outrage.

"Back off, leech."

"Not until you hear what I have to say."

Her lips flattened, but she stopped struggling. "What?"

Basq nodded toward the building behind her. Through the rough stones he could hear the sounds of demons shouting and cheering. Indications of a fighting pit.

"These places aren't like the cheap clubs you're used to," he told her. "The demons who come here are hiding from justice or they're so violent they've been banished from the world. They destroy each other for fun."

Chaaya sniffed. "I'm invincible."

Basq's blood turned to ice at the flippant words. This female's blithe assumption that nothing could destroy her was the reason that Chiron had a guard following her at all times. Well, that and the fact that she wreaked havoc wherever she went.

"No, you're not," he denied between clenched teeth. "You don't understand your powers or your potential weaknesses. It's possible something you least expect might kill you." He paused, then continued in an effort to drive home his point. "Or force you to suffer unending pain."

Chaaya blinked, then she tilted back her head to laugh. "Oh, Basq, you were doing so good until the whole unending pain thing." She clicked her tongue. "That was over the top."

Could his head actually explode? Basq was beginning to think it was not only possible, but likely.

"Chaaya."

Without warning, Chaaya flickered out of sight only to reappear in the middle of the lane.

"I got it." She told him as he whirled to face her. "And I truly didn't mean to start the fight. It just happens."

"You are...." His hands clenched into impotent fists as her lips twitched with evil amusement. "We need to get out of here and get help," he snapped.

She folded her arms over her chest. "Can you find this place again?"

Basq parted his lips to lie. Not only did they need backup to locate Brigette, but he needed space from this aggravating female. But the knowledge that what little trust she had in him would be forever destroyed forced him to reluctantly shake his head.

She narrowed her eyes. "I'm not leaving until I find Brigette."

He hissed in frustration. "Why are you being so stubborn?"

He expected her to ignore the question. Or flip him off. That was her usual response. This time she glanced away, as if hiding her expression.

"Do you know how I became the sacrifice?"

Basq stilled. "No."

She kept her face averted. "I was sound asleep when the witches came to my village and dragged me out of my bed." Her voice was hard. Empty.

As if she'd stripped the memory of all emotion. "I was paraded out of my home in front of the entire village, who stood silent as I was tossed into a wooden cart and hauled away."

The words battered into Basq. It was all too easy to picture a young, frightened girl being ripped from everything and everyone she knew.

"Your family?" he demanded.

Her humorless laugh echoed through the narrow lane. "It was my mother who chose me as the one to be taken."

Basq flinched. "Why?"

"She didn't bother to say. She just waved goodbye as I screamed for her help." She paused to wet her lips, as if they were dry. "Less than an hour later I was in the burrow and the witches were slitting my throat."

"I'm sorry."

"I don't want your sympathy." She turned back to glare at him with a smoldering gaze. "I want you to understand why I'll do anything necessary to make sure Brigette isn't allowed to spread the beast's evil toxin."

"Shit." Basq conceded defeat. He'd lost this battle, but that didn't change his determination to get Chaaya out of this place and back to the safety of Vegas. "We need to find someplace to stay while we consider our options."

"Why?" Chaaya shrugged. "As you said, this place isn't that big. If we search building by building, we're bound to run across her."

"After our bar fight there's going to be people looking for us." As if to prove his point, the sound of a baying hellhound ricocheted between the buildings.

It was close. Too close.

Chaaya scowled. "What people?"

"The bar owner. The orc." He waved a hand. "Whoever's in charge of this place."

She continued to look unconvinced. Aggravating ghost.

"I thought you were telling me it's like the Wild Wild West with no rules except violence?"

"Every society has some sort of power structure," he insisted. He'd traveled to a dozen bullas over the centuries, and they all had one thing in common: greed. "The local chieftain will maintain whatever laws they want, but their primary responsibility is demanding a tithe from demons who enter their bulla," he told her. "Now that they know strangers are in their city without paying the entrance fee, they aren't going to be happy."

"Oh. Can't we just pay?"

"With what?" he asked. "I have a few coins, but not enough to satisfy a chieftain. Plus they usually want something besides money."

"Like what?"

He deliberately allowed his gaze to travel from the top of her shaven head to the tips of her leather boots.

"Like you."

Chaaya grimaced. "Point made," she muttered. "We'll find someplace to crash. At least until the demons settle down."

Basq closed his eyes, allowing his senses to flow outward. He could feel the heat of the numerous demons stuffed into the building next to them and catch the nasty scent of the sewer beneath their feet. Behind them the streets were littered with packs of demons, probably searching for them. Ahead was an empty building that was one stiff breeze away from collapse. Perfect.

"This way."

Chaaya easily kept pace with his long strides as they moved down the lane to enter the back courtyard.

"Why do you know so much about these places?" she asked.

Basq concentrated on their surroundings, refusing to be caught off guard. Too many demons possessed the ability to cloak their presence for him to accept there was nothing lurking in the shadows.

"I used them to stay hidden."

"Hidden from who?" She wrinkled her nose. "Or is it whom? I never remember."

"From the previous Anasso."

She looked genuinely startled by his answer. "Isn't the Anasso the title for the King of Vampires?"

Basq halted at the edge of the building, peering through a broken window. "He was never my king," he told Chaaya. "I was pledged to Tarak until he decided to join with the Anasso."

"You didn't want to be a part of the revolution?"

Basq wasn't surprised that she knew so much about the history of vampires. During the endless centuries she'd been locked in the hell dimension, she'd had the ability to peer into the world. There were few events that she hadn't tucked away in that clever, constantly curious brain.

"I choose Tarak to be my master because I was weary of war."

"Isn't that what the Anasso wanted? To unite the vampires?"

Basq curled his lips at the memory of the first King of Vampires. He'd been a massive, powerful creature who could make the earth tremble when he walked past. It was no wonder that the vampires had flocked to his side. He had the strength to demand their obedience. But Basq had seen something beneath the male's seeming determination to halt the vampire wars by creating one clan beneath his rule. There was a restless hunger in his eyes that had sent Basq fleeing from his promise of peace.

"That was his claim, but we all know what happens when you give a demon unlimited power." Basq shook his head in disgust. "It was only a matter of time before the Anasso went from benevolent leader to tyrant."

"And you were right."

"Unfortunately."

Basq leaned his head through the busted window, scanning the long room that was filled with broken furniture and shattered glass. There was the stench of charred wood, as if there'd been a fire. Or maybe it'd been caused by magic. Whatever the case, he couldn't sense anyone or anything inside.

Still, he carefully plucked out the remaining shards of glass from the window. In this sort of place you never entered a seemingly empty building through the front door. Not unless you were eager to fall into a trap.

"In here," he said, grabbing the frame and pulling himself into the building.

He braced himself for an attack, but there was nothing but a thick silence. Chaaya quickly followed behind him, landing so lightly she didn't even stir the dust coating the floor. Basq's heart clenched. Sometimes he wondered if she was even real. Or just a figment of his imagination that might suddenly evaporate in a puff of smoke.

Shaking away the strangely painful fear, Basq crossed the long room to push open a narrow door. As he'd hoped, there was a flight of stairs that led to the cellar below.

"This should do."

Motioning toward Chaaya, he headed down.

Chapter 8

Chaaya reluctantly entered the cold, damp cellar. The space was long and narrow with a dirt floor and stone walls. There were empty wooden barrels stacked at the far end and dried herbs hanging from the low ceiling. Closer there was a shelf covered in layers of dirt, indicating that no one had been down there for years. Maybe centuries.

Basq moved to grab a tablecloth that was tossed on a broken chair. Carefully shaking it free of dust, he placed it around her shoulders.

"It doesn't smell very good, but it should keep you warm."

Her mouth opened to inform him that she never noticed the temperature, no matter how extreme it might be, only to have the words die on her lips. It wasn't that she was pleased he was worried about her comfort. Of course not. That was just…lame. She was simply tired of squabbling. At least for now.

"I've had worse," she assured him, clutching the cloth around her as she plopped down on the hard ground.

It at least kept the dirt off her clothes.

With that astonishing grace that was unique to vampires, Basq sank down beside her.

"Yeah. Me too."

Chaaya leaned against the stone wall, turning her head to study Basq's fierce profile. Just for a second her stomach clenched with excitement. Not the fluttery butterflies she'd read about in her favorite stories but a brutal, all-consuming awareness.

"Tell me why," she abruptly demanded. Anything to keep herself from reaching out and touching that cold, perfect face.

He turned his head to send her a baffled frown. "Why what?"

"Why you went into hiding."

"I told you."

Chaaya shook her head. Ever since she arrived in Vegas she'd heard rumors about the mysterious Basq who'd returned to the Rebel clan after disappearing centuries before. None of the explanations of his leaving or his return had made sense to her.

And now his own explanation had only added to her puzzlement.

"If you didn't want to join with the Anasso's clan, why didn't you just walk away?" she asked. "As long as you weren't fighting against his leadership, I can't imagine he would care. After all, there had to be hundreds of vampires who weren't eager to become a part of the Anasso party crew."

A faint, secretive smile curved his lips. "You're the first to have worked that out. You have the mind of a warrior."

"A survivor," she corrected.

"Yes."

"Well?"

He paused. Not as if he was deciding whether to answer, but rather to choose his words with care.

So very Basq-like. Cautious. Meticulous. Dependable.

Everything that had been missing from her chaotic life.

"You've seen a portion of my power," he said, thankfully intruding into her idiotic thoughts.

"The darkness?"

He nodded. "I can spread it for miles and make it so thick that no demon can see through it."

She considered his words. "Impressive, but I don't understand what that has to do with the Anasso."

"I left my original clan because my sire insisted on using my powers to destroy his enemies."

She frowned. "How could your darkness do that?"

"He would arrange his warriors in hidden locations and then lure the rival clan into an ambush," Basq explained. "When they were at a precise spot, I would smother them in darkness so they could be destroyed."

Chaaya sensed his tension, as if he was recalling the precise moment he'd cloaked the vampires in blindness so his fellow clansman could cut them down with savage fury.

"Like lambs to the slaughter," she murmured.

His lips twisted into a humorless smile. "If you could ever compare lambs and vampires."

"You were tired of death, so you went into hiding?"

"First I joined with Tarak. He promised peace." Basq shrugged. "It was only when he pledged his loyalty to the Anasso that I left."

Chaaya couldn't deny a stab of admiration. Why not remain with his clan and simply do as he was asked? It would have been easier. And it wasn't like the vampires they battled against were some sort of choirboys. But he chose morals over comfort.

"Why did you travel to bullas?" she asked. "That seems a little extreme."

"The Anasso wasn't happy when I decided to leave, so he put out a reward for my return. My eyes make me distinctive enough that it was like walking around with a target on my back."

She studied his glorious eyes. They were more than distinctive. They had fascinated her since the night she'd first seen him in the Dreamscape Casino. And she wasn't the only female who'd sent covert glances his way. There'd been one nymph in particular who'd...

Chaaya shut down the thought as she realized she was clutching the spear at her side. As if she was mentally savoring the thought of punishing the nymph for even looking at Basq.

"Why did you go to Vegas?" she abruptly demanded.

"The new Anasso has proven he's an honorable leader."

Chaaya had met Styx. The huge Aztec warrior had shut down the entire electric grid when he'd discovered Levet had used his credit card to buy a treasure trove of Backstreet Boys action figures.

"He has an awesome sword," she said.

Basq frowned. Was that jealousy in his eyes? "It's big, I suppose," he said in dismissive tones.

"Exactly." She flashed a provocative smile. "Bigger is always better."

Basq leaned forward, wrapping her in his cool velvet power. "If you believe that, then you've been with the wrong sword," he assured her in a soft voice.

Chaaya choked as a white-hot hunger sizzled through her. Oh no. She was in trouble. Big, fat, ugly trouble.

She swayed forward, almost as if she intended to grab his face and kiss him. Then, with a stern effort, she forced her thoughts back to their conversation.

"So you trust the new Anasso?"

He nodded, his gaze wandering over her face as if memorizing each line and curve. "I'm willing to give him the benefit of the doubt."

"And you were tired of hiding?"

He nodded. "We have a lot in common."

Chaaya frowned at his ridiculous words. "The only thing we have in common is our appreciation for black clothes."

She expected him to move back at her rebuff. Instead he lifted his hand to trail his fingers down the Celtic tattoos that decorated the curve of her neck.

"We both spent centuries locked away from the world. We were both prisoners, although I chose my cage." His fingers paused over the pulse that hammered at the base of her throat. "And we're both trying to find our place."

She told herself to push him away. What right did he have to touch her? None. But she couldn't move. Or rather, she didn't *want* to move. Not when his fingers were sparking delicious jolts of desire. She'd never felt anything so intense. As if sparks were dancing over her skin.

"I thought you hated me," she breathed.

He leaned closer, the tips of his fangs visible. "You drive me nuts."

"Because you can't control me."

"In part," he agreed.

"And the other part?"

"You make me remember that there's more than ice flowing through my veins."

* * * *

Troy strolled into the Royal Guard's private command center. Unlike the rest of the castle, this area was blatantly devoid of marble or fluted columns. And there wasn't one fresco to be found. Instead the area had been dug out of the hard bedrock of the ocean floor.

The only concession to comfort was the thickly padded chairs that framed the long table and the fairy lights that danced near the low ceiling. They spilled a warm, golden glow over the room that softened the stark severity. The tang of salt was thick in the air.

Stepping through the door, Troy easily located Jord. The merman was standing at the front of the room, where a large map hung on the wall. He was gesturing to various locations as he spoke to the four guards who were seated at the table.

Jord cut off his words as he noticed Troy strolling toward him, a scowl on his face.

"Are you lost?" he demanded.

Troy flashed a smile. The one that he'd perfected to cause maximum annoyance.

"Ah, just the little fishy I was looking for," he drawled, halting just a few feet from the merman. "We need to speak." He sent a glance toward the younger guards. "Alone."

With a flattering haste, the guards jumped out of their seats and scurried toward the door. It was no secret that Troy had the ear of the queen. Obviously they didn't want to piss him off.

Jord, on the other hand, looked like he wanted to skewer Troy with his trident.

"I'm busy," the male snapped. "In case you haven't noticed, we're attempting to locate the missing prisoner."

"Oh, I noticed." Troy lifted his hand to inspect his polished nails. "You're certainly making a good show of searching."

"Show?" Jord took an impulsive step forward. A strategic mistake. Troy was at least three inches taller than the merman. It made it all the easier to tower over him. "What are you implying?"

"If you must know, I find it curious that you were so reluctant to ignore your fellow guard's warning."

"What guard?"

"Riza," Troy reminded the male. "He insisted that there was something strange happening with Brigette, but you refused to believe him. In fact, if I remember correctly—and I always remember correctly—you tried to prevent him from sharing his concern with the queen."

"Oh." The guard shrugged. "Riza is young and has a wild imagination."

A convenient excuse, Troy silently acknowledged. "Why do you say that?"

"He swore that he'd seen a real-life kraken, even though they're a myth. And a few weeks ago he was convinced that he'd seen a strange shimmer in the air."

"Where?"

Jord waved an impatient hand. "It was always moving from place to place. Once it was in the ballroom. The next time he claimed to see it in the kitchens."

Troy narrowed his eyes. They'd seen a shimmer in the throne room just seconds before the portal had appeared. Did that mean Zella had been moving the portal around, waiting for an opportunity to rescue Brigette? Or maybe some other creature had created the portal. Or just as likely, this male was lying.

Deciding to play the game, Troy arched a brow. "You do know that was probably the portal used by Brigette to escape?" he pointed out. "Which only proves you should have listened to the male."

"I couldn't know that." Jord acted offended. "It sounded crazy."

"Hmm." Troy polished his nails on his shirt, his expression one of deep skepticism.

The merman instinctively grabbed the hilt of his trident strapped around his waist.

"Is that all?"

"How did you know that Brigette wasn't in her cell?"

Jord paused, clearly caught off guard by the question. "Excuse me?"

"You ran into the throne room announcing that the prisoner had escaped," Troy clarified. "How did you know?"

"It was time for me to go on duty." Jord tapped his foot, as if to emphasize his impatience. "When I went down to the dungeons, I discovered the two outer guards were unconscious."

"Then what?"

"I unlocked the door to the inner dungeon and found Riza on the floor."

"He was unconscious?"

"Yes."

Troy tried to imagine what'd happened. Had the attacker come from inside the dungeon? Or from outside? At last he shook his head.

"Who could overpower three armed guards?"

"It must have been some sort of spell." The explanation was smooth. Too smooth. As if it'd been rehearsed.

Troy held the guard's gaze, allowing him to see the ruthless hunter beneath his frivolous exterior.

"I thought it was impossible to use magic in the dungeon?"

Something that might have been irritation flared through the male's blue eyes. Obviously, he assumed that Troy would be oblivious to the dampening spell that protected the lower floors of the castle.

"I only know they were knocked out," he muttered.

Troy studied the guard. Either he had an appalling attention to detail for a trained warrior, or he was hiding something.

"What happened next?"

"I found the cell door open and the prisoner was gone."

Troy mentally retraced the guard's supposed footsteps. Jord was preparing to go on duty, so he bebops down the stairs and enters the dungeons. The first things he sees are the two guards lying on the floor. He opens the inner door and finds Riza unconscious and the cell empty. Then he supposedly dashes out of the dungeons and travels across the entire castle to make his dramatic appearance in the throne room.

"Why did you leave?" he abruptly demanded.

Jord frowned. "Leave where?"

"The dungeons."

"I thought the queen should be told what had happened."

Troy sent him a skeptical frown. "You don't have an alarm system that you could use to alert Rimm and the other guards that there'd been a prison break?"

The male hesitated. He wanted to lie. Troy could see it hovering on his lips. Then, perhaps afraid that Troy might be familiar enough with the security system to know whether there was an alarm or not, he grudgingly nodded.

"Yes."

"But you decided not to use it?" Troy pressed.

"I suppose I panicked."

"A trained guard panicked because a prisoner escaped?" Troy tapped his chin with the tip of his finger, as if considering the possibility. "That seems unlikely."

A dark, dangerous emotion crawled over the male's narrow face. A poisonous shadow.

"I don't have to answer your questions."

Troy slowly smiled. "You just did."

Chapter 9

Levet perched on a narrow ledge that protruded from the stone wall.

They were still in the sewers, but they at least had found one that was dry. It was still stinky, and there was a nasty layer of moss on the floor, but it was the least awful option to stop and rest.

Directly below him, Brigette had curled into a ball on the ground, like a tired puppy. She'd been asleep for hours, snoring loud enough to wake the dead. And even the undead.

Obviously breaking out of the mer-folk dungeons and being whisked through a portal was exhausting business for a Were. He, on the other hand, had merely dozed. Now he leaned forward, studying the female.

She'd changed since the first day she'd been captured by Ulric and Rainn. Oh, and Chaaya. Not her looks. She was still a beautiful beast with flame-red hair and pale, perfect features. But the arrogance had been stripped away, along with the smoldering anger that had burned in her eyes.

Now she was…not vulnerable. At least, not exactly. But anxious. *Oui.* That was the word. As if she was struggling toward some destiny that remained just out of reach.

He leaned forward, sucking in a deep breath. At the same time, Brigette's eyes snapped open and she glared at him in suspicion.

"What the hell are you doing?"

Levet sucked in another deep breath. "I smell Were, but no wolf," he said. "What happened to your animal?"

With a muttered curse, Brigette shoved herself to her feet and tossed back her long hair.

"None of your damned business."

The air crackled with heat, but there was no hint of the wolf. "Did Zella kill it?" he asked, worry tugging at his heart.

A Were without their animal was like a gargoyle without his wings.

"No." Her jaw tightened until Levet could hear her teeth grinding together. "It's hibernating."

Levet furrowed his brow. There had been a time when the Weres had struggled against a wicked spirit who was draining the strength of their animals, but he hadn't known they could go into hibernation.

"Because it was wounded?" he guessed.

She glanced away. "Not physically."

"Ah." Levet bobbed his head up and down. Now he understood. "Her soul was injured."

Brigette wrapped her arms around her waist in an unconsciously defensive gesture.

"Stop staring at me," she groused. "It's creepy."

Levet didn't look away. He'd noticed a flicker of power dancing around her. Not the black evil that had pulsed around Zella, but a softer, more pervasive sort of energy.

"I see something else."

"There's nothing else," she snapped, brushing the dirt from her clothes. "And I'm starving. I need to find some breakfast."

Mmm. Breakfast. It was Levet's favorite meal. Well, every meal was Levet's favorite meal, but breakfast was extra special. Eggs, pancakes, a roasted pig or two.

His stomach rumbled.

"I am starving as well," he murmured with a dreamy sigh. Then with an effort he shook his head, dismissing the image of pancakes. "Hey, you will not distract me with my tummy. I see an aura around you, but no darkness."

"I don't know what you're babbling about."

Levet leaped off the small ledge to land at her feet. "It was not Zella who released you from the dungeon. It was…"

Brigette stiffened, gazing down at him with an unexpected intensity. "It was what?"

Levet tilted his head to the side. Aha. He knew there was something khaki about this entire situation. No wait…wacky. *Oui*, wacky.

He pointed a finger at her. "You do not know, do you?"

She hunched her shoulders. "Tell me."

"First I wish you to explain how you escaped."

There was a long silence. Distantly, Levet was aware of the footsteps hitting the cobblestone streets above them, and even farther away the trickle of brackish water as it dribbled through one sewer to another. A reminder that the sensation they were alone in the world was just an illusion.

At last, Brigette cleared her throat. "A few days..." She stopped, as if considering her words. "Maybe it was weeks, I can't seem to keep track of time anymore. It doesn't matter." She shook away her confusion. "I heard a voice whispering in my mind."

Levet was instantly fascinated. And at the same time, thoroughly annoyed. Why was everyone else always hearing voices? No one ever attempted to lure him into a delightful adventure. Which was quite unfair considering he was a most excellent adventurer.

"What did it say?"

"It promised me freedom," she said with simple honesty.

Of course it did, Levet silently acknowledged. What better way to negotiate with a prisoner?

"You did not find it odd a strange voice was whispering in your mind?"

She shrugged. "At first I assumed it was Zella, but I eventually realized there was something different about it."

"Different, how?"

"It coaxed rather than demanded. Zella hammered until she got what she wanted," Brigette said. "And it didn't offer me power or riches. It promised me..."

Levet waited for her to finish. "What?" he finally prompted. You couldn't just leave a gargoyle hanging. It was rude.

"Freedom."

"And what else?"

She glanced away. "Nothing."

Levet clicked his tongue. "That cannot be true."

"You don't know anything about me or what I was promised."

"I know that you already have your freedom," Levet told her. "So why are you so desperate to find your mystery voice?"

She stepped back as if his words had struck a physical blow. "Shut up, you ugly lump of concrete."

Levet sniffed at her sharp tone. "No need to be testy. And I am not concrete."

Her jaw clenched, then with an obvious effort she regained command of her fiery temper.

"You said you smelled something," she said between clenched teeth. "What is it?"

Levet shrugged. "Druid."

* * * *

Basq had surprisingly managed to sleep in the cool darkness of the cellar. Perhaps it was the certainty that he was going to need his strength later, or more likely, the fact that while they'd been napping, he'd pulled Chaaya's slender body into his arms with her head resting against the center of his chest. The sensation of having her nestled against him was intensely satisfying. As if she was filling a restless void he hadn't even realized was gnawing at him.

Still, he wasn't stupid.

He knew Chaaya would be furious if she woke to find herself snuggled against him. Not because she didn't want him. He could catch the scent of her desire whenever they were near each other. But she was determined to pretend that he was nothing more than an undead lump of boredom. Basq grimaced. All right, maybe she didn't have to pretend. He could be a lump of undead boredom, but that didn't keep her from wanting him.

Careful not to wake his companion, he arranged her on the floor with the tablecloth pulled over her slender form. Unlike most humans, her body temperature never changed, but it made him feel better to know she was covered.

Moving soundlessly out of the cellar, Basq paused to glance around the building above them. Empty. He quickly exited through the broken window and headed up the narrow lane. There was a grayish light filtering from the sky, but he wasn't worried about daylight arriving to ruin his complexion. Bullas were created by magic. There was no true sun to turn him to ash. Yet another reason he'd often chosen to hide in them.

The streets were thankfully empty of the drunken crowd that had spilled from the bar after the fight, although there were a handful of demons who were busy cleaning the front windows of their various businesses or wandering the street in search of entertainment. Basq remained in the shadows of an alleyway as he watched the ebb and flow of traffic. There was one male imp who leaned against the pole of a streetlamp, his expression bored.

A gopher.

It was a name used by creatures who were willing to barter and sell anything in the bulla.

Like human pawn dealers, only with fewer morals and the ability to use magic.

Just what Basq needed.

Stepping out of the shadows, Basq crossed to stand directly in front of the fey creature.

He was tall and slender, with reddish gold hair that hung in a long braid down his back and a thin face with bright green eyes. He was wearing a long gray robe that could no doubt change colors to allow him to blend into any background. Like a chameleon.

At Basq's approach the imp straightened, his nose twitching as he sensed a customer.

"Master Vampire." The creature offered a deep bow. "How may I serve you today?"

Basq got right to the point. The sooner he finished his business, the sooner he could return to Chaaya.

"First I need blood."

"But of course." The male lifted a slender hand as if about to wave toward a hidden covey of females. "Imp? Fairy? Something more exotic?"

Basq released a trickle of his power. Just enough to make the white in his eyes shimmer and the air thicken with warning.

"I want it in a bottle, and I have the ability to detect if it's been diluted or tainted in any way." An imp possessed the power to enchant objects including blood so that the buyer became addicted. They would be forced to return to this particular seller over and over to get their magical fix. "The price of trying to cheat me is a slow, painful death."

The green eyes widened with faux outrage. "Why, master. You wound me."

"Not yet." Basq tapped his elongated fang with the tip of his tongue. "But it's a distinct possibility if you try to screw with me. Got it?"

The male's amiable charm faded. It was replaced by a shrewd, ruthless entrepreneur.

"Fine, but it's going to cost you."

"I'm not done."

"What else?"

"Human food." Basq rummaged through his memories of watching Chaaya consume her meals with unabashed gusto. He didn't know if she needed it for substance, but she loved to eat. "Preferably a chicken pot pie," he finally said, recalling she was always stealing them from the kitchen despite the fuming protest from the chef. "And a dessert," he added, well aware she had a sweet tooth. His eyes narrowed. "As a reminder, I will know if it's tainted."

The imp arched his brows, surveying Basq from head to toe as if trying to determine his worth.

"You ask a great deal."

"I'm not done," Basq told him.

"What else?"

"I'm looking for a Were."

The imp looked confused. "There's no Weres in this place. Not at the moment."

"She just arrived along with a tiny gargoyle."

The male's eyes lit up at the mention of Levet. Obviously he'd heard rumors about the aggravating creature. Then, mentally sifting through the various ways he could make the most money off the information, he offered Basq a cagey smile.

"Really?" he drawled. "It sounds like a peculiar pair."

Basq grimaced. "You have no idea."

"Why are you searching for them?" The creature kept his tone offhand, as if he was only mildly interested in the answer. "Is there a bounty on their heads?"

Basq had his answer ready. He knew that as soon as he revealed his interest in the two, there would be a stampede to find them. There were always demons eager to make easy money. Which might not be a bad thing if it didn't spook Brigette into fleeing. He had to make sure that no one was willing to go near the Were and gargoyle until he had a chance to get his hands on them.

"The Were is carrying the plague," he stated in grim tones.

As expected, the imp pulled back in horror. Even demons could die during an outbreak.

"Plague?"

Basq nodded. "An extremely virulent strain that has wiped out more than one bulla. I'm trying to contain her before she can spread the disease any further. I could use some help if you're interested."

"Certainly not." The imp shivered from head to toe. "You should warn the chieftain."

Basq leaned closer, as if sharing a secret. "I prefer not to cause a panic. If I can locate her quickly, I have the ability to wrap her in a stasis and remove her without a fuss."

The imp looked dubious. "If you say so."

"Do you know where I might find them?"

The imp flattened his lips, clearly disappointed there wasn't going to be a huge reward. At least not one that was large enough to make him risk the plague. Still, he was a businessman. He wasn't going to release any information without squeezing some value out of the deal.

"As I said, it will cost you." Basq reached into his pocket to remove the few gold coins he had left, but the imp shook his head. "Not money. That." Without warning the male pointed to the golden amulet beaten into the shape of an eagle that hung around Basq's neck.

Instinctively Basq lifted his hand to cover the talisman. He'd worn it for centuries, keeping it as a reminder of a time when he'd held on to the hope of a better future.

"This has no value," he protested.

The imp leaned closer, studying the intricate design. "It was crafted by the Visigoths and charmed by a human witch."

Basq couldn't sense the power that had been beaten into the metal, but he'd known it was there.

"It's useless to demons," he told the male.

The imp shrugged. "I collect magic."

Basq hesitated; then, reaching up, he grabbed the amulet and tugged it off the gold chain.

"The blood, the food, the information," he commanded, holding out the last connection to his old life.

Chapter 10

Chaaya woke at the sound of footsteps heading down the stairs. With a blur of motion she was on her feet, the spear clutched in her hand. It wasn't until she caught the cool, fiercely male scent that she realized that Basq wasn't in the cellar with her.

He'd somehow managed to sneak out while she was sleeping.

Well, that was embarrassing. She prided herself on her warrior skills, but she'd been dead to the world when Basq slipped away.

Heat stained her cheeks as he entered the cellar and crossed toward her.

"Where have you been?" she demanded, her voice sharp.

He held up a small basket. "Bartering for supplies."

The scent of something delicious wafted through the air, and Chaaya forgot her annoyance as her stomach rumbled in encouragement.

Gingerly she reached to take the basket, pulling off the red and white checkered towel to peer inside.

"Is that chicken pot pie?" She blinked. "And waffles?"

"It was the only sweet thing I could buy." He sounded defensive. "There's not much demand for cakes and pies in this bulla."

She glanced up, studying his pale features with his stark features and extraordinary eyes. She'd never been the sort of girl who was infatuated with bad boys. Who wanted a lover who treated them like crap?

But when she met Basq, she told herself that nice guys were bores. Over and over she tried to pretend that she found his unwavering loyalty, his devotion to duty, and his refusal to compromise his morals something to be mocked.

And all because... Because he was battering against the barriers that she wasn't ready to have breached.

"It's perfect," she breathed.

In silence she settled back on the floor and set the basket in her lap. Then, with the pleasure of someone who'd been denied food for countless centuries, she consumed the pot pies in huge bites. Next, she demolished the waffles and licked the sticky syrup off her fingers.

Mmm. Ambrosia.

Once she'd eaten every bite and chugged the bottle of wine that was hidden in the bottom of the basket, Chaaya glanced toward Basq, who was seated beside her.

He looked the same as always, although she thought she could detect the faintest flush on his cheeks. As if he'd just fed. A strange sensation clenched her heart.

Jealousy?

She tried to squash the stupid thought, but that didn't keep the question from spilling from her lips.

"What about you?"

He frowned in confusion. "What about me?"

"Did you eat?"

He reached into his pocket to pull out a glass flask that was half filled with a ruby liquid. Blood.

"I'm reserving some in case I need it later."

Relief as sharp as a dagger sliced through Chaaya, and with a muttered curse she rose to her feet. She was going to start acting as flighty as a dew fairy if she wasn't careful.

"We need to return to the hunt. Eventually Brigette is going to realize we followed her." She tossed aside the cloth wrapped around her shoulders, another reminder of Basq's honorable nature. "Next time we might not get lucky enough to be close when she jumps into a portal."

"I have information that a strange gray creature with fairy wings was spotted entering the sewers," he smoothly informed her.

"Seriously?" Chaaya jerked in surprise. How long had the male been gone while she was snoozing? And just what had he been doing? "Where did you get your information?"

He shrugged. "I bought it."

"I thought you had only a few coins..." Her words trailed away as he instinctively reached up to touch the gold chain around his neck. Only it was missing something. "Oh no. Basq, where's your amulet?"

He abruptly dropped his hand, his expression chagrined as he realized he'd given away more than he intended.

"I bartered it."

His tone was clipped, his expression guarded. He didn't want to talk about the cost.

Chaaya stepped forward, a hard lump of emotion stuck in her throat. "No. You shouldn't have done that."

He waved aside her protest. "We needed food and information. We have both."

"Who gave you the amulet?"

"It doesn't matter."

"Tell me." She pressed her hand against his chest, over the precise spot the amulet had once rested. "Please."

There was a long, painful pause. "Tarak," he finally admitted. "He gave it to me when I joined his clan. He said it was a promise that we would always be family."

The simple words crushed down on Chaaya, as if she was suddenly carrying an unbearable weight.

"Why would you give it up?"

He glanced away, his features set in stoic lines. "We need to find Brigette."

Her hand slid up his chest, wrapping around the back of his neck. "Why, Basq?"

Icy power thundered through the air as Basq's eyes sizzled with the same awareness that zipped and zapped through her. Like an electric shock caught in a loop.

"You sacrificed your life. The least I could do was sacrifice a small bit of metal," he reluctantly confessed.

"It was more than a small bit of metal," she muttered. Then, without giving herself time to consider her impulsive need for more, Chaaya slid her fingers into his dark hair and yanked his head down.

Basq made a sound of surprise, but before he could demand to know what she was doing, Chaaya was on her tiptoes so she could claim his mouth in a fierce kiss.

With quicksilver speed, Basq's arms were wrapped around her, hauling her tight against his body. As if her kiss had triggered a response so deeply ingrained inside him that he reacted on pure instinct. Chaaya parted her lips, savoring the sharp press of his fangs. She'd heard rumors that a vampire's bite could cause an orgasm.

She twined her arms around his neck, arching her back to press against his hard muscles. Weeks ago she'd seen him leaving the spa area of the casino. He'd been wearing a loose pair of jogging shorts and nothing else. She'd nearly drooled at the sight of his broad chest and sculpted six-pack.

At the time she'd been overwhelmed with the desire to know if his rich, creamy white skin was as silky smooth as it looked.

About to appease her curiosity, Chaaya was distracted when Basq lifted his head, studying her upturned face with a brooding gaze.

"You don't owe me anything, Chaaya."

It took her a second to realize what he was implying. "Is that why you think I kissed you?" she demanded in a dangerous voice.

"Isn't it?"

She narrowed her gaze. "I don't pay my debts with my body, leech," she snapped. "If I kiss someone it's because I want to taste their lips." Her gaze moved to his chiseled mouth. "And feel their body. And—"

She had plenty more to say, but her words were cut short as he swooped his head down and kissed her with an earth-shattering urgency. His arms tightened until they would have crushed her if she'd still been human. She gripped his hair, hanging on tight as the maelstrom of sensations battered through her.

Heat seared through her body, clashing against the sharp chill in the air. The contrast was deliciously erotic, spreading a rash of pleasurable goose bumps over her skin. A moan rumbled in her throat, the taste of his lips as heady and addictive as any drug.

This was what she'd sensed was waiting for her. And why she'd gone to such an effort to keep him at arm's length. She'd spent most of her life trapped in a hell dimension—did she really want to become a prisoner of her emotions? Even if this male was the most extraordinary creature she'd ever encountered.

The unnerving thought was just penetrating the desire that clouded her mind when Basq moved his mouth to nuzzle along the line of her jaw before he scraped his fangs down the curve of her neck.

Chaaya gasped, tilting her head back to offer him complete access. Oh yes. She shivered in anticipation. Was she about to discover if a vampire bite really could cause an orgasm? She was 99 percent certain that the answer was yes.

Lost in the dreamy-steamy pleasure cascading through her, Chaaya nearly missed the faint click from overhead. But even as she pressed against the hardening length of his erection, she froze. That was the sound of a door opening.

And a new smell had filtered through the air.

Orc.

"Wait," she breathed.

"I heard." The white center of his eyes expanded. Was he using his power to determine how many demons were above them?

"Is there any other way out of here?" she asked.

"No."

Chaaya stepped out of his arms and grabbed her spear. "Then we fight."

His face was grim. "No, Chaaya."

She twirled her spear, sending him a warning frown. "We're both in charge, remember? If you think you're going to leave me behind while you…"

"Hush." He brushed his fingers over her closely trimmed hair. It was an oddly affectionate gesture. "I'm trying to tell you that there's no need to fight. Once we get to the top of the stairs, I'll use my darkness. Head for the window."

"Oh." She smiled wryly. "Okay."

He stepped back, his face still grim. "Don't you dare die again."

She held his gaze. "I can say the same to you."

"Let's go."

* * * *

Troy at last tracked down Rimm in the throne room. The tall, slender man was wearing the traditional scale armor with a trident belted at his waist. His long, blue tinted hair was held back by a leather strap, and the medallion around his neck revealed his status as the Captain of the Royal Guards.

At the moment he was standing near the dais, watching Inga as she paced from side to side. The queen had changed into a new muumuu, this one in a violent shade of yellow with red poinsettias splotched across the cheap fabric. Her tufts of hair were standing straight up and her eyes were more crimson than blue, a sure indication she was upset.

At Troy's entrance the guard's handsome features pinched into a sour expression.

"We're in conference. You can return to speak with the queen later," he announced in stiff tones.

Troy sashayed forward, halting directly in front of the male. "I'm not here to see the queen. I have some questions for you."

Rimm scowled. "I don't answer to you, imp."

Inga came to an abrupt halt, sending her captain an impatient frown. "I've asked the *prince*." She emphasized Troy's title, although she rarely remembered that Troy had royal blood running through his veins. He rarely remembered it himself. His pedigree was worth less than the thigh-high leather boots he was wearing to complement his lime green spandex pants and sheer white shirt. "He's going to assist in my search for the truth."

Rimm stiffened, looking as if someone had rammed a stick up his ass. "If Your Majesty believes I'm incapable of performing my duties—"

"Stop," Inga interrupted. "This has nothing to do with your lack of competence, Rimm."

The male sniffed. "If you say so."

Troy snapped. For the past months he'd obeyed Inga's command to bite his tongue when she endured the various slights, snubs, and outright insults from her people. She was convinced she could win them over with her hard work and diligence.

Troy wasn't nearly so certain. And right now he wasn't in the mood to put up with the shit.

"She's telling you the truth." Rimm parted his lips to make a snide comment only to snap them shut when Troy pulled a hidden dagger from his boot and pointed it in the male's face. "Just keep your mouth shut and listen, fish," Troy commanded. "There isn't a mer-folk in this castle who would have blamed Inga for tossing you in the dungeon after Riven was removed from the throne. Or even killing you as a traitor."

Inga made a strangled sound of protest. "Troy."

Troy kept his gaze locked on the captain of the guards. "But she didn't because she believed in you. And your loyalty to the throne."

His jaw clenched. "I am loyal."

Troy ignored the male's protest. "And despite the warnings from me and the King of Vampires and dozens of others, she trusted you more than any other demon she could have brought in as the head of her Royal Guard."

"Enough, Troy," Inga pleaded.

"No, this is way overdue." He kept the dagger in the male's face, his voice sharp with frustrated anger. "I want him to acknowledge the faith you placed in him, despite his obvious lack of gratitude."

The scent of salt was suddenly thick in the air, and Troy braced for a fight. He wasn't scared of the merman, but he sure the hell wasn't going to get caught flat footed. Not when that trident could shoot out nasty projectiles.

But Rimm didn't attack. Instead he abruptly whirled toward Inga and fell to his knees.

"He's right, Your Majesty." He bent his head in apology. "I have neglected to offer you my deep appreciation for allowing me to maintain my position."

Inga flushed, looking as uncomfortable as an ice sprite in the middle of the Sahara Desert.

"That's not necessary."

"It is. I would have been..." Rimm tilted back his head to reveal his pale face, which had lost its arrogant expression. "Broken if you would have chosen to remove me. And it's only my shame at having failed you once again that makes me resent having the imp's help."

Inga impatiently waved for the merman to rise to his feet. "I promise you, Rimm, we're all on the same side."

Rimm nodded, flowing upright and turning toward Troy. "Ask your questions."

Satisfied that a temporary cease-fire had been called, Troy slid his dagger back into his boot.

"What can you tell me about Jord?"

"Jord?" Rimm looked puzzled. "You need to be more specific."

"Do you trust him?"

Rimm hesitated, as if considering how to answer. "He's dependable."

"I hear a 'but' in there," Troy said.

"But he was Riven's most devoted soldier," Rimm admitted. "And he's made no secret that he resents having an ogress holding the Tryshu."

Troy shared a glance with Inga. "Interesting."

"Why are you asking?" Rimm demanded.

Troy returned his attention to the captain. "Jord was the one I overheard trying to stop Riza from warning the queen that there was something strange going on with Brigette. He was also the first one to burst into the throne room shouting that the prisoner had escaped."

Rimm's puzzlement only deepened. "I thought the evil spirit had released the Were?"

"That's one possibility, although we've found no trace of the darkness," Troy told him. "The other possibility is that one or more of the mer-folk are responsible."

Rimm jerked, the teeth he'd filed to sharp points snapping together. But even as he clearly ached to deny that any mer-folk could be a traitor, he bit back the denial.

"And you suspect Jord?"

"He's the most likely culprit."

Rimm didn't argue. Instead he asked the obvious question. "Why would he release the prisoner?"

Troy shrugged. "My guess would be that he wanted to undermine the queen's authority. Not only among her people, but among the vampires and Weres who trusted her to keep Brigette locked away from the world."

"I suppose that's possible," Rimm slowly agreed. "He was always eager to take on the dirtiest jobs for Riven. He was ambitious for more power and willing to do anything to get it."

"Or maybe Brigette was able to manipulate him into helping her," Troy continued, unwilling to close his mind to the other possibilities. "She destroyed her entire pack to gain power. She's obviously capable of evil even without the power of the dark beast."

Rimm frowned, as if considering the various implications of an inside job. "Jord would no doubt be eager to humiliate the queen," he slowly admitted. "And he's capable of creating a portal—" His words broke off as he gave a sharp shake of his head. "No, wait. I don't think it's possible."

"Why?"

"I was at the entrance to the royal quarters when I saw Jord race past," Rimm explained. "I followed him as he headed down the corridor."

Troy shrugged. "He could have put Brigette in the secret passage and then made his way to the royal quarters to make sure you saw him."

Rimm turned to point where the hidden panel was located. "The entrance is on the other side of the castle. He would have to travel down four flights of stairs to return to the main corridors and then circle back to the entrance where I was standing. It would have taken several minutes. By then the other guards would have been awake and sounding the alarm."

Troy scowled, trying to picture in his mind the route the male would have to take. At last he heaved a frustrated sigh. The captain was right. The throne room consumed the entire floor in this section of the castle. The only way to get from one side to the other was to go down the stairs and then back up. Even for a merman with considerable speed, it would take time.

Still, he wasn't ready to give up.

"He could have told Brigette where to find the hidden passage," he suggested.

This time it was Inga who shot down his theory. "No, the doors to the passages are protected by my grandfather's magic. They can't be opened by anyone but a mer-folk."

"Damn," Troy muttered.

Chapter 11

Chaaya was prepared as they reached the top of the stairs and Basq spread his darkness through the room. There were shouts of alarm from the gathered demons, but Chaaya ignored them. She had the position of the window firmly fixed in her mind as she sprinted across the wooden floor.

For all her preparation, however, it was disconcerting to be utterly blind. Even when she was in her hell dimension there was an ambient light that allowed her to see what was around her. Now she had to trust her other senses as she plowed forward.

Next to her, she could feel the pulse of Basq's icy power and hear the soft thump of his footsteps. That was how she knew the precise moment he leaped through the air. Trusting she wasn't about to slam her head into the wall, she jumped behind him, thankfully flying through the opening to land on the hard cobblestone lane.

For a hopeful second she thought they might actually have escaped. Then Basq's agonized shout was followed by the collapse of his protective darkness.

It was still dark, but it was the shadows of night, not magic.

Chaaya tensed, her narrowed gaze taking in the circle of demons that surrounded them. They were a motley collection of mongrels, but they wore matching maroon and gold uniforms.

The city guard?

Dammit.

She didn't know how they'd found them, and right now it didn't matter. The only question was how they could escape.

Chaaya glanced to the side, discovering Basq on his knees wrapped in a net made of silver. It was easy to see the pain etched on his face and the way his shoulders hunched, as if his strength was being drained away. And it probably was.

A tall, slender male with long, golden hair approached. He had the features of a fairy but the tusks of an orc. As he neared, he pulled a sword from the scabbard at his side and waved it in Basq's direction.

"Come along like a nice girl, and we won't have to slice open the leech and eat his heart."

Chaaya narrowed her gaze. "I don't do nice."

"Hmm. Spunky." The male smiled, revealing his pointed teeth. "I'm going to have some fun once the chieftain is finished with you." He glanced toward the gathered guards. "Bring him."

Chaaya's hand strayed toward her spear, but out of the corner of her eye she could see Basq shaking his head. He was warning her not to do anything stupid.

Stepping aside as two of the guards grabbed Basq and started to drag him down the lane, Chaaya muttered a string of curses she'd perfected over the long centuries. She didn't have time for this. Not when she had no idea where Brigette was or if the female had a way to travel out of the bulla.

More importantly, she was terrified that the silver was going to permanently damage Basq if she didn't find a way to get him out of the net.

They walked to the very center of the city where a large, lavish palace dominated several blocks. Chaaya lifted her brows in surprise. Unlike the rest of the city, which was built with gray bricks and mortar, this structure was created out of stone and covered with a white stucco. The large windows held brilliant stained glass, and four turrets soared toward the star-speckled sky.

It looked as if it'd been plucked out of the sun-drenched deserts of Morocco and plopped in the middle of this drab city.

Bemused, Chaaya passed beneath the arched gateway and watched the heavy double doors of the palace swing open. As a group they moved forward, climbing a sweeping staircase that led to the second floor. They were met by another set of double doors.

Coming to an abrupt halt, the fey mongrel guard held out an imperious hand. "Weapon."

Chaaya arched a brow. "No."

The male snapped his fingers. "Give me your weapon or I'll take it."

Chaaya spread her arms wide. "Take it."

The guard lost his arrogance as he glanced down at the spear. "Is it cursed?"

"Touch it and find out." Chaaya flashed a wide smile. "I double-dog dare you."

The male jutted his tusks, clearly torn between caution and pride. Did he risk a nasty curse to save his street cred? Or did he toss pride to the netherworld and save himself from having his manly bits wither and die?

He was spared the difficult decision when one of the doors was pushed open and an officious-looking imp in a long maroon robe waved an impatient hand.

"Just let it be," he commanded in sharp tones. "She's going to need it anyway."

Chaaya grimaced. That didn't sound good. Before she could ask what the hell he was talking about, the original guard poked his sword into the center of her back.

"Get in," he snapped.

Chaaya forced her feet to carry her through the open door and into the long, cavernous room. She blinked, nearly overwhelmed by the explosion of color and heat and smells.

The high, vaulted ceiling was coated by layers of gold and precious gems. In the very center a massive chandelier spread a bright glow of light over the richly upholstered furnishings and intricately mosaic tiled floor. The walls were hidden behind crimson tapestries, and a dozen fluted columns marched neatly from one end to the other.

There were at least thirty to forty mongrel demons spread around the room. Some were dressed in delicate satin and lace, some in uniforms, and others in rough leather.

A soft groan yanked her attention back to the guards, who were tossing Basq into a corner.

"I'm in," she rasped, pointing toward Basq. "Now let him go."

"In time," a low, cultured voice with a hint of a British accent drawled.

Chaaya spun on her heel, eying the male who was strolling between the columns to stand next to a tall, velvet-covered chair.

He was short for a male, barely an inch taller than her, with a round head that was not only bald but waxed to reflect the overhead light. His ears were oversized, and the lobes hung nearly to his shoulders, revealing his brownie blood. Weirdly, however, he was wearing a three-piece black suit with a pocket watch and spats over his shiny black shoes. He was even carrying a cane.

He looked like a Victorian banker who might invite you over for tea and crumpets. Until you looked into his black, soulless eyes. Then you realized that after serving you tea, he would chop you up and eat you for dinner.

A shiver raced down Chaaya's spine. "Who are you?"

The male gave a small dip of his head. "Chieftain Dabbler."

"Dabbler?" Chaaya snorted, deliberately taunting the male. She'd discovered that pissing off people made them sloppy. Right now she needed any edge she could get. "Seriously?"

The male heaved a long-suffering sigh. "I know. A hideous name given to me by my parents. Only one of the reasons I killed them." He motioned her forward. "And you are?"

"Chaaya." She strolled toward the male, whistling as she glanced around. "Wow. This is...something."

"Yes, my father designed it himself."

"I assume before you killed him?"

His smile was tight-lipped. "We came here to prevent my human mother from aging. She was a human, you see. Soft and fragile." He motioned his cane around the room. "His palace was his gift to her. A tangible symbol of his love."

"A charming story."

"It was." He heaved a sigh. "Unfortunately they were utterly unreasonable when I suggested that we open our personal paradise to other demons. They were convinced that their privacy was more important than wealth."

"You disagreed?"

"Fervently."

Chaaya pretended interest in the demon's personal history even as she cast a covert glance around the room.

The demons who were wearing the elegant robes and fancy suits were huddled near the walls. Not out of fear, she realized as she caught sight of the braziers emitting clouds of smoke. The incense was no doubt enchanted. That would explain the dreamy look on their faces. The uniformed guards were spread strategically around the exits, ensuring there was no easy way to escape. Dammit.

Her gaze started to skim back toward the strange cluster of leather-clad demons when she was distracted by the golden-haired imp that was tied to a column. Not because he looked terrified. He was probably a captive being punished for some misdemeanor. No, it was the amulet that lay against his gray robe that captured her attention. The last time she'd seen it, the eagle-shaped metal had been around Basq's neck.

"Cha Cha," a rough voice called out, pulling her attention toward the towering orc who'd stepped forward.

"You remember my old friend, Tur?" the chieftain asked.

"Turd?" Chaaya tilted back her head to laugh. "That's a worse name than Dabbler."

The orc growled but Dabbler studied her with a mysterious smile that didn't reach his soulless black eyes.

"Tur warned me you were a feisty thing," he purred. "I'm happy to discover he didn't exaggerate."

Spunky. Feisty. She sounded like a heroine from a fairy tale. A shame this place wasn't filled with princes and funny dwarves instead of smelly orcs and weird-ass brownies.

"Why am I here?"

"It has come to my attention that you arrived in my quaint town without bothering to stop by and introduce yourself."

Chaaya shrugged. "I was busy."

Dabbler clicked his tongue. "Bad manners are never in fashion, my dear."

She took a step backward. Could she get to Basq and drag him out of the palace before they were stopped by the guard? It seemed unlikely.

"We were planning to come today, but your goon squad attacked us," she told the male.

"Were you?" The smile widened. "Ah, delightful news."

"So if that's all cleared up..." She continued to back away, hoping to reach Basq and at least get the silver net off him.

With a flick of his hand, Dabbler sent two guards to stand between her and the vampire.

"There is still the small matter of my tithe," the chieftain reminded her.

Chaaya grimaced, returning her full attention to Dabbler. She was beginning to suspect that this male had gone to a lot of trouble to set up this encounter. But why?

Hiding her fear behind a mocking expression, she shrugged. "I'm afraid I don't have my purse on me. Tell you what, I'll drop a check in the mail."

Dabbler rubbed his fingers over the ivory handle of his cane. "That won't be necessary."

Her smile remained even as her mouth dried. "It won't?"

Dabbler glanced toward the orc. "Tur came to see me with a highly entertaining story."

"Well, he's a highly entertaining sort of dude," Chaaya murmured.

"Indeed he is. Not particularly bright, but he has his uses." Dabbler glanced back at her. "Shall I reveal what he told me?"

"I'm on pins and needles."

"He told a tale of a slender woman who looked human but managed to overpower an entire horde of demons."

Chaaya rolled her eyes. "An entire horde? Turd-head has a vivid imagination."

"That's what I thought, but then the whispers spread through the city. They spoke of a beautiful warrior." The black, empty eyes drifted over her, leaving behind the sensation of being slathered in evil. "Of course I simply had to discover the truth for myself."

She squashed her shiver. There was no way in hell she was going to give Dabbler the satisfaction of knowing how much he unnerved her.

"Discover what?" she asked.

Dabbler spread his arms. "If you fight as well as they claim."

Chaaya blinked. "You want to fight me?"

"Oh, not me. I'm a businessman, not a warrior." The male quickly destroyed her brief hope, pointing toward the orc. "I have another opponent in mind."

Chaaya pulled her spear. She should have guessed that was the reason the orc and his leather-clad buddies were in the elegant palace. They certainly didn't fit with the décor.

The question was whether it was just Tur or the backup band as well.

"I've already beat Dirty Turdy," she said, deliberately goading the oversized lump of muscle. Orcs weren't famous for their even temperament. "I don't do encores."

Tur's eyes flashed a fiery crimson. "Not fair fight."

"There, you see?" Dabbler said in regretful tones. "He says it wasn't fair. I fear I must insist on a rematch."

Chaaya watched the orc stomp forward. "And if I say no?"

"The vampire dies." Dabbler's cold eyes held no emotion. He would kill everyone in the room without the slightest remorse.

That made him far more dangerous than the orcs.

She stroked her fingers along the hilt of the spear, igniting the magic etched into the glyphs.

"What do I get if I agree?"

Dabbler looked surprised by the question. "You live."

She shook her head. "Not good enough. I'm not fighting until you remove the net from my companion."

"These aren't negotiations," he chided.

"Then find someone else to amuse you."

The chieftain hesitated, as if stunned by her audacity. Obviously, he'd been the big cheese for so long he'd forgotten what it was like to have his orders questioned. Still, his affable manner remained firmly intact as he nodded toward the guards.

"Remove the net but keep a close eye on him. If he tries to escape, then stake him."

Chaaya watched in silence as the guards warily untangled Basq from the net. In the bright light she could easily see the angry red wounds burned deep into his flesh, but it was the limp, boneless way he sprawled on the floor that clutched at her heart. How badly was he hurt?

She started to take a step toward him when Dabbler slammed his cane against a small gong set next to the chair. The sound echoed through the room loud enough to make several demons flinch.

"Ready?" He motioned Chaaya toward the center of the room.

"What are the rules?" she asked, feeling the familiar tingles of magic from her spear as she strolled toward the starburst created by the gold and amber mosaic tiles.

"The rules are that there are no rules," Dabbler informed her.

"Ah. My kind of fight." She twirled the spear, crouching low. "Let's play, Turd-head."

The orc released a bark of annoyance, but he wasn't so infuriated that he forgot to grab a heavy wooden cudgel from one of his ugly cohorts.

"Tur," he growled, stomping toward her. "Me Tur. You Cha Cha."

The orc rambled to the center of the room, loosely holding the cudgel in one hand. He looked big and awkward and stupid as a box of rocks. But Chaaya wasn't fooled. The moment he started his fierce charge, he moved with a fluid speed that caught most demons off guard.

Twisting aside, she easily avoided his attack. At the same time, she carefully watched the cunning expression that settled on his blunt face. He had a strategy. One that had no doubt worked a thousand times before.

With a hungry grin, he charged again, acting as if it was going to be the same as the last one. Then, at the last possible moment, he swung his cudgel.

There was a whistling sound as the weapon sliced through the air, aimed directly at her head. The crowd gasped, no doubt expecting to be splattered with blood and brains. But already anticipating the move, Chaaya easily leaped over the cudgel, slashing her spear to slice off the tip of his ear.

The orc skidded to a halt, his hand raised to cover his wounded ear. The skin of orcs was too thick for most blades to penetrate, but her spear was enhanced with magic. She still needed to stab him in the heart to kill him, but he was definitely distracted. And pissed off.

Exactly what she wanted.

"Cha Cha," he snarled.

"Did you say you want to cha-cha?" she taunted. "I prefer a partner who doesn't have two left feet, but I suppose you'll do."

He raised the cudgel over his head. "Me bash you."

Chaaya wiggled her fingers in a "come here" motion. "Let's dance."

He charged again, this time swinging his club in an upward motion as he anticipated Chaaya leaping over it. That was the problem with orcs. They had no imagination.

Waiting until the last possible second, Chaaya ducked low, sticking her spear between his legs. The oversized creature cried out as he tripped over the weapon, falling on his face with a ground-shaking impact.

Chaaya swiftly straightened, intending to leap on the orc and put an end to the fight. But a flicker out of the corner of her eye warned her that an idiot from the peanut gallery was about to do a sneak attack.

Spinning with blinding speed, Chaaya kicked out, catching the mongrel on the side of the head. The creature was knocked to his knees, and without hesitation, Chaaya sliced him open from stomach to throat. The creature's skin wasn't nearly as thick as a regular orc's, and the blade slid through like a hot knife through butter.

The room went silent as the mongrel gazed down in horror. Blood and a few vital organs spilled out of the wound, landing on the marble floor with an audible plop. The creature gave a keening cry as he leaped to his feet and dashed for the nearest exit. Chaaya glanced around, silently daring the rest of the booster club to jump in. As one, they all stepped back.

Slowly she turned to see Tur advancing with wary steps. "Tired of game," he muttered.

So was Chaaya. Although she continued to smile and weave the spear in an elegant series of figure eights, she could feel her strength draining away. The sooner she could end the fight, the better.

But how?

The orc might be stupid, but he wasn't suicidal. He wouldn't use a direct assault that might leave any vulnerable spots available to her spear. Not when he could simply use his cudgel to keep her at a distance and wait for a lucky strike.

It was the near-blinding glitter from the tiled floor that offered a sudden inspiration.

"We just started," she taunted, stepping back.

Tur scowled. "Me bash."

"Yawn. I heard you the first time." She spread her arms wide. "If we're going to banter, at least try to be inventive."

With an angry roar, Tur swiped the cudgel in her direction. She leaped to the side, then with a loud cry, she pretended to lose her balance and fell to her knees.

Tur grinned, taking a long step toward her as he anticipated a quick end to the battle.

"Not so smart-mouth now, eh, girlie?"

Rolling to the side, Chaaya clenched her muscles and threw the spear with every ounce of power she had left in her. It sailed upward, but it missed the orc who jerked out of its path. That was fine with Chaaya. She wasn't aiming at Tur. Her target was the chandelier above their heads.

It was a risky gamble, but it paid off as the blade connected with the iron chain that attached the massive light to the ceiling.

There was a shrill creak, then a strange crackling sound as the layers of gold and gems were pulled away with the weight of the chandelier. En masse they plummeted downward. Tur looked confused, as if he didn't understand what was happening. Chaaya, on the other hand, was desperately scrambling backward.

She'd barely managed to reach the edge of the danger zone when the tons of metal and flames and thick iron chains smashed Tur on the head. Dazed, he stumbled backward, slamming into a column with enough force to snap it in two. More of the precious gems cascaded from the ceiling.

Knowing it was now or never, Chaaya surged to her feet and dashed across the shattered tiles of the floor. She snatched her spear out of the rubble and leaped forward in full Xena mode. Tur's crimson eyes widened at the sight of her, but it was too late for him to react. Her spear was already piercing his lower stomach to puncture his heart before he could move.

"How many times do I have to tell you?" she asked between clenched teeth, twisting the spear until the screaming stopped. "My name is Chaaya."

Yanking her spear free, Chaaya turned to discover Dabbler surveying the destroyed room with wide-eyed horror.

"No!" Dabbler cried out, pointing a shaking finger in her direction. "You...you..." Words seemed to fail him.

Chaaya shrugged. "This was your idea, not mine."

The words had barely left her mouth when a heavy object smashed into the back of her head, nearly cracking her skull. Chaaya felt an explosion of pain, then a welcome darkness rushed up and crashed over her.

That was the last thing she knew.

Chapter 12

Basq paced the cramped cell. Back and forth. Back and forth. He was on his 733rd circuit—yes, he'd counted each one—when there was a faint groan from across the narrow space. Rushing to kneel beside the shabby cot, he grabbed Chaaya's hand as her lashes fluttered and she slowly opened her eyes.

A funny sensation tightened his chest. As if his unbeating heart was being squeezed in a tight vise.

After being trapped in the silver net, he'd been nearly comatose. The shocking pain had driven his demon into a protective hibernation, but he'd been distantly aware that Chaaya was being forced into a battle. The fear and sense of helplessness had been brutal. Much worse than any torture he'd ever endured.

Now he wanted to wrap her in his arms and never let her go.

Unfortunately they were currently locked in a dungeon far below the palace with a heavy iron door and silver lock that ensured he was effectively trapped. They needed to get out of there before the chieftain decided exactly how he wanted to punish Chaaya for not dying.

Her eyes at last focused and he ran the tips of his fingers over her cheek. "What part of *don't cause trouble* didn't you understand?"

She wrinkled her nose. "It wasn't my fault."

He skimmed his hand over her shaven scalp, surprised to find how soft the shorn strands of hair were beneath his palm. Then he traced the delicate tattoos that ran down the side of her neck.

"How badly are you hurt?"

"A few aches and pains." She shoved herself to a sitting position. "Nothing serious. What about you?"

He shrugged. "I drank the blood I had in the flask to regain my strength."

She studied his face, as if searching for any lingering wounds. Then, finally satisfied that he was fully healed, she swiveled her feet off the cot and glanced around the barren cell.

There wasn't much to see. A stone floor that matched the stone walls and stone ceiling. Two cots. And a door. That was it.

"How long was I out?"

"Two hours," Basq said before giving a faint shrug. He'd been too busy worrying to pay any attention to the passing time. "Maybe three."

Her eyes narrowed with fury. She shoved herself off the cot. "That bastard. I'm going to…"

"Chaaya." Basq grabbed her shoulders, keeping her from disappearing. "I can't get out of here."

"Oh." She made a visible effort to control her burst of anger, offering him a tight smile. "No problem. Escaping prisons is my specialty."

His grip softened as he smoothed his hands down the curve of her back, cupping her hips as he stepped close enough to savor her warmth.

"Not your only specialty," he assured her.

"True." She lifted her hand to run her fingers through his hair. "I'm also awesome at kicking orc butt."

She was teasing, but her words hit him like a sledgehammer to the gut. Suddenly he was back in the net, the pain searing through him as he heard the roar of the orc as he tried to kill this female.

"I hated being helpless," he ground out, his fangs aching. "I never want to feel like that again."

She cupped his cheek in her palm. "I had it under control."

His lips twisted. This female would face a horde of marauding trolls without batting an eye.

"Always in charge."

"It's how I roll."

He tugged her against him, desperately wanting to shut his eyes and pretend they were alone in his lair with nothing to think about but the glorious desire weaving a spell between them.

"I thought we were in charge together?"

Her thumb stroked along his jaw before tracing the tip of his fang. "That means having each other's backs, doesn't it?"

Basq shivered as the image of sliding his fangs into her soft, yielding flesh seared through his mind. The hunger for her taste had been simmering inside him since her arrival in Vegas. Now it felt like a wildfire, scorching through him with a ferocious intensity.

With a jerk, Basq dropped his hands and stepped back. He was treading in dangerous waters. The eternal, everlasting, forever and ever sort of danger.

"Yeah, that's what it means," he said, giving himself a mental shake. This wasn't the time for distractions.

No matter how tempting.

Chaaya studied him, perhaps sensing his inner conflict. Then, with a cocky little smile, she sauntered toward the door.

"I'm going to get some keys."

"Be careful, Chaaya," he urged. "The chieftain might act like a fool, but he's a cunning demon."

"A dead demon once I get out of here," she assured him.

"Not without me," he insisted. "I want in on the fun."

"Hold tight."

Chaaya pressed against the door, her body fading from sight as she oozed through the thick metal. Any other time, Basq would have been fascinated by her amazing talent. He'd never met anyone who could walk through solid walls. But now he resumed his pacing, his hands clenched in frustration.

It was annoying as hell to have Chaaya once again risking her neck while he was trapped. When he got his hands on the chieftain... No. Not his hands. His fangs.

He was on his sixth circuit when there was a faint click and the door swung open. Rushing out of the cell, he found Chaaya standing in the center of the passageway, a heavy set of keys dangling from her fingers.

"That was quick," he congratulated her.

"The guards were busy with a strange dice game that included lots of swearing and stomping their feet. If we hurry, we might be able to sneak past them."

He nodded, taking a step toward the closed door at the end of the dungeons.

"Wait," an urgent voice called from the cell across the walk space. "Master Vampire."

Chaaya sent him a puzzled glance. "A friend of yours?"

The torches shoved into the brackets along the dirt floor flickered as Basq's anger thundered through the air. "He's the bastard that sold us out."

Her eyes narrowed, as if she'd been struck by a sudden realization. Before she could speak, however, the imp continued his pleas for help.

"That's not true," he whined. "I would never betray a client. It's bad for business."

"Then how did they find me?"

"I was attacked just minutes after you left. I assume they followed you."

Chaaya rolled her eyes at the smooth words. "Do you believe in leprechauns?" she asked Basq.

"About as much as I believe this imp had nothing to do with our capture," he retorted.

"Wait. Okay." A desperate edge entered the imp's voice. "I might have heard the chieftain was searching for two intruders in the city."

"So you cashed in," Basq snapped.

"It's what I do."

Basq wanted to smash through the door and rip out the imp's heart, but he leashed the impulse. No use wasting his energy. Not when it'd been his own fault for trusting the imp in the first place. No need to compound his stupidity.

Plus, there was the sudden sound of a door being pulled open.

"Uh-oh. I think the guards are finished with their dice game," Chaaya warned.

"I'll deal with them," Basq assured her.

"You go ahead."

Basq sent her a curious glance. "What about you?"

"I have a small task to take care of. I'll join you before you reach Dabbler." Her lips twisted as he arched a brow. "That's the idiotic name of the chieftain." She nodded toward the far end of the dungeon. "Go."

Confident that Chaaya could take care of herself, Basq wrapped himself in darkness and silently moved through the door that had been opened. He found two mongrel goblins roaming around the cramped guard chamber, their heavy steps shaking the ground as they grunted in annoyance.

Basq was momentarily puzzled. What the hell were they doing? A second later realization hit.

They were searching for the keys that Chaaya had stolen.

He smiled in anticipation. Time for some fun.

Invisible to his enemies, Basq flowed into the chamber and grabbed the first guard.

The battle was short, brutal, and not nearly satisfying enough.

Within a minute both mongrels were sprawled on the stone floor, their unseeing gazes staring at the low ceiling.

Basq stepped over the dead demons and through the door on the other side of the chamber. He discovered a roughly carved tunnel that wound upward, taking him to the main floor of the palace.

He paused in a shadowed corner, releasing his power as he allowed his senses to flow through the massive building.

There were dozens of demons spread through the various rooms, mostly mongrels or fey creatures. No vampires or Weres. Good. He concentrated specifically on the smell of brownie that scented the air. That had to be the chieftain.

Once he got the trail, he moved across the marble floor and headed toward the narrow opening to the nearest turret. He didn't bother to use his powers of concealment as he raced up the narrow steps. He would be a blur to anyone except the most powerful demons.

The stone stairs spiraled upward, at last ending with a heavy wooden door that was defended by two large uniformed guards.

Basq halted just out of sight. Chaaya would never forgive him if he destroyed the chieftain before she could join him. A second later she appeared from around the bend in the staircase.

"Here," she murmured, tucking something in his hand.

Basq glanced down, catching sight of the amulet that was still warm from her skin. The strange sensation in the middle of his chest returned as the metal glinted in the moonlight that slanted through the narrow slots in the stone walls.

When Tarak had offered him the hammered eagle, he'd been honored. It not only sealed their relationship as clansmen, but it'd revealed the older vampire's trust in Basq.

Now the amulet was even more precious. Chaaya had obviously sensed how much it meant to him and had gone into the imp's cell to get it back. It proved that she cared more than she wanted to admit.

Of course, he wasn't stupid enough to embarrass her by making a big deal out of her thoughtful gesture. She liked the reputation of being a badass loner who didn't need anyone or anything.

He slipped it back on the gold chain that lay against his chest. He could barely sense its weight, but he realized that he missed the feel of it. As if he'd lost a piece of himself.

"Is the imp dead?" he asked, his voice pitched too low to carry.

"No." She shrugged. "I thought I would leave him to rot in his cell. It allowed me the pleasure of savoring his screams of despair as I left the dungeon."

He brushed his fingers over the amulet. "Thank you."

Another shrug. "We all need our good luck charms."

"What's yours?"

She kissed the copper blade of the spear she held in her hand. "This."

He nodded, then pointed above his head. "The chieftain has two guards on duty outside his private lair."

"I can take care of them."

He nodded. "I'll surround us in darkness. We'll be on them before they know we're there."

She flashed a smile. "You're just a handy-dandy dude to have around, aren't you?"

He sent her a dry smile. "Just stay close and don't make a sound."

"Got it."

Releasing his powers, Basq wrapped them in a small cocoon of darkness and headed around the curve. Chaaya was pressed tight against his back as he took the last steps to the top of the turret.

Once they were in striking distance, Chaaya stabbed her spear through the heart of the largest guard and was turning to deal with the second one before the first hit the floor. Basq concentrated on silently pressing open the door and stepping inside to make sure there were no other warriors waiting for them.

A quick glance revealed a cavernous room shrouded in shadows. There was a domed ceiling with intricate frescoes and walls that were lined with glass cabinets filled with treasures. Gems, coins, golden goblets. And in the center of the marble floor was a large bed draped in maroon satin. No guards.

Basq moved forward, his fangs lengthening at the scent of brownie that drenched the air. The chieftain was tucked beneath the covers. Just waiting to be killed. Very accommodating of him.

"Make sure no one sneaks up on us," Basq whispered to Chaaya, who appeared next to him.

There was a brief hesitation before she turned to walk back to the door. No doubt she sensed his fierce need for revenge. He'd been humiliated by the damned brownie, something he didn't forgive or forget.

Moving in silence, he reached the side of the bed just as the demon began to stir. Basq plunged the room into darkness. There was a rustle of satin, then a muttered curse as Dabbler realized he couldn't see.

"Who's there?" the brownie called out. "Rince?"

"Guess again," Basq mocked.

There was a long silence. Was the male hoping this was nothing more than a nightmare? Probably.

"Leech?" Dabbler finally forced himself to speak. "What have you done? I'm blind."

Basq's hand shot out, his fingers wrapping around the male's neck. "Luckily you don't need to see. Just listen."

The male froze, smart enough to know his life was hanging in the balance. "What do you want?" he asked. "Money? Females? Males? Name your price."

"Information."

"Yes." The sharp tang of sweat mixed with the earthy scent of the brownie, making Basq wrinkle his nose in distaste. "I have that," Dabbler assured him.

"There's a pureblooded Were in the city," Basq said.

"A Were?" The chieftain pretended shock. "In my bulla?"

With casual ease, Basq tightened his grip on the male's neck and lifted him off the bed.

"I can find her with your assistance, or I can find her without you." The temperature in the room plummeted and layers of frost coated the furnishings. "One means you're still alive, the other means you're dead."

"Fine. Yes." The brownie squirmed, the nasty stench of his sweat nearly overpowering. "The imp did mention the Were and some strange gargoyle creature."

Basq continued to dangle the creature over the bed, restraining his fierce urge to rip out his throat. Capturing Brigette so he could return Chaaya to the safety of Vegas was more important than avenging his damaged pride.

"Where are they?" he demanded, his fingers digging deeper.

Dabbler squealed like a pig. "He claimed they were in the sewers," he managed to choke out.

"And?"

"I sent my guards to fetch them, but they came back empty-handed. They said the sewers were empty."

Basq cursed. He'd hoped the male could confirm the rumor that Brigette was hidden in the sewers as the imp had claimed. Instead he'd revealed that they were too late.

Again.

Infuriated, Basq pulled the brownie toward him, viciously pleased to feel the fear that quaked through the demon.

"So you can't lead me to them."

Dabbler didn't miss the icy edge in Basq's voice, or the threat of what would happen to him if he proved to be useless.

"No, I told you—" There was another piggy squeal as Basq pressed the tips of his fangs into the male's flesh. He didn't want to taste his blood. He could already smell the taint of drugs coursing through his veins. He was assuming it came from the incense that filled the palace with clouds of smoke. "Wait," Dabbler pleaded.

"You just admitted you're of no use to me."

"I don't know where the Were is, but I'll have the guards scour the city until they find her."

As if Basq would willingly hang around the palace waiting for the guards to wrap him in a silver net and tie it with a bow.

"Not good enough," he growled. "I can scour the city myself. A lot quicker than your guards."

"I can…" Dabbler's words faded as the air thickened with Basq's icy fury.

"Die," Basq finished for him, fingers tightening until he could feel the slender bones begin to fracture.

"No." Dabbler reached out to grab at Basq's wrist, his legs kicking in a futile effort to escape. "There's a way."

There was an edge of terrified sincerity in his voice. As if he was certain that he had an answer, even if he didn't want to share it.

"Talk fast," Basq warned.

"Kgosi."

"Kgosi?" Chaaya abruptly moved to stand next to Basq. "What the hell is a Kgosi?"

Chapter 13

Brigette squatted on the ledge of the tower, scanning the city below. From her vantage point she could easily keep watch on the narrow streets while avoiding any unwanted attention.

"I was right, was I not?" Levet inquired. The tiny demon was perched next to her, loudly munching on a roasted chicken he'd managed to grab after she'd knocked out a goblin guarding the back door of a pub. She'd finished her own meal in less than two seconds. She was burning through energy at an alarming rate. "This is a much better location to hide."

She sent him a fierce glare. "I'm not hiding."

He furrowed his brow. "Then what are we doing?"

"Waiting."

"Ah." Levet swallowed the remainder of his chicken in one gulp before noisily licking his fingers. "You must admit that it smells nicer up here. Plus we can see the stars."

Brigette stared at her companion in bafflement. She'd never encountered another creature like him. It didn't seem to matter that she'd kidnapped him and hauled him to this weird-ass place. Or that they were leashed together by a magic neither of them understood. He was irrationally good-humored. As if nothing could possibly rattle him.

Brigette didn't know whether to be annoyed or impressed.

"You are…" Words failed her.

Levet flashed a winsome smile. "*Oui*, I know. A charming companion and a ravishingly attractive knight in shining armor. Females find me quite irresistible."

She paused before asking the question that had been teasing at the back of her mind since they'd been sucked through the portal.

"You said you knew what it was like to want to be a part of a family, but always alone." She tried to sound bored. As if she was simply passing the time.

"Ah, indeed, mine is a tragic tale," Levet agreed, pressing a hand to the center of his chest. "Like all proper heroes."

"Did your family die?"

The fairy wings fluttered, as if confused by her question. "*Non.* They are all alive and residing in Paris." Levet tapped a claw against his chin. "Well, all of them except for my aunt Bertha. She is like me, a wandering soul who never stays in one place too long." *Tap, tap, tap.* "I think it is because she once fell asleep in the Swiss Alps and woke centuries later to discover she was encased in a glacier. It took me months to chisel her out. Since then she never sleeps in the same place for more than a few days."

"Then why aren't you close to them?"

"My mother tried to kill me when I first hatched."

Brigette stared at the gargoyle. Was he being serious? "She tried to kill you?"

"*Oui.*"

"Why?"

He wrinkled his tiny snout. "She did not appreciate my uniqueness. Like most gargoyles, she has a depressing lack of imagination and a habit of smooshing things she does not understand."

There was no bitterness in his voice. Just a blithe acceptance that his mother intended to smoosh him for being different.

It made her resentment toward her family seem even more shallow. "How did you survive?"

"I was small enough to hide in cracks in the walls of our lair," he told her. "Eventually she grew tired of attempting to catch me."

"That's awful."

"That was not so bad. It became a game of sorts, and it kept me from becoming bored. There is nothing quite as refreshing as darting around a room while being chased by a gargoyle the size of a freight train." Without warning his wings drooped. "I will admit, however, my heart was broken the night I was driven out of Paris."

There was something weird niggling in the center of her heart. Sympathy? No. that couldn't be right. She was an evil bitch who tried to destroy the world, right?

She didn't get all soppy over a stunted lump of granite.

Brigette cleared her throat. "Do you hate them?"

"*Non.*"

"But…" She shook her head in disbelief. "They tried to kill you."

"All families are complicated."

"Complicated, not homicidal."

"I suppose that is true." He reached up to rub one stunted horn, as if considering his relationship with the mother who'd tried to end his life and then forced him to flee. "Still, if they had not driven me from my home, I would never have enjoyed the wonderous adventures that have been enormous fun. Nor would I have become a knight in shining armor and saved the world. More than once." He shuddered. "I would be stuck in the Guild castle, scabbing with my brothers."

"Scabbing?" Brigette had a crazed thought that he might be referring to some creepy gargoyle game. Then she rolled her eyes. "You mean squabbling?"

He waved aside her question. "And watching the moss grow on my very fine *derrière*."

With a shake of her head, Brigette leaned forward, staring down at the cobblestone street below her.

"If you could change the past, would you?"

Levet made a sound of surprise. "Certainly not. My past has molded me into the extraordinary creature that I have become. And as a bonus, there is not a smidge of moss on my *derrière*." He glanced over his shoulder in sudden concern. "Is there?"

About to inform him that she wasn't going to check his ass for lichen, Brigette abruptly shoved herself backward. Doing a flip, she landed in a crouched position, peering over the ledge of the tower at the vampire and slender female dressed in black strolling down the sidewalk directly beneath them.

"Shh," she hissed. "It's Chaaya."

"Really?" Levet rose to his feet, his wings quivering with excitement. "We should say hello. I do not like that bad-tempered leech, but Chaaya is always fun. She is my sister from another mustard."

"Mister," Brigette corrected before she could help herself.

"*Oui*, mister. *Bonjour*—"

"Stop, you idiot." She yanked on the leash connecting them, tugging him off the ledge. "She wants to kill me."

Levet looked confused before he widened his gray eyes. "Oh, I forgot."

"How could you…" Brigette shook her head in defeat. "Never mind." She returned her attention to the female, who had halted on the corner. The leech was standing beside her, along with another male who was wearing a long, gauzy robe that looked like a woman's nightgown. He had the floppy ears of a brownie but the features of a human. "I wonder what they're doing?"

Her question was answered when the man in the nightgown raised his hand and waved it in front of an empty alley. Suddenly a shimmer of light appeared, growing large enough for the vampire to step through, quickly followed by Chaaya and the unknown male.

"A secret entrance," Levet breathed beside her, obviously enchanted by the sight. "We should investigate."

She gave the leash a sharp tug as he spread his wings and prepared to follow them. "Are you out of your mind?"

Levet scowled, then a cunning smile curved his lips. "What if they are going to meet with a demon who can open a portal?" Levet asked, obviously trying to tempt her into entering the hidden passage. "Do you not wish to escape so you can resume your hunt for the mystery voice?"

Brigette grabbed the ledge in a white-knuckled grip, caught between the fear of being lured into a trap and the knowledge that she couldn't wait in this dreary gray place forever. Not only was her connection to the voice blocked, but her strength was fading.

"You're right," she reluctantly conceded, sending the gargoyle a warning frown. "We're going to follow them. But if you give one hint you're about to betray me, I'll—"

"*Oui, oui.* You will eat me." Levet hopped onto the ledge and motioned for her to join him.

Brigette straightened. "This is such a bad idea."

* * * *

Troy strolled into the barracks next to the dungeons that were reserved for the guards. There were a dozen soldiers gathered in the long room. Most of them wore the unique mer-folk scaled armor with tridents holstered on their hips, as if they were just coming off duty or preparing to relieve another guard. A few were seated around a table playing cards, others dozed in the shell-shaped chairs, and a couple stood in the back throwing small daggers at a target carved in the shape of an orc.

The scent of salt was thick in the air, along with a hefty undertone of suspicion as the mer-folk turned their heads to study Troy. There had always been some wariness, but this was intense. As if someone had deliberately poisoned them against him.

It didn't take a genius to guess who might be responsible.

Jord.

Pretending indifference, Troy wandered toward a male who was leaning against the wall with his arms folded over his chest. He had a sash around the hilt of his trident, a symbol that he was more than just another soldier, he was the officer in charge.

The male narrowed his blue eyes as Troy halted in front of him. "Are you looking for someone?"

"Riza," Troy revealed.

The male shrugged, his hostility barely concealed. "I haven't seen him."

Mmm. Troy arched a brow. Was the soldier prejudiced by Jord? Or was it something else? Maybe he just didn't like him.

He wouldn't be the first.

Or the last.

"What about Koral and Lusca?" he asked, referring to the two guards who'd been on duty in the outer chamber of the dungeons.

The officer cast a covert glance toward the male and female who were playing darts at the back of the room before he parted his lips to deny having seen them.

Troy walked away, in no mood to soothe the male's prickly resentment. Later he would discover exactly what Jord had said to ensure the guards wouldn't cooperate with his investigation.

He sauntered past the crowd gathered around the card table, resisting the urge to send them a finger wave or maybe blow them a kiss. He was powerful—far more powerful than anyone in the mer-folk castle could possibly imagine—but he wasn't capable of defeating a dozen armed warriors.

Besides, he wasn't there for shits and grins. After his conversation with Jord, he'd read through the reports offered by Riza, and then by Lusca and Koral. Not one of them had matched the others.

So who was lying?

Or were all of them lying?

He intended to find out.

Reaching the pair at the back, he glanced toward the target. "Is this a private game or can anyone join in?"

The male—Troy assumed he was Lusca—scowled, as if to make double sure Troy realized he wasn't welcome.

"What do you want?"

"Answers."

The male gave a toss of his head, his long, golden hair tinted with blue rippling down his back.

"What sort of answers?"

Troy smiled wryly. He'd perfected the hair flip. This male was an amateur. "About Brigette's escape," he said.

The female, Koral, tossed a small dagger from hand to hand. Her face was thinner and her teeth chiseled to narrow points. Troy sensed she was the more dangerous of the two.

"We already gave our report to Rimm."

Troy spread his fingers, offering a smile of faux regret. "I'm sorry, but there are few details I want to clear up."

Lusca folded his arms over his chest. "We're off duty."

Troy considered his options. He couldn't force the guards to reveal what they knew. Not unless Inga threatened them with the Tryshu, and he was trying to avoid that. The mer-folk would never respect her if she ruled with the same ruthless oppression that Riven had used.

So how...

It was the glint of the dagger's blade as Koral flipped it over and over that gave him the perfect solution.

"How about a little wager?" he drawled.

"For money?" Lusca demanded.

"I'll pay you one gold coin each time one of you hits closer than me to the bull's-eye."

Koral's eyes glowed with a sudden anticipation. Troy suspected she was the local champion.

"And if we lose?" Lusca asked, obviously not as confident that the outcome was predetermined.

Troy shrugged. "You answer my question."

The two guards exchanged a glance before Koral sent him a warning frown. "No cheating?"

"I can't use magic down here, can I?" he demanded. "Is it a deal?"

"Okay."

Koral grabbed several silver daggers from a basket and dropped them at Troy's feet. Then, with far more care, she opened a velvet-lined case to choose three daggers with mother-of-pearl handles. They were obviously her private collection.

Lifting her hand, she released the first dagger with a snap of her wrist. It flew end over end, the silver shimmering in the light of the nearby torches. With a thud it hit the target, sinking into the porous material. It was a near-perfect throw, hitting a breath from the bull's-eye.

Troy reached down to scoop up the daggers; then, straightening, he tossed one with nonchalant motion. It flew straight as an arrow, hitting the exact middle of the bull's-eye.

Shocked silence. Troy rolled his eyes. Did they really think he'd propose a wager if he wasn't sure he was going to win?

"How were you knocked out?" he asked.

Lusca reluctantly turned his attention from the target to Troy. "We were standing guard in front of the door to the dungeon."

"Which way were you facing?"

The male paused to consider the question. Obviously no one had asked him before.

"Toward the dungeon," he said in firm tones.

"You were hit from behind?"

Both guards nodded.

"You didn't sense anyone approaching?" Troy pressed.

"Obviously not," Koral snapped.

"You didn't smell anything?" Troy demanded.

They gave another shake of their heads, their expressions resentful. They were insulted by his questions, without even recognizing why he was asking. A disturbing realization. Mer-folk weren't the toughest or the most skilled soldiers. There was no need since they were protected behind the powerful magic that guarded their isolated lair. But even untrained fey should have been able to sense a stranger sneaking up behind them. A certain sound. A smell. A change in the temperature in the air. *Something.*

That meant whoever it had been was so familiar to them that he or she hadn't set off any alarms.

"What were you hit with?"

Lusca touched the back of his head, as if recalling the painful blow. "I don't know. Some sort of club."

"Or a trident?" Troy suggested.

Koral released a low hiss of anger. "Jord warned us you were trying to pin the Were's escape on one of the guards. Obviously he was right."

Ah. So that was what the merman had been telling them. Troy held the female's angry gaze.

"If I intended to do that, why would I be down here asking questions? I could simply make my accusations." He shifted his glance to Lusca. "I'm here for the truth. Nothing more, nothing less. Could it have been a trident?"

The male offered a grudging nod. "Yes."

Koral clicked her tongue, as if angered that Troy had made them admit their attacker might have been one of their own.

"I'm not answering any more questions until we throw again."

Troy waved a hand toward the target. She grabbed a dagger and positioned it in her fingers, taking several seconds to adjust her aim before throwing it toward the target. It twirled end over end, hitting next to his dagger in the bull's-eye. Troy threw his own, hitting just outside the circle. With a shrug, he reached into a hidden pocket in his tight pants and pulled out a slender gold coin. Casually he tossed it toward the female.

She grabbed the money, eying him with suspicion. Did she realize he'd deliberately allowed her to win? Probably. She wasn't stupid.

Taking another dagger from the case, she tossed it toward the target. This time she missed by a sliver. Troy barely waited for her dagger to reach the target before he took his turn. This time it was a direct strike.

Koral gaped in disbelief, but Troy was already turning his attention toward Lusca. "How long were you out?"

"Just a couple of minutes," the male said.

"What did—"

"You asked your question," Koral interrupted. "Throw."

"Fine." Troy impatiently tossed the dagger, hitting the bull's-eye with enough force to cause the other daggers to clatter to the stone ground.

Biting her bottom lip, Koral concentrated on the target, eventually throwing her dagger. It was good enough to hit the edge of the bull's-eye, but not good enough to beat Troy.

"What did you do when you woke?" Troy asked Lusca.

"The dungeon door was wide open, so we went in to check on the prisoner, but she was gone."

"What about Riza?"

Lusca lost a bit of his frosty suspicion. Was he becoming curious about the direction of Troy's questions? Troy hoped so. He needed information.

"What about him?" the male asked.

"Was he still unconscious?"

"Oh." Lusca glanced toward Koral as if he couldn't remember.

"He wasn't there," the female said, her tone firm.

"Wasn't he on duty inside the dungeon?" Troy asked.

"Yes." Koral visibly shuffled through her memories. "I guess he must have woken before us."

Troy arched a brow. "And he didn't try to help the two of you?"

The guards exchanged another glance. Clearly they hadn't considered the missing guard until this moment.

"Maybe he was chasing after the prisoner," Lusca at last suggested.

"What did you do next?"

Koral shook her head, grabbing a dagger to throw it at the target. Troy didn't even look. Keeping his gaze locked on Lusca, he tossed the dagger over his shoulder, allowing Koral's gasp of disbelief to assure him that he'd hit the exact center of the bull's-eye.

"Well?" he urged the male to answer his question.

Something that might have been admiration softened the male's expression. Obviously, the way to earn the male's trust was throwing a tiny dagger.

Odd.

"We set off the alarm and went in search of Rimm."

Troy nodded. "Was that standard protocol?"

Koral answered. "Yes."

"So why didn't Jord and Riza sound the alarm and go in search of Rimm?"

The two studied him with a matching expression of confusion. They didn't have an answer. Which was all the answer Troy needed.

There was something funky going on with Jord and Riza.

He reached into his pocket to pull out another gold coin and tossed it toward Koral.

"Here."

"I didn't win," she protested.

"You gave me what I needed."

Unexpectedly, the female tossed the coin back at him. "I don't want your money."

Troy caught the coin. "No?"

She nodded toward the target. "I want you to teach me to throw like that."

"Later," he promised.

Troy turned to stroll out of the guard room, already plotting his next move.

Jord had claimed that Riza was on the ground when he'd found the cell empty. But if that was true, why hadn't the younger male followed the protocol when he woke?

Something he intended to discover.

Chapter 14

Basq grimaced as they stepped into the alley only to be whisked into a vast desert. Instinctively he flinched as the illusion of golden sand drenched in sunlight surrounded them.

Dammit. He hated magic. Especially magic that sucked him from one place to another.

Glancing around to make sure that Chaaya was nearby and unharmed, he abruptly froze. Standing next to him, she was bathed in the dazzling sunlight that made her...glow. Her skin was as pale and smooth as ivory with soft lips that looked as if they'd been kissed by a rose. Her dark eyes held a hint of copper and the Celtic tattoos held a metallic glitter.

In the moonlight she was a ghostly beauty. In the sunlight she was gloriously, vividly alive.

Reluctantly he looked away, studying the vast sky above. The bright crystal blue didn't captivate him with the same enchantment as the sight of Chaaya. Oh, it might have if it'd been real. Of course, it would also have turned him into a pile of ash. Next he surveyed the rolling dunes that appeared to have no end. And perhaps they didn't.

Far in the distant he could make out the silhouette of a sprawling structure. It looked like a castle rising out of the sand with the traditional curtain wall and towering central keep. But the stylized décor on the gate reminded him of an ancient Persian fortress.

Basq pointed toward the castle. "Let's go."

With a strangled sound, Dabbler dug his feet into the sand. "No way. I've brought you to the lair of Kgosi. All you have to do is start walking. He'll find you."

Basq narrowed his eyes. "That wasn't a request. Go."

"No."

Frustration bubbled through Basq. He didn't like this place. Not only was the sun unnerving despite its inability to hurt him, but he could feel his power draining at an alarming rate. As if something—or someone—was sucking it out of him.

He bared his fangs. "Do you honestly think I won't kill you?"

Dabbler quivered, his fear sullying the air with an earthy stench. "If I go a step farther, I'm dead."

Chaaya moved to stand next to him, studying the brownie with a hard expression.

"It's a trap."

Dabbler shook his head, his earlobes flapping. "No. I swear."

Basq reached to wrap his fingers around the demon's throat. They were too exposed out here. Vulnerable. He wanted to find the mysterious Kgosi and get the hell out of there.

"I'm done with games."

"Listen." Dabbler held out his hands in a pleading gesture. "I can explain."

"Start talking," Basq commanded.

"My father didn't actually create the bulla," the demon admitted, licking his fat lips. "He was searching for a place to keep my mother from aging when he stumbled across an empty space between space."

Basq eyed the brownie in disbelief. "He just happened to stumble across an unclaimed bulla?"

"We thought it was unclaimed," Dabbler corrected. "My father built the palace for my mother, and we settled in to molder in dull isolation. After my parents died—"

"After you killed them," Chaaya interrupted.

"Fine, yes," Dabbler muttered. "After I killed them and started to create my city, I happened to discover this opening."

Basq studied the brownie. There was no mistaking his genuine fear, but the probability that the words spewing out of his mouth were true was zero to none. This male had lived in his own delusion of grandeur for so long, Basq doubted that he was capable of recognizing fact from fiction.

"You'd never noticed it before?" he asked.

Dabbler shook his head, flushing at the mocking disbelief in Basq's voice. "I don't know if I missed it or if it deliberately concealed itself, but one day it was simply there."

Basq let it pass. He was more interested in what they'd walked into than when Dabbler had found it.

"So you entered?"

"Of course." Dabbler hunched his shoulders. "Who wouldn't?"

"Most sane creatures," Chaaya muttered.

The brownie looked defensive. "I wanted to see if it was a portal in or out of my city."

"Ah." That claim made sense to Basq. "You were afraid that demons might be coming and going without paying your tithes."

"I'm a businessman."

Basq had several names for a male who murdered his own parents for profit. None of them were *businessman*. He didn't bother sharing them. This male was beyond shame.

"What did you find?" he instead asked.

"An oracle."

"Oracle?" Chaaya snorted in disgust. "They're fake."

"That's what I thought," Dabbler said. "But he hasn't been wrong about anything."

Chaaya folded her arms over her chest. "Like what?"

"He foresaw my city would grow and prosper."

Chaaya rolled her eyes. "Could he have been a little more vague?"

The brownie scowled, obviously annoyed by Chaaya's disbelief. "He said that my most trusted companion would betray me."

"Did he?" Chaaya asked.

Dabbler looked confused. "I'm not stupid. I killed him before he could try."

"That's it?" Chaaya snorted. "No tall, dark, and handsome man in your future? Maybe an unexpected windfall?"

Dabbler pressed his lips together. "He warned me that next time he saw me, I would die."

As if his words were some sort of magical cue, the sand behind them began to swirl, rising in the air to form a slender tornado. Basq stepped to the side, putting himself between Chaaya and the whirlwind.

His protective stance, however, did nothing to stop them from being sucked into spinning sand. One minute they were standing in the middle of the desert and the next they were consumed by the maelstrom. Blinded by the fierce wind, they were tumbled around like a load of laundry and then spat out into a...

Harem?

Basq quickly regained his balance as he glanced around the dark, opulent room. It was as large as a football field and shaped in an octagon with a soaring ceiling that was tiled with gold and rubies. The walls were carved out of stone and the windows were covered by delicate trellises. The floors were hidden beneath woven carpets and the air was thick with jasmine.

At the very center of the room was a massive pile of satin pillows in all shapes and colors, and above them Basq could make out a vaporous form drenched in silk and gold and decadence.

Jinn.

Basq hissed in shock. The elusive creatures rarely meddled in the affairs of other demons. Thank the goddess. Their power was greater than that of the dragons, and their tempers volcanic at best.

As he watched, the form went from wispy to a solid male who sprawled on the pillows. He was tall and slender and wore nothing more than a golden cloth tied around his waist. His chest was broad and his midnight skin glistened with waves of iridescent color, almost like a mirage shimmering in the sun. His black hair was worn in long dreadlocks threaded with gold, and his eyes were a brilliant green.

Basq felt the undeniable tug of attraction toward the male, and he knew both Chaaya and Dabbler would be feeling it as well. It wasn't personal. Just the potent sensual allure of a jinn.

"Welcome back, Dabbler," the jinn murmured with a vicious smile.

"Kgosi." Dabbler fell to his knees.

The jinn's smile widened. "So you decided to ignore my warning?"

"It wasn't my fault." Dabbler pointed toward Basq. "The leech forced me here."

The emerald gaze never strayed from the desperate brownie. "There's no use trying to appeal to my better nature. First, I don't have a better nature. And second, I have no control over fate." He waved his hand in a laconic motion. "I see what I see."

Dabbler licked his lips. "There has to be a way to change it. There always is."

"You've wasted your life hoarding money and power, but it will be no use to you now."

"You can't do this to me. You can't."

Jumping to his feet, Dabbler ran toward the open doorway across the room, his scream reverberating through the air.

Kgosi turned his attention toward Basq and Chaaya. Basq clenched his hands, his fangs instinctively lengthening at the power that thundered through the air. The male was doing nothing more threatening than lounging on his back as his slender fingers brushed the tassels of a pillow, but the echoes of his magic rippled through the room.

"I did warn him," Kgosi murmured.

Basq glanced out the opening, watching the brownie disappear over a sand dune.

"Perhaps you were premature," he warned. "It looks as if he's escaping."

The jinn shrugged. "Just give it time."

"An oracle's answer to everything," Chaaya muttered, moving to stand next to Basq. "That way people forget all the prophecies that are wrong in the hope that eventually one of them will get fulfilled. Then they're all like 'Ta-da. Aren't I amazing?'"

Basq froze, prepared for a blast of nasty magic. The jinns were infamous for their wiliness to kill over the slightest offense. Instead, the male chuckled.

"A disbeliever, Chaaya the Gatekeeper?" he drawled. "What of you, Basq?"

* * * *

Brigette stood in front of the alley, watching the gargoyle gingerly press his hand against an unseen barrier.

"I sense the magic, but I can't see it," she said in frustration.

"It is beautiful," the gargoyle murmured.

Brigette grimaced. There was nothing beautiful about the illusion of a nasty alley filled with trash between crumbling gray stone buildings. It reminded her of her old village. Well, without the coating of evil gook.

"What do you mean beautiful?"

"The sparkles are like stars." There was an expression of wonderment on the gargoyle's lumpy face. "As if the entire universe is swirling across the doorway."

Brigette squashed her stab of envy. So what if she couldn't see the sparkles? She was looking for a way out, not imaginary stars. Besides, she'd learned her lesson about wallowing in jealousy. It never led to anything good.

"Are they dangerous?" she asked.

"I do not sense evil. It is more…" Levet wrinkled his snout.

"Yes?"

"Indifference."

Brigette squared her shoulders. She was going to trust the gargoyle. It didn't make a damned bit of sense, but she was convinced that he wouldn't deliberately lead her into a trap.

"Okay. Let's get this over with."

They stepped forward together, and Brigette felt the magic brush against her skin. She smelled jasmine and heat and…sex.

That was weird.

Bracing herself for an attack, Brigette grunted in surprise as she was dumped into the middle of an empty desert. She shielded her eyes, blinded by the searing sunlight. If there were any enemies nearby, she couldn't see them.

Eventually her eyes adjusted and she glanced around.

Lots of sand. And nothing else.

"Ah, sunlight." Levet tilted back his head as if absorbing the golden rays.

"It's not real," Brigette informed him. She didn't have a lot of magic, but what she possessed was deeply rooted in nature. This desert was void of life, revealing it was nothing more than an illusion.

Levet nodded. "*Oui*, but I turn to stone in daylight. It is a treat to feel the warmth on my skin."

Brigette blinked. The creature truly was the oddest thing. With a shake of her head, she returned her attention to their surroundings.

She couldn't see anyone, but she caught a familiar scent. "Chaaya and the leech are here." She turned in a slow circle, searching for footprints in the sand. "Somewhere."

Without warning, Levet abruptly pressed against her leg, as if something had frightened him.

"Oh no."

"What?"

"I smell jinn."

Brigette glanced down at his worried face. She'd heard of jinn, but honestly, she'd thought they were a myth. Like the Loch Ness Monster. Or a comfortable bra.

"Is that bad?"

"It is not good."

Brigette clenched her hands. If Levet was eager to retreat, then the jinn must be dangerous. Really, really dangerous.

"Maybe we should leave and reconsider our options," she suggested.

"A very wise notion."

About to turn to locate the portal, Brigette was distracted by a distant scream.

"Wait. What is that?"

Levet cocked his head to the side. There was another scream, and at the same time, a small form appeared over a distant sand dune.

"The brownie mongrel."

Brigette's stomach did a strange flop as the brownie floundered through the sand, his harsh screams hammering her delicate ears.

"He sounds like he's dying," she muttered.

Levet gave a tug on her robe. "We were leaving, were we not?"

"Yeah."

They cautiously backed toward the portal, keeping a wary eye on the demon, who was waving his arms in a wild gesture.

"Get out of my way, idiots," the brownie shouted.

"Hey, this is our exit. Find your own," Levet shouted back.

There were more wild gestures from the brownie before the sand beneath Brigette's feet started crawling up her leg. As if it'd come to life.

"Levet," she growled, trying to pull her leg free. The tendrils of sand were not only creepy, they were threatening to trap her.

"I got this."

The gargoyle lifted his hand, holding his palm flat as he muttered a magical word. There was a sputter, then a puff of smoke, and Brigette had a flashback to the last time the gargoyle had used his magic.

He'd nearly killed them both.

"No, don't," she snapped.

In his typical fashion, Levet ignored her, concentrating on his spell. There were more sputters, then with a wave of his hand, a large fireball formed in midair.

"There, see?" He beamed with pride.

Brigette reached out, but before she could grab the ridiculous creature, the brownie barreled by, knocking her aside. Turning her head, she watched the demon leap toward the portal. At the same time, Levet launched his fireball. They met at the portal at the same time.

Predictably, the fireball exploded as it hit the barrier. Just as predictably, the brownie screamed. A shrill, earsplitting scream.

Brigette covered her ears and braced herself. She'd already been in a portal with Levet's magic. She knew what was coming next. Or at least she thought she knew.

There was a rumble, as if an earthquake was rising beneath their feet. Then, with a concussive impact, the portal blew apart. Wind sheared past Brigette, forcing her to her knees and nearly stopping her heart. Worse, it picked up the loose sand that surrounded them and scoured it across her skin.

She was being flayed by the miniscule projectiles.

She didn't know how much time passed before the ground stopped shaking, but it felt like an eternity. At last convinced she wasn't going to be ripped apart, she shoved aside her hair that had been tugged from its braid. Sand sprayed out of the thick curls, sticking to her damp skin to form a crusty layer.

Brigette grimaced. She needed a shower in the worst way. Unfortunately, that was probably not going to happen. At least not in the near future.

Slowly turning, her mouth dropped open at the sight of the charred, gaping hole. It looked as if a nuclear bomb had struck. Perhaps a meteorite.

There was no sign at all of the portal or the brownie.

Her gaze swiveled back to stab Levet with a glare of disbelief. "What have you done?"

The fairy wings drooped. "Oops."

Chapter 15

Chaaya tried not to stare. The jinn was a dark, luscious temptation as he inspected her with a lazy gaze. Everything about him oozed sex and desire and…hunger. And she had a suspicion she'd be crawling over him in mindless need if he released the full effect of his magic.

Thankfully he was content to study her with an unwavering emerald gaze. At least until the distant screams echoed through the air. Then he offered her a smile that made her heart slam against her ribs.

"As I said." Kgosi waved a languid hand. "Just a matter of time."

Chaaya shook off the bewitchment. If she'd still been human there would have been no way she could break free of the magic, but her current reincarnation—or whatever had happened to her—offered immunity to most magic. Plus, there was a large part of her that would never be swayed by a jinn, no matter how gorgeous he might be. A part that belonged to another male, even if she wasn't prepared to admit it.

"How do you know my name?" she asked, ignoring Basq's warning frown. She didn't know much about jinns. No one did. But it didn't take an expert to suspect that only a fool pissed them off. That didn't stop her, of course. She didn't know how to be anything but an in-your-face sort of gal. "Have you been watching us?"

"I've caught glimpses of you over the centuries," Kgosi claimed. "I know you were sacrificed to halt the evil tide from corrupting the earthly magic."

Chaaya narrowed her eyes, but it was Basq who pointed out the obvious. "Her story isn't a secret."

The emerald gaze drifted over Basq's tightly clenched features. "But yours is, isn't it, vampire? You have hidden in the shadows, both real and metaphorical."

Chaaya's brows snapped together. Dabbler had claimed Kgosi was an oracle and that he could help her locate Brigette. But she wasn't nearly so confident. In fact, she suspected that Dabbler had hoped to dump them here in the belief the jinn would be angry enough to kill them for intruding.

Instead, it sounded like the brownie had died a painful death.

Bonus.

"Can you see the future?" she asked.

He pursed his full, sensual lips. "I can see several futures."

She made a choking sound. "I hate the mumbo jumbo of oracles."

Basq stepped closer, as if expecting the jinn to strike out. Instead Kgosi arched a brow.

"Have you known many oracles?"

She wanted to tell him she'd known a hundred. Maybe a thousand, but that ruthless emerald gaze warned her that Kgosi would know if she was lying.

"Just the one in our village," she admitted. "Sybil was always predicting disaster. Either the harvest would fail, or a plague was coming." She wrinkled her nose. Sybil had craved constant attention as she'd drifted around the village dressed in flimsy robes, her face covered by a veil. Every so often she would stop in the center of the market and start spouting nonsense while she waved her arms in dramatic motions. "Once she predicted that the moon was going to fall from the sky."

Kgosi appeared unimpressed. "She sounds more like a charlatan than a true oracle."

"That's what I tried to tell everyone, but would they listen to me?" Chaaya spread her fingers in a gesture of defeat. "No."

A silence filled the vast space as Kgosi studied her with his unnerving gaze. "She didn't get anything right?" he at last demanded.

"A few rainstorms. Some deaths."

His eyes narrowed. "And?"

Chaaya snorted. "And she told me that she could see darkness in my future."

Kgosi tapped a slender finger on the pillow next to him. "Didn't you have darkness?"

Chaaya grimaced at the reminder of her endless centuries spent in the hell dimension.

"That could mean anything," she protested. "Besides, I think it was more a fervent hope for something bad to happen to me than an actual prophecy. She hated me."

"Shocking," Basq softly murmured.

She widened her eyes with utter innocence. "I know, right? I'm oozing with charm."

There was a rustle of silk and a soft breeze scented with jasmine as Kgosi rose to his feet.

"If you have no belief in oracles, then why did you seek me out?"

Chaaya tilted back her head, keeping her gaze locked on the male's perfectly carved face. His broad, naked chest was more than a mere ghost girl could handle.

"Dabbler promised a way to find the Were I'm trying to capture. He didn't say you were an oracle."

"Ah." Kgosi tilted his head, as if listening to a silent voice. "The Were. And a tiny gargoyle."

Chaaya jerked in shock. Could he actually be a for-real oracle? One that did more than prance around for attention?

"You know where they are?"

"I thought you didn't believe."

She planted her fists on her hips. "Tell me."

The male smiled. "Closer than you imagine."

Disappointment flooded through her. "See?" She sent a disgusted glance toward Basq. "Mumbo jumbo."

A ripple of magic slammed against Chaaya, a less-than-subtle reminder that this male might act like a lazy, self-indulgent, reasonably harmless demon, when in reality he was one of the most powerful forces in any dimension.

"If you want the right answer, you must ask the right question," he told her.

Chaaya's mouth went dry as she warily returned her attention to the jinn. "You claimed to see Dabbler's future, and our past."

Kgosi nodded. "I can see both."

"What about the present?"

"Time has no meaning for an oracle." Kgosi waved his arms in an expansive gesture. "When I have a vision it could be from yesterday, today, or a thousand years from now."

"That's...unhelpful," Chaaya muttered before she could halt the words.

The emerald of his eyes began to swirl, as if they were caught in a whirlwind. Or perhaps they were about to shoot out tornadoes that would rip her to shreds. Hard to say.

"I have remained polite because this meeting was destined to occur, but don't try my patience, Chaaya."

Basq moved with blinding speed, placing his larger body in front of her. "Don't threaten her."

Chaaya's gut clenched with terror. She didn't particularly want to be shredded by a tornado, but that was a lot better than seeing Basq hurt. The mere thought was enough to send her into a panic.

No tornadoes appeared, however, and the jinn's voice was more curious than threatening as he studied the vampire.

"Does she know?"

Chaaya stepped to the side, watching Basq's face pale. He slowly shook his head.

"Know what?" she asked. No answer. "Basq?"

"Later," he promised.

Her lips parted to demand an explanation when the jinn abruptly returned his attention to her, his eyes still swirling.

"Ask the question," he barked.

Chaaya's flippant attitude was decidedly absent as she searched her brain for the right words. She wasn't afraid. At least, not for herself. But she wasn't going to put Basq at risk because of her smart-ass mouth.

"Is the Were infected with the same darkness that I battled before?" she cautiously asked.

"No."

Chaaya grimaced. She didn't know whether to be relieved or disappointed. The devil she knew or the devil she didn't—which was worse?

"But she is infected with some new power?" she pressed.

"No. She's being manipulated, but she's not infected."

Chaaya grunted in shock. Was it possible she'd been chasing after the stupid Were for no good reason? Typical. One day she'd cure her impulsive...

No. That was a lie. She would always be impulsive. But perhaps one day she'd have a partner who could whisper words of caution in her ear. She hastily shoved aside the weird thought. This wasn't the time or place for such nonsense.

"So there's no danger to the world?" she asked.

Kgosi held up a slender hand. "I didn't say that."

"But—"

The hand sliced through the air, warning Chaaya she was near the end of the jinn's patience.

"The question," Kgosi snapped.

Running her fingers down the shaft of her spear, she allowed the tingles of magic to bolster her courage. She knew the question.

She just didn't want to ask it.

At last, she squared her shoulders. This was important. She didn't know why. She just knew.

She forced out the words. "Can you take me to the power who is manipulating Brigette?"

A smile of triumph curved Kgosi's lips. "At last."

Basq wasn't nearly so pleased. Whirling to face her, he studied her in horror. "Chaaya, no."

She shrugged, already prepared as the jinn waved his hand and a tiny cyclone formed above her head. The wind battered her, tugging at her hair and forcing her to squeeze her eyes shut.

Then, just as she felt herself being sucked off the ground, a familiar hand reached out to grab her arm.

Shit.

* * * *

Inga was always nervous when she sat on the throne. Not only did she fear that it might shatter beneath her massive weight, but it made her the center of attention. Something she hated. Even worse, she had to wear her crown. The stupid thing poked painfully into her skull, and it would never stay straight. No matter how many times she pushed it into place, it would inevitably slide to the side, making her look like a drunken sailor.

The only thing that made her feel better was the heavy Tryshu she gripped in her hand. People might laugh at the sight of her on the throne, but they wouldn't do it to her face. Not as long as she carried the huge trident.

"Are you ready?" Troy asked.

He stood on the dais next to her, his expression impatient. She heaved a gloomy sigh.

"As ready as I'll ever be."

He smiled, patting her shoulder. "You'll be brilliant."

She shook her head. "I'm not clever or subtle like you, Troy. You can convince anyone to tell you what you want. If I need information from someone, I bash them over the head."

He gave another pat on her shoulder. "Just ask him to recount what happened the night Brigette escaped." He started to turn away, only to glance back. "And make sure it's a detailed account. We need to discover if he's been lying."

Yeah. No problem. Inga forced herself to nod. "Okay."

Leaping off the dais, Troy motioned toward Rimm, who was standing across the long room. Then, with a last glance at Inga, the imp disappeared into the secret passageway.

Inga released a shaky breath, concentrating on the young guard who entered the throne room with a wary expression.

Showtime.

"Welcome, Riza," she said, inclining her head in what she hoped was a regal manner, at the same time motioning for Rimm to close the door. She didn't want anyone overhearing this particular conversation.

Slowly the merman walked toward the throne, his scaled uniform gleaming and his fingers nervously tugging at the belt that held his trident in place. Once he was standing in front of Inga, he performed a deep bow.

"You asked to see me, Your Majesty?"

"Yes."

There was an awkward pause. Riza cleared his throat. "Is something wrong?"

Inga sucked in a deep breath. She'd rehearsed this encounter with Troy, she reminded herself. She knew what she was supposed to say.

"On the contrary. I believe I owe you my personal gratitude," she assured the man, careful not to smile.

For some reason the mer-folk found her smile intimidating. Maybe because of her razor-sharp teeth. Or more likely because it usually looked like a grimace rather than an expression of happiness. Not her fault. She hadn't had much practice smiling.

Riza looked confused. "Gratitude?"

"You were the only guard to be alarmed by the Were's ramblings," Inga clarified. "If we had listened to your concerns sooner, then Brigette might still be locked in her cell."

"Oh." Riza shifted from foot to foot. He was obviously nervous, but that didn't mean he was guilty. "I did nothing."

Inga clicked her tongue. "There's no need to be modest."

He stretched his lips into a smile. "Thank you, Your Majesty. If that is all…"

Riza started to back away, but Inga waved the Tryshu in his direction. Immediately the male froze in place.

"Actually, we have need of your services," she told him.

The guard glanced behind Inga, as if expecting to see Troy. "We?"

Inga nodded toward Rimm, who stood silently by the doors. She'd tried to tell the older male that she didn't need his protection, but he'd insisted on being in the throne room.

"My captain continues to insist that the dungeons are adequately protected, but I'm not convinced."

Riza's gaze darted back to her, his expression defensive. Was he trying to decide what nefarious reason Inga might have for asking her questions? Or just baffled why he would be included in a debate between his captain and his queen?

"They are extremely well guarded, my queen," he assured her.

"Obviously not," Inga protested. "My prisoner was speaking to shadows and no one noticed but you."

"I'm sure they just dismissed her babbling as that of dungeon fever."

Inga lifted her shaggy brows. "Dungeon fever?"

"It happens to prisoners when they're driven mad from the isolation."

She pretended to consider his explanation. At last she heaved a gusty sigh. "Perhaps, but that doesn't prove the dungeons are secure."

Riza glanced toward Rimm. The older male gave a shrug, as if warning Riza that he was on his own.

"I'm not sure what you want from me, Your Majesty," Riza hesitantly admitted.

Inga settled back in the throne. "I want you to tell me what happened."

"Happened?" the guard furrowed his brow. "When the prisoner escaped?"

"Yes."

"I made my report." He waved a hand toward Rimm. "I'm sure the captain can—"

"The queen would like to hear it from you," Rimm interrupted.

A salty-sour tang filled the air. For whatever reason, Riza didn't like the direction of the conversation.

"I was on duty guarding the dungeon," he said, hesitantly.

Inga nodded. "Alone?"

"There were two guards in the outer chamber."

"And then?"

"I was struck from behind and knocked unconscious."

Inga pursed her lips, as if considering her next question. "You didn't see who it was?"

"No."

"And when you woke, the cell was open?"

Riza's expression remained defensive, but he responded without hesitation. Probably because he'd told this part of his story a dozen times.

"It was. And the prisoner was gone."

"What did you do?"

Again there was no hesitation. "I went in search of her."

"What about the other guards?"

Riza faltered. "Which ones?"

Inga leaned forward. "The two in the outer chamber."

"Oh…I…" He looked confused, obviously caught off guard. Mention of the other guards hadn't been in his report. "They were gone," he finally said.

"Gone?" Inga pretended to be baffled. "Weren't they knocked out at the same time?"

"Well…" He hesitated before seeming to be struck by inspiration. "That's what they said. I never did see them knocked out, so I can't say for certain what happened to them."

Inga hid a grimace. What was that human saying? Throwing someone under the train? A bus?

"Are you suggesting that they might have been responsible for Brigette's escape?"

Riza spread his hands, trying to appear regretful. "I'm not suggesting anything. I just know they weren't in the outer room when I woke and went in search of the prisoner." He paused, clearing his throat. "Forgive me, Your Majesty, but I really should return to my post."

Inga stroked her fingers along the shaft of the Tryshu before giving a grudging nod. They had what they needed.

"Of course," she agreed, waving her hand toward the doors. "Thank you again for your very brave service to the throne."

"Your Majesty." The male backed toward the door that Rimm was pulling open. Then, with a jerky bow, he turned and fled down the corridor.

Inga remained seated on the throne as Troy strolled out of the hidden passage and halted next to the dais.

"Gotcha," he murmured, a smug smile curving his lips.

Inga frowned. The younger guard had been twitchy and obviously eager to be away from the throne room, but that didn't prove guilt.

"You're sure?"

Troy sent her a startled glance. "Koral and Lusca swore that they woke to find Riza gone," he reminded her. "Now Riza is saying that they were gone, with the implication that they might be responsible."

"Koral and Lusca could be the ones who are lying."

"I don't believe in coincidence." Troy's voice was hard. He'd made up his mind who was responsible. "It was Riza and Jord who made a show of Brigette talking to shadows. And Jord who rushed in to reveal that the Were had escaped."

Inga slumped back in the throne. Troy was right. The two guards had been manipulating them from the beginning.

"I still don't understand why," she muttered.

Troy's green eyes glowed with ruthless determination. "That's what I'm about to find out."

Chapter 16

Levet flapped his wings, attempting to shake off the layers of sand. The fine grains were everywhere. In every nook and cranny of his body. He grimaced. He was going to be chafed raw by the time he got back to Vegas.

"The portal is gone." Brigette was staring at the big hole in the ground, her expression one of disbelief.

Levet cleared his throat. He'd hadn't fully thought through the danger of tossing a fireball after the fleeing brownie. Styx's mate Darcy often told him that he needed to think before he acted, but it seemed a wasted opportunity. How did you know how anything was going to turn out until after it was over?

He would have missed some spectacular adventures if he stopped to think what might happen.

"*Oui.*" He scratched the tip of his snout. "But on the bright side, the brownie is also gone."

"Bright side?" The Were whirled around, her hands balled into tight fists. "There is no bright side."

"Of course there is," Levet protested. Really, werewolves could be so crabby. It had to be all that hot blood pumping through their veins. He spread his arms wide, offering his best smile. "You wanted to be out of the bulla, and here we are."

She refused to properly appreciate his awesome efforts. Or even his smile.

"Yeah, stuck in a strange dimension with a jinn." She glanced around the empty desert as if expecting the powerful creature to pop out of a nearby dune. "Perfect."

"The jinn is unfortunate," Levet had to agree. "But if we are careful, it is possible we will survive."

She blinked. "That's your bright side?"

"It's better than always being a gloomy butt." He dropped his arms, studying the tight line of her jaw as she struggled to contain her temper. "Does nothing make you happy?"

She released a growl. "Certainly not being stranded in the middle of a desert."

"That is not an answer. What will make you happy, Brigette?"

She flinched, as if his soft words had rubbed against a raw nerve. "I don't know," she admitted. "I thought power would fill the hole inside me."

"There is only one thing that can fill that hole."

She pointed a warning finger in his face. "Don't say it."

"Love."

"I told you not to say it," she snapped.

Levet lifted his hand in a helpless gesture. "It is true."

Brigette turned, gazing blindly over the rolling sand. "I was loved."

"Not by yourself."

She snorted, her lips twisting into a self-derisive smile. "I loved myself. Too much."

Most demons no doubt would agree with the female. She'd sacrificed her home, her family, and her pack all for the promise of power. How could she be anything but a selfish bitch?

Levet, however, wasn't so easily fooled.

"*Non.* You judged yourself so lacking you destroyed everything in an effort to prove yourself worthy."

She made a small, choked sound. As if she'd almost swallowed her tongue. "How could you possibly know what I felt?"

"Because I did the same."

"You made a deal with an evil spirit to destroy your clan?"

He shook his head. "Not precisely, but I have occasionally rushed into situations that were not entirely safe."

She pointedly glanced toward the gaping hole in the sand. "Occasionally?"

Levet heroically ignored her mocking tones. The female had not had the best life. She'd been infected by an evil spirit, sacrificed her family, and then ended up in a dungeon. It was no wonder she was a gloomy gussy. Hmm. That didn't seem right. He shrugged.

"I have a need to prove I am as heroic as any other demon," Levet confessed.

He didn't like revealing his secret lack of confidence, not to anyone. The world depended on his bubbling enthusiasm. But this female was clearly in need of a pep talk. And since he was the only one available, he had to do his duty.

Perhaps sensing they shared more in common than she wanted to admit, Brigette's anger drained away and she held up her hands in a gesture of defeat.

"What are we supposed to do now?"

"We find a portal," Levet told her.

"Can you sense one?"

"In that direction. But…" He wrinkled his nose.

Brigette rolled her eyes. "Let me guess. That's where the jinn is?"

"*Oui.*"

"Nothing else?"

Levet closed his eyes, allowing his senses to spread through the desert. The power of the distant jinn was like a tidal wave, beating against him and making it almost impossible to determine if there was any other magic in the dimension.

At last he firmly shook his head. "*Non.*"

"Damn." Brigette narrowed her eyes against the blinding blaze of the overhead sun. "What about Chaaya? Is she here?"

"I do not sense her or the leech."

"I suppose that's one small miracle," Brigette muttered in resigned tones.

"Do not fear." Levet reached up to pat her hand. "I will distract the jinn and then you can escape."

Brigette jerked her head down to study him with a startled expression, as if she couldn't believe anyone would sacrifice themselves to save her.

"Are you insane?"

Levet blinked. What an odd question. "I am a hero."

She scowled. Then, before Levet could assure her that he was indeed noble enough to martyr himself, she lifted her arm and shook it.

"Nice, but I think you forgot something."

"Did I?" Levet was confused, but not necessarily surprised. "Unfortunately I have forgotten many things," he confessed. "Styx, the King of Vampires, told me that I have a hole in my head. Or perhaps he said he intended to put a hole in my head. To be honest, I was not really listening. He babbles about the most uninteresting things. Like the night he was yakking about the importance of not selling his big sword on eBay, even though he never uses the thing and I needed the money to buy a new—"

"This!" Brigette rudely interrupted, giving her arm another shake.

Levet frowned. "I was supposed to remember your arm? How odd."

Spitting out curse words, the female grabbed the glowing strand that held them together.

"This."

"Oh. The tether?"

"I couldn't escape even if you were able to distract the jinn," she reminded him. "Not as long as we're bound together."

"Actually." Levet cleared his throat. "It is possible I was not entirely honest with you."

Brigette looked puzzled. "About what?"

"About the magic that has bound us together." Levet whispered a soft word of magic and the leash disappeared.

Brigette's eyes widened and her mouth fell open as she studied her arm in disbelief. At last she sent him a glittering glare.

"You lied?"

"Lied is such an ugly word," he protested.

She took a step forward, the already hot air becoming an inferno as her anger lashed out in a physical wave of heat.

"Levet."

"I did not wish you to do something you would later regret," he protested.

She bared her white teeth. "Like eating you?"

"That would have been at the top of the list."

The female snarled in fury, her muscles tensing as if she was preparing to leap on him.

"I'm going to—"

Whatever she was about to say was lost as the sand behind her began to spin. Faster and faster, the fine grains twirled in a whirlwind that grew over seven feet tall. Hastily, Levet backed away. He'd already felt the thunderous magic that beat inside the cyclone. This wasn't good. It wasn't good at all.

The wind battered at them as the cyclone drifted closer, then without warning, a tall form stepped out of the spinning sand.

Brigette gasped, her hand pressing against the center of her chest as she ogled the half-naked male who stood in front of her. Levet sniffed. The jinn was gorgeous, of course. They always were. And his stunning emerald eyes smoldered with a sensual promise. But still. There was no need to gape at him as if he were some sort of god.

Especially when the jinn was regarding them with an expression of extreme irritation.

"Enough of your squabbling," the jinn chastised. "The two of you are giving me a headache."

* * * *

Chaaya glanced around the black…nothingness that surrounded them. It was like they were trapped in outer space. Or maybe wedged somewhere between dimensions.

The thought should have terrified her. She had no ability to create portals to escape the strange void. Instead she was furious.

Whirling around, she glared at the male who was calmly investigating their surroundings. As if he hadn't just ruined everything.

"You just can't help yourself, can you?" she snapped.

The aggravating male arched a brow. "Excuse me?"

"Why did you grab me?"

He turned to face her, his arms folded over his chest. "The question is why did you ask the jinn to take you to the power controlling Brigette?"

"It's what I do." She waved her arms in a dramatic motion. She couldn't help herself. She was a little…emotional. "It's my duty."

He stepped toward her, his own emotions tightly controlled. Well, not so tightly, she acknowledged as a savage shiver raced through her body. The temperature was coating her in a layer of ice.

"No. You sacrificed your life to halt the evil from entering the world," he reminded her. As if she'd somehow forgotten. "You've done your duty."

She wrapped her arms around her. It wasn't that she was actually cold, but her mind told her that she *should* be.

"That's not how it works."

His eyes narrowed. "According to who?"

Chaaya snorted. It was a stupid question. So she gave him a stupid answer. "Destiny."

He didn't roll his eyes, but he looked skeptical. Still, he didn't argue. "Fine, then we do it together."

Chaaya stomped her foot. It wasn't childish. It was…demonstrative.

"I didn't ask you to get involved in any of this," she reminded him.

He studied her for a long moment. Was he deciding what to say? Or debating the pleasure of walking away and leaving her to stew in her own impulsive folly?

"Do you want me to tell you what Kgosi meant when he asked me if you knew?" he abruptly demanded.

The word *no* hovered on her lips. Now wasn't the time for that sort of conversation. Then curiosity overcame any claim to logic, and she nodded.

"Yes."

"He sensed you were my mate."

Chaaya hissed, as if she'd taken a blow to her stomach. It didn't matter that she'd sensed the emotional bonds weaving them together. Or Basq's fierce need to protect her. Or her own need to protect him.

It was still a shock to hear the word spoken out loud.

"Mate?"

He stepped toward her. "Do I truly have to explain what the word means?"

"I know what it means, but…" Her words trailed away as another shiver raced through her.

He moved until he was close enough to lightly brush his fingers down her cheek. At the same time, he deliberately leashed in his powers to allow the air to warm above freezing.

"Yes?" he asked.

She tilted back her head, becoming lost in the striking beauty of his eyes. "How can you be sure?"

He cupped her cheek in his palm, wrapping his other arm around her waist. "Like you said. Destiny."

Destiny…

The word had always been a curse to Chaaya. Somehow her destiny always meant pain and loss and loneliness.

It never meant being partnered with a sexy, brooding male who made her heart thump and her blood hot with hunger.

"I drive you nuts," she muttered.

"True. But that is exactly what I need." His voice was husky as he splayed his fingers against her lower back, urging her to arch against his hardening erection. "Otherwise I become a dull lump who wouldn't recognize fun if it bit me on the ass."

"Don't." She reached up to press her fingers against his mouth. She'd said the words, but having them thrown back in her face made her wince in regret.

He nibbled at the tips of her fingers. "You bring excitement to my very boring life."

Chaaya snuggled closer, moving her finger until she could press it against the tip of his large fang.

"Is that a good thing?"

The white center of his eyes glowed with a sudden hunger. For blood or sex? Or both? A groan was wrenched from her throat at the vivid image of having him pumping deep inside her at the same time as those fangs were buried in the flesh of her neck. Oh, yes. She was fully on board with both.

His nose flared as he easily caught the scent of her desire. Allowing his fingers to skim down her neck, he swiftly slid her leather coat off before slipping his hands beneath the white tee.

"It took me a while to recognize it, but yes, it's a good thing," he assured her.

Chaaya stood still as he peeled off the undershirt to reveal her bare torso.

"Basq," she rasped in shock. "What are you going?"

The darkness around them swirled. Was it reacting to the vampire's intense desire?

Impossible to know for sure.

On the other hand, Chaaya didn't have to guess if *she* was reacting to his touch. Her knees nearly buckled as he cupped her breasts in his hands.

"What I've wanted to do since you arrived in Vegas." His thumbs swept over the tips of her nipples, teasing them to tight nubs. "Perhaps from the moment I was created."

Chaaya arched her back, pressing hard against his thick erection. She wanted this male. No, *wanted* wasn't a big enough word. She ached for this male. As if he'd ignited a fire that had been smoldering for centuries, not just a few weeks.

Maybe Basq was right. Maybe they'd been waiting for this moment from the moment they'd been created. And now the promise of an explosive orgasm clenched her gut with anticipation.

But as much as she wanted to rip off his clothes and nip and nuzzle her way from the tips of his pointy fangs to the bottom of his feet, she wasn't going to put the male at risk. He was hers to protect.

Wrapping her arms around his neck, she sent him a frustrated frown. "You have painfully awful timing, vampire."

His fingers headed downward, skimming over her rib cage before they grasped her narrow waist.

"You're my first mate," he reminded her. "I don't have a lot of practice."

The word hit her again, but this time it didn't make her flinch. Instead she quivered with pleasure.

"Mate," she breathed.

He held her gaze. "Does that frighten you?"

"Yeah," she admitted without hesitation.

She felt him stiffen at the soft word. "Do *I* frighten you?" he demanded.

"No."

"Then what are you afraid of?"

She grimaced. Her awareness of this male was snuggled in the center of her heart. Like a secret treasure she wanted to hoard for an eternity. And now his every touch was enslaving her more firmly than if he'd bound and shackled her to his side. No doubt most females would be enchanted to tumble into love with such a worthy male. But she...

"I just earned my freedom," she protested.

He didn't look shocked. Or annoyed. Instead he offered an understanding nod.

"And you think I intend to imprison you?"

She struggled to breathe. She wasn't sure it was entirely necessary since she was a ghost thingy, but it felt weird to not to do it.

"Do you?" she asked.

"Never." The word came out with a fierce insistence. "I've spent endless years in my own prison. We are going to rejoice in our freedom together."

The breath returned to her lungs. Was it possible? Could she share her life with this male without feeling as if she was being smothered?

She tangled her fingers in the lush satin of his dark hair. "Even when I want to go to the Diablo Club?"

His lips twitched. She was well aware he detested when she spent her evenings at the rough, demon-filled bar. Then, bending his head, he scraped his fangs down the side of her throat.

"Even then," he assured her.

Chaaya pressed against the back of his head. She wanted those fangs in her flesh almost as much as she wanted to sink down on the steel-hard arousal that he was stroking against her lower stomach.

Almost.

"And when I want to gamble away your fortune?" She continued to test his tolerance.

"As long as you aren't playing strip poker." His fingers moved to unzip her leather pants. "That's going to be our private game."

"You know how to play poker?"

"You can teach me."

His lips traced the line of her collarbone, his hands tugging her pants over her hips. Bending down, he paused to pull off her boots before he finished stripping her bare. He might not know much about cards, but he obviously knew exactly how to get a woman out of her clothes.

He kissed his way back up her body, pausing to explore each line and curve with diligent care. Chaaya groaned, her toes curling in bliss.

"Now, that's a temptation I can't resist," she admitted.

He stroked his fangs over the upper curve of her breast, his icy touch far more erotic than the heat from any other demon.

"And me?"

She shivered, relishing in the ruthless pleasure that jolted through her. Had she always known that beneath Basq's solid dependability was a male who could create magic with his touch? That might explain why she went to such lengths to try and smash through his façade of calm control. She wanted the fiery male he kept buried.

"A temptation I don't want to resist," she rasped.

"Exactly the words I longed to hear."

She dug her nails into the flesh of his nape, the need inside her becoming a physical ache.

"Basq…wait."

Chapter 17

Basq swallowed the rancid curse that hovered on his lips. His entire body trembled with hunger for this female, but the last thing he wanted was to pressure her into a decision that she was going to regret. Especially when it was a forever and ever and ever decision.

Eternity was a long time for regret.

With a heroic effort he lifted his head, gazing down at her with a wary expression.

"Is something wrong?"

She glanced around the darkness that surrounded them. "Where are we?"

"Ah." He occasionally forgot that Chaaya had spent most of her existence trapped in a hell dimension. Her ability to peer into the world meant she had kept up with the changes to modern culture, but she was still learning and discovering hidden magic. "It's a warp."

"Wharf?"

"A warp," he gently corrected. "It's the space between space between space—"

She placed her hand over his mouth. "I get it, but why would Kgosi bring me here?"

It was a question that was nagging at the back of Basq's mind. Jinn were notoriously cruel to lesser demons. And they considered any creature not a jinn as lesser. But it was possible that Kgosi's role as an oracle overcame his natural desire to cause pain.

"A warp is usually connected to a doorway," he told her.

She furrowed her brow, once again glancing around. There was a long silence before she sucked in a shocked breath.

"Oh. I see it. It's just a faint shimmer, but I'm sure it must lead somewhere." She returned her attention to Basq. "I still don't understand why he brought me here. Unless you did it?"

Basq shook his head. "I can't control magic. My guess would that he's giving you the opportunity to decide that rushing into an unknown danger with nothing but a spear and outrageous belief in your invincibility isn't the smartest decision."

"He's a terrible oracle if he thinks anything would make me decide not to rush into danger," Chaaya dryly pointed out.

"True."

"So this is some sort of hallway?"

Basq shrugged. "Basically."

"And anyone can walk in?"

Basq shook his head. "The warp is like a private bubble that surrounds us. Nothing can get in or out except us."

"So we're all alone?" she pressed.

Basq slowly smiled, belatedly realizing where their conversation was leading. He skimmed his hands down the curve of her back to grasp her slender hips.

"All alone," he assured her, his cock fully extended as he urged her closer.

"Good." She pressed her mouth against his, allowing his fangs to scrape against her lower lip. "It would be a shame to waste this rare seclusion."

He groaned in aching anticipation. She wasn't a soft, delicate creature who had to be handled with gentle care. Instead she was a fierce warrior who could meet him kiss for kiss. Thrust for thrust. And the feel of her warm, battle-hardened body rubbing against him was better than any aphrodisiac.

"A sin," he agreed in a rough voice, sweeping his mouth over her cheek before nuzzling the hollow beneath her ear. There was a faint tingle as his lips brushed over the tattoos that ran the length of her neck. "Who did these?" he asked.

"My mother." Her voice was distracted, as if she was having trouble concentrating. "She was the head druid priestess of our village."

He used the tip of his tongue to trace each intricate design. The tingles were strange, but oddly sensual. As if the magic was a part of Chaaya.

"Do they have meaning?"

"They match the hieroglyphs on my spear. My mother told me they were for protection." She snorted. "Another lie."

Basq didn't miss the edge in her voice. Slowly he lifted his head, staring down at her beautiful face.

"Another?"

Chaaya glanced away, as if to hide some deep emotion. "She also told me she loved me."

Regretting his unintentional reminder of the female who'd been willing to sacrifice her own daughter, Basq gently cupped her face in his hands and urged her to look at him.

"Chaaya."

She reluctantly met his steady gaze. "What?"

"Do you trust me?" He waited for her slow nod before continuing. "You have enchanted me," he told her, each word filled with the emotions that churned inside him. "Even when I am gritting my fangs in frustration, my heart is filled with so much love it feels like it's going to burst. And there is nothing that I wouldn't do to ensure your happiness. Nothing."

Her lips parted, her eyes softening at the sheer intensity of his promise. "You…"

"Yes?"

She helplessly shook her head. "I don't have the words."

"Then show me."

A wicked smile curved her lips. "I can do that."

She impatiently tugged at his black sweater, nearly ripping it off his body as her mouth explored the hard planes of his chest. Basq eagerly kicked off his boots and dealt with his slacks while she nibbled and licked a path downward, as if savoring the taste of his skin.

His fangs throbbed. Chaaya wasn't the only one eager for a taste.

The mere thought of plunging his fangs deep into her flesh and drinking the intoxicating sweetness of her blood was creating a near-unbearable hunger. In fact, the only thing keeping him from tossing her on the ground and completing the mating was the intense pleasure she was creating as she lowered herself to her knees.

Nothing, not even an attack by an enraged dragon, a jinn, and a unicorn, would induce him to distract Chaaya from her avid investigation of his aching body.

Her slender fingers glided down the tight ripples of his stomach before lowering to grasp his erection in a firm grip. Ancient words of pleasure tumbled from Basq's lips as she examined his cock from root to tip, seeming to take pleasure in his shudders of painful bliss.

Then, when he thought that the sensations thundering through him couldn't get more intense, she leaned forward to take him between her parted lips.

Basq's head fell back, his body clenched as she sucked him deep into her mouth before she slowly, excruciatingly pulled back.

Oh…hell.

He reached down to touch the downy hair that covered her head, his knees threatening to buckle as she used her teeth and tongue to create erotic chaos. He wanted to spend the rest of eternity savoring the sensation of her wet mouth surrounding his cock. But he was just a vampire, not a superhero.

There was only so much a poor male could endure before he lost complete control of the situation.

Grasping her shoulders he tugged her upward. "Enough, Chaaya."

"I wasn't done showing you," she protested with a smile of pure female satisfaction.

He wrapped his arms tight around her waist, circling the base of her throat with openmouthed kisses.

"You do it very well," he assured her, continuing to brand her soft skin with kisses as he headed down to the curve of her breast.

She circled her arms around his shoulders, moaning softly as he reached the tip of her nipple.

"You're not so bad yourself," she assured him.

He chuckled. "I'm glad to know my efforts are appreciated."

Her nails dug into his flesh as he laved her nipple with his tongue before sucking the tip between his lips.

"Much appreciated," she assured him.

The sweet taste of her was like nectar on his tongue, tempting him beyond all reason. He had to have her. It was that simple. And that complex. She was his mate, and he had to claim her in the most basic, primitive way possible.

Lifting his head, he gazed down at her. "Chaaya, are you ready?"

Her face was flushed and her eyes smoldering with the same hunger that echoed deep inside him.

"Can't you tell?"

The scent of her desire drenched the air, making his cock twitch with impatience. But that wasn't the question he was asking.

"Are you ready to become my mate?" he clarified.

"Yes." The word came without hesitation.

Still, he had to make certain. "You're sure?"

Her eyes narrowed. "Do you want me to beg?"

He flinched in horror at the mere thought. This female's pride was an integral part of her, as important as her tattoos and leather and badass attitude. He would never do anything to compromise it or demand that she become less to satisfy some male need for dominance.

"Never," he swore in a harsh voice. "Not unless you're begging for more of this."

He captured her lips in a kiss of savage need, and without warning she jumped up, wrapping her legs around his waist.

Basq cupped her ass in his hands, angling her over the straining head of his erection. Then, lowering her inch by luscious inch, he speared deep inside her. They groaned in unison, both taking a moment to absorb the shockingly intense impact of this moment.

After all the bickering and teasing and wary refusal to accept the inevitable, they were one.

Finally.

Chaaya wiggled against him, clearly impatient. "More," she demanded, tangling her fingers in his hair.

He chuckled, moving his hips in a slow, ruthless pace as he scraped his fangs along the base of her throat.

"More," Chaaya rasped, meeting him thrust for thrust with a strength that sent sparks of bliss shooting through him.

Yes, he silently acknowledged. He needed more. Pulling back his lips he bared his fangs, and with one smooth strike he plunged them into the yielding flesh of her upper breast.

He sucked deep, a dizzying explosion of emotion bursting through him as her blood slid over his tongue and down his throat.

She was just as sweet as he imagined, with a hint of sage. But it was more than that. There was a wild, reckless power that coursed through him.

This magical warrior woman. This creature of pain and sacrifice and untold loyalty.

She filled him until his heart overflowed and he couldn't contain himself any longer. Pumping into her at a ferocious pace, he continued to drink deeply until she clutched her legs around him and screamed in a shattering release.

His own orgasm hit in unison, his muscles contracting as the ecstasy erupted through him like an earthquake.

"Mine!" he cried out, his joy reverberating through the darkness.

* * * *

Brigette opened and closed her mouth a dozen times. Like a beached fish.

This dazzling, exotic, outrageously gorgeous male was a jinn? She'd somehow expected a blob of smoke that floated around causing disasters. Instead he was…male perfection.

Her eyes lingered on the bare torso, mesmerized by the shimmers of color that swirled over his midnight skin. She could stare at them all day. And night. With an effort, she tilted her head back to meet the emerald gaze.

"I…" She stopped as the word came out as a squeak. Well, that was embarrassing.

"Did you forget how to speak?" Levet asked.

Brigette flushed, clenching her teeth. Her humiliation was complete. "No, I didn't forget how to speak," she snapped.

Levet sniffed. "How was I to know? My aunt Bertha forgot how to speak after she was struck by lightning."

"Stop," the jinn commanded.

Amazingly there was a shimmer of magic that sealed the gargoyle's mouth shut. Levet squealed in annoyance, but Brigette returned her attention to the male who towered over her.

A rare occurrence considering she was over six foot in her bare feet.

"Who are you?" she managed to ask without squeaking or squawking.

"Kgosi." The word reverberated through the desert, as if the demon inside was as vast as the universe. "I've been expecting you."

Brigette stilled. Was this the creature who'd been whispering to her? How else would he know her? Then she grimaced. No. It'd been a female voice. And she'd called herself Greta, not Kgosi.

Besides, this male had the sort of power to crash through any barrier. He wouldn't have needed to use mer-folk to release her from the dungeons.

"You're not the voice," she said, a lame part of her nurturing the hope that he would confess to being the one who'd freed her from her prison.

He shook his head. "No."

Disappointment speared through her. Of course she couldn't be so lucky as to have her mystery helper be a tall, dark, yummy jinn. Life was never that good. At least not to her.

"Then this is a trap." Her jaws clenched. If she could still reach her animal, she would have shifted into a wolf and run away. At least he'd have to catch her before he could do whatever horrible thing he had planned. But she didn't even have that satisfaction.

All she could do was stand there and wait for fate to kick her in the teeth.

"There's no trap." The emerald gaze darkened as it swept over her stiff form. "I foresaw your arrival because I'm an oracle."

She scowled. "I don't believe in oracles."

The male cocked a dark brow, his expression unreadable. "I'm getting a lot of that lately. Do you want to touch me and prove to yourself I'm real?"

His words wrapped around her, stroking over her skin like a physical caress. Brigette was suddenly convinced that she had never wanted anything more in her entire life than to stroke her fingers over his chest. And abs. And...

Her mouth went dry and her heart did somersaults in the middle of her chest as she allowed the fantasy to fill her mind.

Beside her, Levet at last managed to pry his lips free of the spell. "She does," he chirped in bright tones. "I can smell it."

"Shut up," she hissed, heat scorching her face even as the jinn studied Levet in astonishment.

She could have warned him that no power was great enough to keep the tiny gargoyle silent.

Levet flapped his wings, holding out his hand. "Very well. I will touch."

Sand swirled as the jinn held up his hand. "Stay back."

The gargoyle halted, but his wings flapped as he continued to study Kgosi with a curious gaze.

"I know a jinn," he said. "Well, she is not a full jinn. Her name is Laylah and she is my FFB."

Brigette rolled her eyes. "BFF."

"*Oui.*"

Kgosi looked baffled, his gaze moving from Levet to Brigette. "Does he belong to you?"

"No."

Levet puffed out his narrow chest. "I am my own agenda." He paused, wrinkling his snout. "Agent."

The sand continued to swirl around the male's large feet and the ground shook as he took a step forward.

"Then you don't mind if I kill him?"

"Hey," Levet protested, sticking out his lower lip.

Despite the fact that Brigette had just denied any connection to the aggravating gargoyle, she found herself moving to stand between Levet and the towering jinn.

Why? Because she was obviously as crazy as a luna sprite.

"I'm looking for a way out of here," she said, hoping to distract the male.

It worked. The emerald gaze returned to her, his beautiful face impossible to read.

"No, that's not what you're seeking."

She stared at him in confusion. "Yes, it is."

He leaned forward, capturing her in the glowing depths of his gaze. "Tell me what you seek."

She licked her lips, feeling the world melt away. Long ago, when she was just a little pup, she used to visit the human village to play with the children. They told her about an old gypsy woman who lived in an isolated cottage who would put them in a trance and lead them away from their homes. She'd laughed. Maybe humans were weak enough to be hypnotized, but she wasn't.

Not until this moment.

"The voice," she breathed.

He nodded. "A promise."

"Yes." Kgosi was right. The mysterious female had offered her a promise. And her greatest desire.

The jinn reached out to touch her cheek. His touch was light, nothing more than a brush of his fingertips, but it sent fire cascading through her body.

"Be careful what you wish for," he whispered.

His soft words sent a chill down her spine despite the blazing heat that threatened to choke her. With an effort, she asked the question that had plagued her since she'd escaped from the dungeon.

"Can you take me to the voice?"

The fingers drifted downward, resting over her racing heart. "Remember, Brigette, there is more than one way to redeem a soul."

She gasped in shock. "How did—"

The words were torn from her lips as the sand beneath her feet began to shudder, as if there a massive earthquake threatened to destroy the strange dimension. Fear squeezed her heart, but as she reached out to grab the jinn, the ground split open and she was falling through empty space.

Spinning round and round, Brigette felt her stomach heave. She had no idea where she was or what was going to happen when she finally landed, but she assumed it was going to be awful.

Squeezing her eyes shut in the hopes of blocking out the dizzying sense of vertigo, Brigette was astonished to hear the flap of wings followed by the unmistakable scent of granite.

Levet was falling next to her.

"Argh!" the tiny demon cried out.

Chapter 18

Chaaya snuggled in Basq's arms, her leg thrown across his hip in a gesture of pure ownership.

Not that she needed further proof. She stretched out her arm, revealing the crimson tattoo that ran the length of her inner forearm. For the hundredth time she waited for the flare of panic. This was the point where she realized that she was permanently tied to this male and freaked out.

Only there was no freak-out. No panic.

Instead a smug sense of satisfaction purred through her. Like she was a cat that had just found the biggest, best bowl of cream.

Recovering from their latest bout of intense sex, Basq trailed lazy fingers over the vivid tattoo.

"You're marked."

She turned her head to study his bemused expression. "You sound surprised."

"I didn't know since…"

She snorted as he swallowed his impulsive words. "Since I'm a weirdo?"

He chuckled, his hands gliding up her arms and down the curve of her back. "Don't worry. I have a fondness for weirdos."

She leaned forward to nip at his lower lip. "Just a fondness?"

"Maybe more than that." He cupped her ass in his hands and pressed her tight against the thick length of his erection. Chaaya arched her brows in surprise. They'd already made love a dozen times. It was impressive that he was ready to go again. "Do you want me to demonstrate?" he asked.

She did. Already she could feel the intoxicating intensity of his hunger as it pulsed deep inside him. The mating had created more than just a tattoo. The very essence of this male was scorched into her soul.

Unfortunately there was a voice in the back of her head whispering that her duty was waiting for her. And outside the warp, time was ticking away. Who knew what evil might be released if she didn't stop Brigette?

"Later." Licking the tip of one fang, Chaaya forced herself to rise to her feet and pull on her clothes. "I need to finish what I started."

With a fluid motion Basq was on his feet and fully dressed. She raised her brows. He looked perfect. There wasn't one wrinkle in his black slacks or soft sweater, and not one strand of hair out of place.

Amazing.

"What *we* started," he insisted, reaching out to run his fingers down the tattoo on her arm. "Mate."

She slowly nodded, shivering as the mark tingled beneath his light touch. "I've been alone a long time. It's going to take a while for me to get used to the whole mate thing."

"I'm patient," he assured her.

She smiled wryly. "With me you're going to need the patience of a saint."

His eyes shimmered with a white fire as his gaze lowered to her lips. "I'm not a saint."

Chaaya grinned, recalling all the ways he'd proven his lack of saintliness. The things he could do with those fangs made her melt in sensual pleasure.

"Thank the goddess," she said in husky tones.

His fingers circled her wrist, as if preparing to tug her against him. Then, with blatant regret, he loosened his hold and stepped back.

"Okay, let's get this over with." His expression was grim. "Then you owe me several centuries of uninterrupted peace."

She sent him a regretful glance. There was no way in hell she could stay out of trouble for centuries.

"That seems highly unlikely."

"A week?"

She grimaced. "We'll see."

Turning to head toward the shimmering doorway, she halted abruptly as Basq brushed his fingers down the curve of her back.

"Chaaya. It will destroy me if you die," he warned in low tones. "Please be careful."

She pulled out her spear, glancing over her shoulder to meet his worried gaze. "I swear."

* * * *

Brigette couldn't judge how long they fell through the darkness. It might have been a second, or several centuries. Time had no meaning in the space between dimensions. She did know that she was unprepared when the void spat her out and she landed flat on her back.

The impact was enough to knock the air from her lungs and rattle her teeth.

Shit.

For a second she sprawled on the mossy ground, gazing up at the dark, star-splattered sky. Where was she now? Her world? Another dimension? Pluto?

She took a second to absorb her surroundings. There was a distant hoot of an owl, and the soft footsteps of a fox as he scampered away. A warm breeze brushed over her, carrying the scent of rich earth and sage.

It was home. No, wait. It was home before it'd been destroyed by the beast. And her.

With a low growl she shoved herself to her feet and glanced around. She half expected to see her village. It all felt so familiar. Instead it was...

Different.

With a frown she studied the dozen rough huts with peaked thatched roofs that huddled around a large pit that blazed with an enormous fire. Her village had been much larger and created out of stone and mortar. It'd also been built on the edge of a cliff, not in the middle of a flat plain surrounded by mountains.

This place might have been one of the dozen human towns that had been near her home.

"I hate jinns." Levet climbed to his feet, giving his wings a disgusted flap to shake off the clinging moss. "Tricky beasts."

Brigette's body ached from the abrupt landing, but the mere thought of the jinn made her insides melt with a nearly forgotten hunger. Through the long centuries of being infected with the corrosive evil, Brigette had lost the ability to feel like a woman. Or a wolf. The jinn had painfully reminded her of all she'd sacrificed.

And only emphasized her acute need to rewrite the past.

"They're not so bad," she muttered.

"Fah." Levet sent her an annoyed glance. "You only say that because you think he is soapy."

"Soapy?"

Levet wrinkled his snout, as if struggling for the proper word. "Dishy. *Oui*. Dishy."

"He was gorgeous," Brigette admitted without hesitation.

"All jinns are gorgeous," Levet told her. "It is one of their most annoying qualities."

"And sexy," she added, enjoying the melty sensations that continued to ooze through her. Levet snorted. She pointed an accusing finger at him. "Don't pretend you didn't notice."

"*Oui*. I noticed. Just as I noticed he sealed my lips shut and dropped me like a sack of potatoes in this..." He spread his arms wide and glanced around. "Place."

Brigette shook away the memory of the jinn along with the male's last troublesome warning. She had a destiny to change.

"Do you know where we are?" she demanded.

Levet tilted back his head to sniff the air. "Another dimension," he finally announced. "This one is very old. And very small."

Brigette scowled. Why would the oracle bring her here?

"Can you sense Chaaya or the vampire?"

Levet firmly shook his head. "They are not here."

Brigette impatiently drummed her fingers against the side of her leg. "Are we alone?"

Levet started to nod only to stiffen as he glanced toward the narrow road that led over a nearby hill.

"*Non*. There is something approaching."

"Something?" Brigette didn't like the sound of that.

Levet spread his claws as if baffled by what he was smelling. Brigette ground her teeth in frustration. Once upon a time, she would have been able to recognize anyone or anything from miles away. But since her wolf had gone into hibernation, her senses were dulled.

"It is not a demon," Levet at last muttered.

"A witch?"

"Maybe." He pointed down the road. "It is coming from that direction."

Brigette braced herself, prepared for anything to appear over the hill. A troll. An orc. A dragon.

Instead a slender female materialized out of the darkness, marching toward them with jerky strides that hinted at annoyance. A portion of Brigette's fear vanished.

The stranger wore a long, flowing gown that was sheer enough to reveal that she was barely five foot and weighed less than a hundred pounds. It also revealed she carried no obvious weapons. Unless the female possessed some powerful magic, she was no match for a pureblooded Were. Even if Brigette couldn't call her wolf.

Then, as she moved into the reddish glow created by the fire, Brigette gasped in shock. There was no mistaking the delicate features and the large, dark eyes.

"You said Chaaya wasn't here," she growled.

Levet sent her a puzzled glance. "That is not Chaaya."

"You're sure?"

"Positive."

Brigette swallowed her panic and forced herself to study the female as she moved closer. The face was the same, although the clothes were definitely different. Then she moved her head to the side, revealing her hair wasn't buzzed short but pulled into a tight braid that flowed down her back.

Halting in the center of the village, the woman pointed a finger in their direction. "Where have you been?"

Brigette jerked. The voice. It was low and commanding. And shockingly familiar.

"You're the one who has been speaking to me," she rasped, a combination of relief and unease swirling through her. On the bright side, she'd finally managed to locate the creature who'd offered her the promise of redemption. On the less bright side, the female looked exactly like the person most determined to stick a spear through her heart. "Are you Greta?"

The woman narrowed her dark eyes. "I asked you a question."

Brigette jutted her chin to a stubborn angle. "Tell me if you're Greta."

"I am," she snapped. "You destroyed my portal, so how did you enter this place?"

Brigette bit back her snarl. The woman might appear helpless, but she possessed the ability to give Brigette her heart's desire. That meant for now she held the upper hand.

"A jinn," she forced herself to answer.

"Jinn." Greta looked genuinely confused. "Why would they interfere in my business?"

Brigette shrugged. "He's an oracle. He said he foresaw my arrival."

Greta glanced toward the fire as if considering the implications of an oracle being responsible for Brigette's arrival in this dimension.

"What does that mean?"

"I don't know," Brigette admitted, her brows drawing together as Levet moved forward, his snout twitching as he leaned toward the distracted woman.

"Druid," the gargoyle abruptly announced in satisfaction.

Greta jerked back, her gaze locked on Levet. "What is this creature?"

"Levet." The gargoyle performed a deep bow, his wings shimmering in the firelight. "Knight in shining armor, at your service."

"I—" Greta bit off her words as Levet resumed his sniffing of her gown. "What are you doing?"

Levet tilted his head, looking confused. "You smell like Chaaya, but you are not her."

The woman stiffened, eagerly glancing around. "Where is she?"

Brigette blinked. "I assume she's still in the desert with the jinn."

"Why didn't you bring her with you?"

A shiver of unease curled through the pit of Brigette's stomach at the sharp reprimand. The voice that had whispered to her for hour after hour had cajoled her to escape the dungeons and travel to meet her. She'd promised there was a glorious reward waiting for her, and that she had been chosen above all others.

Now, this…Greta acted as if she was utterly indifferent to Brigette's arrival, and instead was far more interested in Chaaya.

"Why would I bring Chaaya?" Brigette narrowed her eyes. "In case you didn't know, she's trying to kill me."

The woman moved with a speed that caught Brigette off guard. Standing directly in front of her, she lifted a hand and slapped Brigette across the face.

"You fool."

"What the hell?" Brigette lifted hand to her stinging cheek, glaring at Greta in furious disbelief. "Who do you think you are?"

"Druid," Levet answered, taking her words literally.

Greta sent the gargoyle a glance of sheer distaste. "I was druid. Long ago."

Brigette continued to hold her cheek. The blow hadn't been particularly painful, but it deepened the mystery. Which was the last thing she wanted.

She was here for her reward, not to be abused by this…druid who looked like her worst enemy.

"Why would a druid want to release a Were from her prison?" Levet asked the question that was hanging on Brigette's lips.

Greta hesitated, as if considering whether or not to answer. Then a smile of cold cruelty spread across her face.

"Because you had the one thing I needed, wolf," she told Brigette.

"What's that?"

"The ability to lead Chaaya to me."

Brigette struggled not to panic. Okay. This was starting to seem like an elaborate hoax. But she wasn't going to give up hope.

If she did…

She squared her shoulders. "I don't understand."

"It's simple." Greta shrugged. "I need Chaaya."

"If you needed her, then why not simply reach out to her?"

The cruel smile widened. "Because she is too smart and too wary to be swayed by an unknown voice whispering in her head."

Brigette flinched at the deliberate insult. "You chose me because I was too stupid and too desperate to ignore you." Her voice was flat, her hands clenching at her side.

"Only in part."

"What's the other part?"

The woman lifted her hands, as if to imply that Brigette was incredibly dense not to already have figured out the reason.

"Your connection to the beast, of course."

That was the last thing Brigette had expected. She frowned in puzzlement. Did Greta think she could somehow use Brigette to tap into the evil magic?

"The beast is locked away," she said. "Along with her power."

"Yes, but the fear of it returning has remained. Which is why you were locked in the mer-folk castle." Greta paused, allowing her gaze to skim down Brigette's tense body before returning to her grim expression. "Well, not the only reason, I suppose. You also betrayed your pack and allowed them to be massacred, didn't you?"

Brigette clenched her teeth. The woman was deliberately goading her. Why? Maybe to keep her off guard. Or perhaps because Greta was just a bitch. The only thing Brigette knew for sure was that she would be a fool to continue to react to the insults.

"What does that have to do with Chaaya?"

The woman reached up to touch a brooch that held the neckline of her gown together. It was made of delicate silver and twisted in the shape of a Celtic knot. Brigette had seen such jewelry before. The humans in the nearby villages had worn them, some as a symbol of their particular clan, and others to ward off disease or misfortune.

Brigette assumed the thing had some sort of magic locked inside.

"I asked myself how I could lure her to join me," Greta murmured. "The obvious answer was to create the proper bait."

"Me?"

"I knew that the demon world would assume it was the power of the beast that had released you from the dungeon," Greta said with a smooth assurance in her own brilliance. "And that they would insist on Chaaya following you to prevent the release of the evil spirit."

A heavy weight seemed to press against Brigette's chest, squeezing the air from her lungs. It felt like a troll was squatting on top of her, but she knew that it was the toxic combination of regret and guilt and hopeless fury that crushed her.

"So I was the bait," Brigette rasped.

"Exactly."

Brigette pounded her fist into the palm of her hand. Dammit. She hadn't been chosen. At least not for any grand opportunity for atonement. It was Chaaya this woman wanted. And Brigette... She was nothing more than fodder.

She wanted to howl in despair. Only she couldn't. Her wolf had been the first to abandon her.

Blinking back the scalding tears, Brigette glared at the woman who'd lured her to this place with false hope.

"And what of my promise?" she demanded.

Greta waved a slender hand. "You failed to fulfill your part of the deal. Why should you be rewarded?"

"Since I didn't know what my part of the deal entailed, I can hardly be blamed for not fulfilling it," Brigette protested.

Greta looked bored. "Why should I care?"

Brigette faltered. A good question. Why should the woman care? The druid clearly had no interest in anything beyond her obsession to lure Chaaya to this weird place. And Brigette didn't have any way of forcing her to give her what she'd promised.

Which meant she was screwed.

The realization had just formed when Levet loudly cleared his throat. "You should care because I will use my ability to speak into Chaaya's mind to warn her this is a trap if you do not fulfill your pledge."

There was a startled silence as both females turned their heads to glance toward the tiny gargoyle. Brigette had nearly forgotten that Levet was there. Now she searched his ugly face in confusion. Was he serious? He'd never mentioned he could speak telepathically with Chaaya.

Of course, that wasn't something he would have confessed if he'd been snitching to Chaaya and the vampire to keep them updated on where they were located, a voice whispered in the back of her mind. And it would certainly explain how they'd managed to follow her.

Then Levet angled his head so he could send her a quick wink.

Brigette swallowed her urge to laugh in disbelief. He was lying. But why? This creature had no reason to try and help her. Just the opposite. He considered her the enemy.

So what was going on?

Greta appeared equally suspicious. Her pretty features were hard as she glared down at Levet.

"Where is she?"

Levet waggled his brows. "Closer than you think," he murmured in what he no doubt hoped was a mysterious voice. "But farther than you can touch."

Greta jerked her head from side to side, as if expecting to see the young female walking over a nearby hill.

"You're lying," she spat out.

Brigette stepped forward, drawing the woman's attention back to her. The gargoyle was presumably trying to help, but his babbling was as likely to get them killed as to save them.

"Are you willing to risk the opportunity to capture her?" Brigette demanded. "All I have to do is say the word and Levet will send her running from this place."

The woman twisted her lips, no doubt preparing to tell Brigette to go to the netherworld. As if Brigette hadn't been stuck in a hell of her own making for the past five hundred years. But before she could speak, she whirled to the side, her hand reaching out.

Brigette sucked in a deep breath. Was there someone coming? She couldn't sense anything. Just the endless hills covered in sage and moss. But Greta might have the power to detect anyone entering this particular dimension. Or maybe she was just crazy.

Right now it didn't matter.

Greta remained staring into the darkness for several seconds, then with a jerky motion she grabbed the brooch at her neckline and yanked it off. The sheer material of her gown ripped, but she didn't seem to notice as she tossed the piece of jewelry toward Brigette.

"Fine. Here's your reward."

Brigette snatched it out of midair, staring at the piece of jewelry in confusion. "What is it?"

"Make your wish with it."

Brigette cradled the brooch in the palm of her hand. It was beautiful. Each strand of silver was delicately interwoven layer by layer to form the symbolic knot. And in the very center was a pale stone that she hadn't noticed when she'd first caught sight of the ornament.

She bent closer. She didn't recognize the stone. It didn't have the fiery brilliance of a diamond or the blueish hue of an aquamarine. It almost looked like a piece of plastic stuck in the middle of the knot.

"I make a wish with this?" she asked, wondering if the woman was trying to fool her with a piece of junk she'd found in a pawnshop.

"That's what I said," Greta snapped.

"But—"

"Begone." With a wave of her hand, Greta spoke a magical spell in a language that Brigette didn't understand.

There was a swoosh of air, as if someone had opened a massive door behind them. Brigette clutched the strange brooch, stumbling as the wind pulled her backward. It felt like a black hole had formed and they were being ruthlessly sucked inside it.

Beside her Levet flapped his wings, his eyes wide as he struggled against the gravitational pull; then, with a cry of frustration, he lost his balance and was inhaled into the darkness.

Brigette watched him disappear a second before she was pulled in behind him.

Chapter 19

Basq wrapped his arms around Chaaya a second before they tumbled out of the doorway and landed on the hard ground. He managed to take the worst of the impact, bruising his ribs and jarring his fangs, but it was Chaaya who gasped as if in pain.

Rising to his feet, his pulled her upright, scanning for any visible injuries.

"What's wrong?" he asked when he didn't see any blood or protruding bones.

Chaaya stepped past him, her gaze locked on the collection of huts that circled a blazing firepit.

"This is my home," she breathed.

"Home?" Basq frowned. A vampire couldn't sense magic, but even he knew they were in another dimension.

She shrugged. "It looks exactly like the village where I lived as a child," she told him. "As if someone scooped it up and placed it in this new spot."

"Are you sure?" he carefully demanded. Glancing around, he could see the rolling hills that appeared barren beneath the midnight sky before returning his attention to the nearby buildings. "It looks like any other village to me."

Almost as if she was in a dream, Chaaya glided forward. She circled the large pit, the glow of the firelight tinting her skin and shimmering against the tattoos snaking down her neck.

Basq watched her in fascination. It was as if he was seeing her in her natural habitat for the first time. A proud Celtic warrior who could face down any enemy.

He shook himself out of his weird sense of fascination as she reached the largest building in the center of the village.

"This was our home," she murmured, touching the heavy wooden door that was scarred with glyphs. "I remember the day my mother carved this. It was her personal protective spell."

"You speak of your mother, but never of your father," Basq pointed out.

She dropped her hand and turned to face him. "I come from a very long line of druid priestesses."

"I assume you still had a father?"

She shrugged. "I never knew him. Not even his name."

Basq was surprised. In the past, human cultures had a long, tedious history of placing the emphasis on the males. It didn't matter if the father participated in the child rearing or not, fathers were always given the reverence for creating a baby while the mothers were often shoved into the background. The fact that Chaaya didn't know who her father was seemed odd.

"Did he come from this village?" he demanded.

She looked confused at his question. "Only females were allowed here," she said. "When my mother decided it was time for her to have a child, she traveled to London."

Ah. That would explain her mother's ability to keep the father a secret. But why?

"She never told you anything about him?"

Chaaya shook her head. "He was incidental after my mother became pregnant."

"Harsh."

She shrugged, as if she'd come to terms with the fact that she would never know anything about the man who'd fathered her. He didn't know why the thought bothered him. As a vampire he'd awoken with no memory of who he'd been when he was a human. That had been fine with him. He had no interest in learning anything about his previous life.

"My mother was focused on her duty as the head priestess," she told him. "Nothing was allowed to distract her. Not even her daughter."

"So true, my dear," a female voice drawled.

With a curse, Basq spun around, his fangs bared as he stepped between Chaaya and the unknown female who was stepping out of the darkness. Why the hell hadn't he sensed her? Was she an illusion or…?

His mind went blank as the woman stepped into the glow of the firelight and he caught sight of her face.

She looked exactly like Chaaya.

He hissed in shock, moving to stand between the mystery creature and Chaaya. It had to be a trick.

"Stay back," he warned, his darkness beginning to spread toward Chaaya. He could keep her hidden while he discovered a way to escape this latest trap.

"There's no need for threats, vampire," the woman murmured, her gauzy gown drifting on a soft breeze as she moved toward him. As she neared, Basq could start to pick out differences between her and Chaaya. The stranger's features were sharper, her nose longer, and her eyes a shade lighter. Plus, she didn't have any tattoos. "I have no intention of harming my niece."

"Niece?" Chaaya moved to stand next to Basq, ignoring his frown of warning. "Who are you?"

The woman blinked, as if startled by the question. "Don't you remember?"

Chaaya furrowed her brow, studying the face that looked so much like her own. At last she sucked in a sharp breath.

"Greta?" She spoke the name tentatively, as if it was pulled out of the deep recesses of her mind.

"Yes." The woman smiled, reaching out her hand as if she would touch Chaaya.

Basq growled low in his throat, fulling exposing his fangs. Greta glared, but she hastily dropped her hand, her lips pinching together with annoyance.

Next to him, Chaaya barely seemed to notice the exchange. In fact, she had a disoriented expression that troubled Basq. He was used to this female being razor sharp and on constant guard. Her distraction was a sign of just how unsettled she was to land in the middle of her old village. And it didn't help to be confronted by a creature who claimed to be a long lost relative.

It had clearly rattled her.

"You were driven from the village when I was barely more than a baby," she finally muttered.

"Driven?" Greta repeated in confusion. "Is that what Keyrah told you?"

Chaaya nodded. "My mother said that you were caught using black magic."

"Foul lies." Greta lifted her fingers to her mouth, looking aghast. "I didn't think even Keyrah would stoop to such depths."

Chaaya simply stared at Greta as if unsure how to respond. Or maybe she was just trying to decide if the woman was a strange illusion sent by the power-controlling Brigette to distract her.

If that was the case, it was doing a hell of a job.

Assuming that Keyrah was Chaaya's mom, Basq took command of the conversation.

"Are you saying that Chaaya's mother lied to her?" he asked.

Greta slowly turned her head, stabbing him with an annoyed glare. Did she hate vampires? Or was she worried that he might interfere in her nefarious plans for Chaaya?

"She did," she finally forced herself to say.

"So why were you forced to leave?"

Greta sniffed in disdain. "I wasn't forced. I fled."

Basq narrowed his eyes. "Why would you flee? A woman alone at such a point in history would have been far too vulnerable to survive."

With a deliberate motion, Greta turned back to Chaaya as if determined to cut him out of the conversation.

"I left because your mother was determined to sacrifice me," she told Chaaya.

Chaaya blinked, stunned by the blunt words. "You were supposed to be the sacrifice?"

Greta grimaced. "Yes. I'm so sorry, dear Chaaya."

Taking a step to the side, Basq wrapped an arm around Chaaya's shoulders. At the same time, he kept his gaze firmly locked on the stranger.

"I don't trust her," he stated in firm tones.

A smoldering fury flared through Greta's eyes before it was quickly hidden. Not soon enough, however. Chaaya instinctively pressed against his side as if seeking the reassurance of his touch.

"Neither do I," she softly murmured.

A strange emotion rippled over Greta's face. Not pain that her niece didn't trust her. Not regret. No. It was something closer to fear. Then, as if aware she was revealing more than she intended, the woman forced a small smile to her lips.

"I understand." She once again held out her hand. "Please, I can explain everything if you will just listen."

Basq hissed in warning, his fangs fully extended. "Talk fast."

If looks could kill, he would be a pile of ash. Thankfully, Greta's vicious glare did nothing more than convince him that she was a danger to Chaaya.

Smoothing her hands down her sheer gown, the woman paused as if trying to regain command of her temper. Then she pasted the smile back on her lips.

"I was older than your mother, but it quickly became obvious she possessed the greater power," Greta said, the words suspiciously smooth. "When the previous head priestess died, the role passed to her."

"That must have pissed you off," he said.

She was too smart to deny her desire to be head priestess. "I was disappointed, but resigned," she admitted. "In our community we all have a role to play."

"And what was yours?" Basq demanded.

The woman waved an arm toward the huts. "To be a source of support to the head priestess. I performed the morning rituals and kept watch over Chaaya." She paused, studying the silent Chaaya with an expression of utter devotion. "She was like my own child."

Basq swallowed his laugh of disbelief. He didn't have Chiron's ability to peek into the minds of others to read their thoughts, but he didn't need to with this woman. She gave a charming performance of a loving sister and aunt, but Basq didn't doubt for a second that she'd spent her life consumed with a burning jealousy toward her younger sister. The ruthless ambition that drove her life had been etched into her narrow face, and the scent of envy was embedded in her very skin.

"So what happened?" he asked.

"My sister never trusted that I had accepted her leadership." She sent Chaaya another one of those melting looks. "Or perhaps she was jealous of my relationship with her daughter. Chaaya considered me her mother, not Keyrah."

Basq glanced toward Chaaya, who was standing as still as a statue. Perhaps she feared the slightest movement might shatter her.

"Is that true?" he asked, his voice gentle.

She shook her head, her gaze remaining locked on Greta. "I don't remember."

"You were so young when I had to leave," Greta cooed. "It's no wonder you don't remember."

Basq pulled Chaaya closer. He had full confidence that she would soon be back to her usual kick-ass self. For now, however, she was vulnerable and in need of his protection.

He glanced back at Greta. "You said you were going to be sacrificed?"

"Yes." She lifted her fingers to touch her neckline, then she frowned as if she'd expected to find something there that was missing. She gave a small shake of her head and continued. "Word came to our village that a great evil was threatening the world. I offered to travel to speak with the other druid villages. I was certain that if we combined our magic, we could defeat any threat."

"And Keyrah?"

"She decided it would be better to work with the local coven."

Basq raised a brow. It did seem odd that Keyrah would choose to work with witches rather than the other druids.

"Did she say why?" he asked.

Greta shrugged. "She claimed that the only way to prevent disaster was to offer one of our priestesses as a sacrifice."

Basq felt Chaaya shudder. Was she remembering being dragged from this very village? Being held down by strangers and having her throat sliced?

The temperature dropped several degrees. He would give everything he possessed to destroy those responsible for harming Chaaya. Unfortunately, he couldn't yank them from their graves. And right now he didn't dare allow himself to be distracted.

He leashed his temper, but a layer of frost continued to coat the landscape, hissing as it hit the flames.

"You didn't believe her?" he demanded.

Greta blinked. Either she hadn't expected the question or she was unnerved by the ice clinging to the hem of her gown.

"I…" She stopped to clear her throat and square her shoulders. "I feared she was seeking a way to get rid of me."

Basq arched a brow. It was a lame excuse. Clearly, she hadn't gone to the effort of practicing a better one. Sloppy.

"Keyrah was the head priestess, wasn't she?" he pointed out. "Couldn't she just order you to leave if she didn't want you around?"

Realizing she'd lost ground, Greta turned back to Chaaya. She no doubt hoped that the younger female would be an easier touch.

"The others in the village would have rioted if I had been hounded out of the village," she insisted. "I was a favorite."

"So you left." Chaaya's tone was flat, her expression impossible to read. It was only because Basq was intimately connected to her that he could sense the emotions churning deep inside.

"Yes." Greta pressed her hands to her heart. "I never dreamed she could be cruel enough to murder her own daughter."

Basq squeezed Chaaya tighter, taking back control of the conversation. "Why would she sacrifice her daughter if she was trying to get rid of you? You were already gone, right?"

The flames in the pit suddenly shot higher. The female was clearly connected to them. She was probably connected everything in this place.

"I assume she saw her as a threat as well. There was no mistaking Chaaya's power, even when she was just a babe." The muscles in Greta's jaw bulged as she clenched her teeth. "It was only a matter of time before she took over as head priestess."

"You're saying Chaaya was sacrificed because her mother feared she would grow up to become the next head priestess?" Basq asked, his voice dripping with skepticism.

"Who knows what was in Keyrah's mind?" With a curse of frustration, Greta whirled toward Chaaya. "Does this vampire speak for you, niece?"

* * * *

Troy slipped into the small, forgotten closet at the end of the dungeons. The air was musty, and salt coated the walls, a sure indication that no one had bothered to open the door in years. Maybe centuries. Thankfully his curious nature insisted that he investigate each nook or cranny. Who knew what treasures might be hidden away? That meant he knew more about the mer-folk castle than most of the residents who'd been there forever.

A bonus he used to his advantage as he followed Riza from the throne room through the maze of corridors. The guard was lost in his dark thoughts, making it a simple matter to stroll behind him, heading lower and lower, until he at last reached the dungeons.

Troy waited until the merman entered an empty cell before he silently darted into the closet, leaving the door cracked so he could see out. Then he waited. And waited. With a grimace, he brushed his hands down his silk shirt. It felt like the salt in the air was eating through the thin material.

At last there was a strange creak, and a hidden door across the narrow hall pushed open and Jord cautiously stepped out. Ah. So that was how the guards had moved through the castle with no one seeing them.

With a quick glance around to make sure no one was watching, the male entered the cell where Riza was waiting.

"I told you we couldn't be seen together," Jord snapped, his low voice easily carrying to where Troy was hidden. "We want that revolting ogress to think we're squabbling over what happened to the prisoner, not realizing we're working together."

Troy grimly controlled his fury. The scent of scorched citrus was sure to warn the mer-folk they weren't alone in the dungeons.

Instead he concentrated on what Jord had revealed.

The two males were working together and had presumably assisted Brigette in escaping from her cell. Plus, his worse fears had been confirmed. They'd done so because of their hatred for Inga.

Bastards.

"She's asking questions," Riza whined, the heel of his boots clicking against the bedrock as he paced around the cell.

Jord made a sound of frustration. "All the more reason to stay away from each other."

"I think she suspects something."

"Why should she suspect anything?" Jord snapped. "You're allowing your imagination to run wild."

The pacing abruptly halted. "Is it also my imagination that Troy was nosing around the guard room, demanding to know what Koral and Lusca saw the night the prisoner escaped?"

Troy smiled. He'd hoped that word of his conversation with the two guards would make the rounds. The more pressure put on Jord and Riza, the quicker they would break.

"He's a nosy bastard." Jord spat out the words. "Always pushing himself into mer-folk business. Perhaps when the Tryshu is in my hands I'll stick it through his impish heart."

Troy's breath locked in his lungs. He'd suspected that the guards had been trying to lure Inga into some sort of trap or perhaps just hoping to embarrass her by allowing a high-value prisoner to escape from her dungeons. Far too many of the warriors had been loyal to the previous King of the Mer-folk, Riven. And now they harbored resentment, not only because Inga had ultimately been responsible for Riven's death, but because she was a mongrel who looked more like an ogress than mermaid.

But to take the Tryshu?

That was impossible, wasn't it? The ancient trident was the very heart of the mer-folk magic. It picked the leader. And it'd chosen Inga.

Period. End of story.

So why did these fools think they could somehow force it away from her?

A question that had to be answered.

First, however, he wanted to make sure that no other mer-folk were involved. He leaned forward, intent on the guards' whispered conversation.

"And when is that going to be?" Riza hissed.

"Soon."

Riza's sharp laugh indicated he'd been told that before. Probably more than once.

"You promised it would be after the Were was released. She's gone. We should have our reward," he reminded Jord. "I think you were tricked into giving that witch everything they wanted without ensuring that you're going to get what was promised."

Troy lifted his brows in surprise. Their partner was a witch? That was...unexpected.

The stench of charred salt lay thick in the air as Jord battled to contain his temper.

"You have to be patient," he insisted.

"Until when?"

"Until I tell you."

"Or until we're revealed as traitors and we end up in one of these cells," Riza muttered.

Assured that there was no other mer-folk involved, Troy left his hiding place and strolled into the cell.

He took enormous pleasure in the guards' mutual expression of horrified shock.

"Traitors don't end up in these cells," he assured them with a mocking smile. "They end up dead."

Chapter 20

Chaaya was in shock. Not the *surprise birthday party* sort of shock. Or an *I can't believe I just lost all my money on the roulette table* sort of shock. This was a soul-deep shock that stuffed her brain with wool and made her limbs far too heavy for her body.

And worse, she couldn't concentrate. She knew they were in danger, but the memories of her childhood that she'd tucked away centuries ago were swirling around so fast they made her dizzy. Everywhere she glanced brought a vivid image of herself and her life in small village.

She remembered dashing around the fire and laughing when her mother tried to catch her. Sneaking away to swim naked in the nearby stream. Being tucked into a warm bed with her spear at her side, like a barbaric teddy bear. The druids dressed in white robes rising early to tend to the sick who waited at the edge of the village.

For endless years the only recollection that stuck in her brain was the night she'd been dragged from her bed and hauled to the burrow to be sacrificed. That sort of thing tended to overshadow everything else. Now a tangle of emotions overwhelmed her.

Then, without warning, Chaaya felt a cool power tingle through her. The mating bond. The delicious energy Basq offered helped to soothe her raw nerves and gave her the strength to square her shoulders and confront the female who was staring at her with a hint of disgust.

"I speak for myself," she assured Greta, stepping away from Basq even as she continued to draw on his strength.

This might be her battle, but she didn't have to face it alone.

The knowledge banished the last of the fog from her mind.

"Thank the goddess." Greta curled her lips. "I was beginning to fear that he had somehow bewitched you."

At last capable of focusing on the female who claimed to be her aunt, Chaaya took in the features that resembled her own. A sharp certainty that she'd encountered Greta when she was very young jolted through her. It wasn't a specific memory, but more a sense of dread that curled through the pit of her stomach at the sight of her.

Instinctively, she grabbed the hilt of her spear. This didn't seem to be a good time to get caught unprepared for...well, for whatever hideous surprise was waiting for her.

And there would be a hideous surprise waiting for her.

No doubt about that.

"Vampires have no magic," she muttered, more for something to say than to make any special point.

Greta clicked her tongue, shooting a malevolent glance toward Basq. "So they claim. I've never trusted leeches."

His own smile was as cold as the Arctic. "The feeling is mutual."

"Stay out of this," Greta snapped.

Basq growled, taking a step forward. Chaaya hastily reached out to touch his arm.

"Let me handle this, Basq," she commanded.

She expected him to argue. He was a male. He was a vampire. And he was mated. Each one of those meant he was 100 percent convinced that it was his duty to protect her. Instead he gave a grudging nod and stepped back.

"Okay."

She brushed her fingers down his arm in silent gratitude before she sent the female an accusing glare.

"You lied."

Greta was instantly wary. "Excuse me?"

"You claimed you were a favorite of the village, but I remember you lived in that hut away from the others." Chaaya used her spear to point toward the distant chimney just barely visible.

Greta shrugged. "I enjoyed my privacy."

Chaaya shook her head. The ancient memories were returning. Not like an old movie playing in her mind, but in strange bursts. Like a flickering bulb that was on the verge of burning out.

"The others suspected you of performing foul rites," she abruptly said.

Greta's lips pinched in annoyance. "Your mother obviously poisoned your mind, sweet Chaaya."

"*Sweet* Chaaya?" Basq snorted.

Chaaya smiled wryly. "He's right. No one who's ever actually known me would ever call me sweet."

Greta grimly ignored the vampire, as if pretending he wasn't there would somehow make him disappear. *Good luck with that*, Chaaya acknowledged wryly. She'd tried that trick herself. Complete waste of time.

"You said yourself you were very young when I left," Greta said. "Obviously your opinion of me was tainted by your mother."

She had a point. It was possible that Chaaya's opinion had been swayed by her mother. But that didn't explain the wariness crawling over her skin. Or the instinct that was screaming at her to stick the spear in the heart of her aunt before something awful could happen.

She didn't believe for one second that Greta had been chosen as a sacrifice. The druid priestesses would never have allowed her to simply walk away. They would have scoured the world until they found her and returned her to fulfill her destiny.

She was careful, however, to keep the skepticism out of her voice. "Where did you go after you left the village?"

Greta frowned. "What?"

"Where did you go?" Chaaya repeated.

"I traveled the world."

Well, that was vague.

"Alone?"

"Mostly."

Even more vague. "How did you survive?"

The older woman waved a dismissive hand. "I used my healing gifts to earn food and a place to sleep for the night."

Chaaya narrowed her eyes. There was enough truth in Greta's words to convince Chaaya that she wasn't blatantly lying, but she certainly wasn't being completely honest.

The question was...what was she hiding?

"And you lived happily ever after?"

"I lived." Greta blinked, as if fighting back tears. "I'm not sure how happily. It was a brutal existence that I barely endured. One I wouldn't wish on my worst enemy."

"Did you have children?"

The pretense of a tragic vagabond forced to wander the world alone was shattered by the abrupt question.

"Children?"

"Do I have any cousins?"

"Oh. No." A visible shudder raced through the woman's body. "I wasn't blessed with children."

Her tone made the thought of children sound more like a curse than a blessing.

"And you never returned to the village?"

"No."

Chaaya waved the spear to indicate the strange void that surrounded them. "How did you end up here?"

A portion of Greta's tension eased. This was a question she'd obviously been expecting.

"I'm not sure. I was battling against a wizard—"

"You were battling a wizard?" Chaaya interrupted. Those weren't words you heard every day. Or ever.

Greta shrugged. "He was the leader of a cult of human magic users. They had a grand plan to take over the world."

"So how did you get involved?"

"I happened to be taking refuge at the wizard's temple when someone snuck in and stole a powerful amulet."

The words were polished to the point of perfection. As if Greta had been rehearsing them for years. Perhaps centuries.

Chaaya studied her aunt's delicate features, which gave nothing away. There were a few possibilities. Greta might be telling the truth. Unlikely. She might have snuck into the temple and stolen the amulet herself. More likely. Or she might have been staying at the temple and colluded with someone else to steal it.

She kept her thoughts to herself. "An unfortunate coincidence," she instead murmured.

"Most unfortunate." Greta sniffed. "Especially when the wizard blamed me for the theft."

"What did he do?"

A genuine expression of horror twisted her features. "I was tied to a post and burned alive."

Chaaya grimaced. No one deserved that. No one.

"That's truly awful. I'm sorry," she murmured.

"It was a ghastly way to die. You can't imagine how I suffered."

"You should have stayed to be sacrificed." Basq mocked the woman's tragic tale. "It's not any worse than being burned at the stake, is it?"

Greta ground her teeth, and Chaaya hid her wry smile. The vampire was deliberately trying to piss off the arrogant older woman, no doubt hoping that he could aggravate her into revealing the truth of why they were there.

Greta grimly refused to glance at Basq. "Perhaps we could speak in private," she suggested to Chaaya.

Basq stepped in front of Chaaya, his arms folded over his chest. "She doesn't go anywhere without me."

"Careful, leech," Greta snapped in outrage. "Druid priestesses bow to no man, whether he has fangs or not."

"We're a package deal," Basq warned in stubborn tones.

Chaaya swallowed a sigh. Things could get very messy very quickly if she didn't take command of the situation. She moved to stand directly next to Basq, sending a silent assurance that she could handle her aunt.

"How did you end up here?"

"I assume the wizard cursed me before he set me on fire."

Chaaya deliberately glanced around. "This is a curse?"

"I'm not sure. One moment I was being consumed by the flames and the next I was trapped here."

"And it just happened to look like your own village?" Basq dryly demanded.

The flames in the pit hissed, as if in reaction to Greta's anger. Still she refused to glance in the vampire's direction.

"It must use my memories to create the illusion."

The words were again said with the quick assurance of someone who had a lot of time to consider her answers to various questions. Chaaya needed to shake things up.

"Why did you lure Brigette here?"

Silence. Well, except for the continuing hiss of the flames. Greta hadn't been expecting that.

She finally licked her lips. "Who?"

"The pureblooded Were."

More lip licking. "I don't know who you're talking about."

Chaaya rolled her eyes. Greta was a remarkably bad liar, probably because she was so accustomed to bullying others she never had to worry about explaining herself.

"She was traveling with a three-foot gargoyle with fairy wings. They're hard to miss," Basq pointed out in dry tones. "Not to mention the fact that their scent is still in the air."

Greta's head snapped to the side, her eyes narrowing. Clearly, she'd reached the end of her patience with the vampire.

"You..."

Basq arched a brow. "Yes?"

Greta glanced back at Chaaya. "How do you bear him?"

Chaaya smiled. "He sneaks up on you. Slow and steady."

Basq's fingers lightly traced the curve of her spine. "That's the only way to capture a ghost."

A white-hot pleasure seared through her, helping to banish the strange darkness that swirled around her aunt. It wasn't the pulsing evil that filled the beast. This was cold and empty and foreboding. Like this void.

Greta held out her hand in a pleading motion. "My sweet Chaaya."

"Stop saying that," Chaaya snapped. She was many things. Sweet wasn't one of them. "Why did you release Brigette from her dungeon in the mer-folk castle?" She pointed the spear at her aunt. "I would suggest you not lie again."

"I was trying to find you."

"Through a Were?"

Greta dropped her arm, peevish frustration marring her face before she smoothed her expression.

"I don't know what went wrong. I called out, hoping to reach you, and instead a Were answered me."

"Crossed wires?" Basq drawled.

"Something like that, yes," Greta managed to grate between clenched teeth.

"How did you get her out of the dungeon?" Chaaya asked. The older woman was off balance. The trick was to keep her that way.

"She swore to me that she would contact you once she was out of her cell."

"That's not what I asked you." Chaaya forced a hard smile to her lips. "How did you get her out?"

The pale brown eyes darted from side to side. Chaaya assumed she was searching for inspiration.

"She said that she had made friends with a guard who would be willing to help," she finally said.

"You do realize that makes no sense?" Basq scoffed. "If she had a guard to release her, then why did she wait until you just happened to contact her?"

"Stupid leech." The flames stopped hissing and started to spiral, dancing together in a fiery fury. The glow lent an orangish cast to Greta's face, emphasizing the angular sharpness of her features. "She needed a means to get out of the castle. I offered her that in return for contacting you."

Chaaya frowned. Okay. That might be true. Brigette couldn't create portals, and that was the only way in or out of the mer-folk castle. But the whole "crossed wires" and "reaching out to you" was a bunch of crap.

"So where is Brigette?"

Greta waved her hand in an impatient gesture. "The Were assured me that you were following her, but she was unreasonably terrified you intended to kill her."

"No, her terror is perfectly reasonable," Chaaya corrected her aunt. "I fully intend to kill her."

"Why?"

"Because she's evil."

"Oh." Greta tried to look stricken by the revelation. The artificial emotion, however, never made it to her eyes. "I had no idea."

Basq released a sharp laugh. "Really? The fact that she was locked in a dungeon didn't give you any hint?"

Greta took a step toward Chaaya, angling her body to block out Basq. "As I said, I reached out in an effort to contact you, Chaaya."

Chaaya sniffed the air. The scent of wolf and the dry tang of granite lingered, but they were too faint for Brigette and Levet to be in the area.

"Where is she?" Chaaya demanded.

Greta hesitated. Chaaya could almost hear the wheels turning in the older woman's head.

To lie or not to lie. To lie or not to lie…

At last she shrugged. "I allowed her to return to her world."

"How?"

Another shrug. "I opened a portal."

Basq made a low sound deep in his throat. "If you can open portals, why do you stay here?"

Greta's gaze remained on Chaaya even as she grudgingly answered Basq's question. "I can open portals, but I can't go through them."

It was Chaaya's turn to hesitate. She'd never heard of a druid being capable of opening portals. But it might have something to do with the magic of this strange place. And it seemed a weird thing to lie about.

"So you're stuck?" she finally asked.

Greta nodded. "Yes."

"Why did you want me here?"

"Beyond wishing to be reunited with my only family?"

Chaaya rolled her eyes. She sensed this woman had as much family feeling as a scorpion. Probably less.

"Yeah, beyond that."

"It's simple." Greta glanced toward Chaaya's hand. "I need the magic of your spear."

Chapter 21

Brigette plummeted out of the portal and landed face first on the hard, rocky ground. It felt like she'd been shot out of a cannon. Or dropped from the top of a cliff. She grunted as the air was knocked from her lungs and her head banged against a stone.

"The bitch did that on purpose," she growled as she shoved herself upright.

Still, Greta had kept her promise, Brigette realized as she slowly glanced around.

There was no mistaking the broken foundations that poked out of the thick heather, and the sense of desolation that lay like a heavy fog over the dark landscape. A chilly breeze whipped around her, bringing with it the tang of salt water. And in the distance a lone owl cried in search of a mate.

The sound pierced her heart, just as the sight of the devastated village crushed something deep in her soul.

When she'd been here before she'd been locked in Zella's evil clutches. The beast hadn't forced her to betray her pack and sacrifice everyone she loved for her own ambitions, but once she'd given into temptation, her mind had been filled with darkness. She accepted the stark destruction that surrounded her, barely able to recall how the place had looked before the attack by the goblins.

Now she allowed the memories to slowly, painfully return. At the center of the village had been a large building with a slate roof where the pack would gather to celebrate holidays and matings and the births of pups. Next to it had been a storage shed and a smaller community center that was used as a nursery for the older pups. Weres were animals at heart, and they preferred to play and nap in big piles.

Finally, there had been a wide circle of stone cottages with thatched roofs. In the summer each home had a window box filled with flowers, and each winter they would build fires and drink warm cider at the edge of the village to celebrate the solstice.

So many traditions shattered. So many loved ones lying in charred ashes…

"*Mon dieu*," Levet muttered, as he rose to his feet and brushed away the clinging dust. Then, as he glanced around, his eyes widened and his tail twitched with horror. "There has been a terrible mistake."

Brigette glanced down at him in confusion. "What are you talking about?"

He waved a stubby arm. "We managed to escape one hell dimension only to end up in this gruesome place. You indeed have the most ill luck."

"No." She shook her head, sadness tightening her chest until it was a struggle to breathe. "For once I have been given exactly what I desire."

"To be here? But…" Levet shuddered. "It is a ruin."

"For now, yes. It wasn't always like this, you know," she said, keeping her voice soft, not so much out of respect for the dead, but to avoid the pain at the echo that resonated through the empty landscape. "Once it was a place of beauty. Peaceful." She sighed. "Serene."

"You hated it," Levet reminded her.

"I hated the gnawing sensation inside me that refused to be satisfied," she corrected. "It made me feel like an outcast."

"So you destroyed everything?"

"Yes." The image of a sleepy fairy-tale village shattered as Brigette forced away the memories and instead allowed reality to return. "I destroyed everything."

There was the sensation of Levet's wing brushing against the back of her leg, as if the gargoyle was attempting to comfort her. Brigette froze. When was the last time anyone had touched her in anything but anger? She couldn't remember.

"And now you have returned. Why?" Levet asked.

Brigette sucked in a ragged breath. "Redemption."

Levet furrowed his brow, casting a doubtful glance around the crumbled stones and stunted weeds.

"Do you intend to rebuild the cottages?"

Brigette shuddered at the mere thought. Not only had the village been burned to the ground by the goblin raiders, but it'd been soaked in evil for over five centuries. The only good thing that could happen to this place would be to have it slide off the edge of the cliff and plummet into the sea.

"No." She firmly shook her head. "New bricks and mortar can't disguise the blood that stains these foundations." She held up her hands. "Blood that is on my hands."

"You can't remain here on your own," Levet protested, his snout wrinkled. "It is unhealthy."

Brigette slowly turned, staring down at the tiny demon who'd become oddly familiar in the short time they'd been together. Almost as if he was...her friend.

"Why do you care?" she abruptly demanded.

He blinked. "Pardon?"

"You bound us together to try and keep me from escaping the mer-folk," she reminded him.

"I thought you were evil."

"I am evil." She waved her arm toward the destruction. "Look."

"You have done bad things," Levet conceded.

"Unforgivable things," she insisted.

"Perhaps." He tilted his head back to regard her with a strange expression. "But you are no longer infected by the beast."

Her gaze moved to the burrow where she'd first heard Zella's whispers. If only she'd walked away. But she hadn't.

Brigette sadly shook her head. "The taint remains. It will forever stain my soul."

"*Oui*, but you can change," the gargoyle insisted.

She grimaced. If only it was so easy. A part of her wanted to believe that she could close the door on the past. The beast was locked away and the evil banished from this world. Why shouldn't she get a second chance?

Then her gaze drifted back to the cracked foundation that had once been her home. The place where her family had been savagely murdered.

"Is that why you convinced the druid that you could reach Chaaya with your mind?" she asked with a humorless smile. "Because you think I can turn over a new leaf? Maybe devote the rest of my life to helping others?"

Levet held up his hands. "I believe it is possible."

"No." The sharp word rang through the empty village like a death knell.

Levet studied her with a searching gaze. "Then you intend to bury yourself here and wallow in self-regret?"

Brigette held out her hand, revealing the brooch that lay in the center of her palm. "I intend to use this."

Levet leaned forward, studying the strange jewel at the very center. "A votum stone?"

Brigette frowned. She'd never heard the name before. "Is that what it is?"

Levet sent her a startled glance. "You intend to use a magical artifact without knowing its powers?"

Brigette ground her teeth. "Are you serious? So far I've colluded with an evil beast to destroy my pack. I allowed myself to be led from my cell by a treacherous merman. I followed a mystery voice into a portal with absolutely no idea where I was going or who would be waiting for me on the other side. And now you think I should be worried about wishing on a strange stone?"

Levet cleared his throat. "Fair point."

She pointed toward the brooch. "Tell me about this."

He shrugged. "It's a votum stone."

"Votum." She tasted the word. She didn't recognize the name or the language. "I've never heard of one."

"They're very rare," Levet told her. "And very expensive. It offers the owner a wish."

Brigette released the breath she didn't know she was holding. Deep in her heart she'd assumed this would turn out to be just another trick. Her entire life she'd tried to game the system only to find herself outmaneuvered. She wasn't clever enough, or maybe just not lucky enough, to avoid a destiny that included getting shit on.

Cautiously, she reached out to touch the stone with the tip of her finger. It felt smooth, and unexpectedly warm. As if there was a living force inside the small gem.

"Why would Greta give it up?"

"No doubt she used her wish," Levet said in dismissive tones. "A votum stone is like a purple light special."

Brigette shuffled through her brain. Being around Levet meant constantly attempting to translate his weird gibberish.

"Blue light special?"

He gave an emphatic nod. "Only one wish per customer."

Hmm. One wish. She would have to be very, very careful to say exactly what she wanted.

"And it will give me anything I desire?" she pressed.

"So it claims." Levet studied the stone with a sour expression. "Long ago my—"

"Don't say your aunt Bertha," she interrupted.

The gargoyle clicked his tongue. "*Non.* This has nothing to do with my aunt Bertha. It was my friend Tamara. She was a sprite who was granted the votum stone by a witch."

Brigette heaved a sigh. She didn't want to hear this story. It was bound to reveal some dire reason she shouldn't use the stone. But she'd discovered trying to keep Levet silent was like trying to stop the waves from crashing onto a beach. An impossible task.

Conceding the inevitable, Brigette did her best to hurry along the tale of tragedy. "And she used the wish?"

"She did."

"Well?" Brigette made a sound of impatience. "What did she wish for?"

"The heart of her lover."

Brigette jerked back, a revolting image searing through her mind. "Don't tell me, he was killed and she got his bloody heart."

"*Non*." Levet lifted his tail, polishing the dust from the tip. "He proclaimed his love and they were wed in a glorious ceremony that I arranged. There were dew fairies dancing and carpets of flowers—"

"Levet, get to the point," she snapped.

He sniffed, but thankfully continued with the story. "The evening of their wedding they were killed in a fire."

Brigette shrugged. "Coincidence."

"And what of Greta?"

Brigette narrowed her eyes. The gargoyle was just babbling now. "What about her?"

"She still had the votum with her."

"So?"

Levet heaved a sigh, clearly implying Brigette was impossibly dense. "If Greta still had a wish, she would have used it to get out of the void. But if she had used her wish earlier, then she would have no need to keep the stone. She would have traded it for something of value."

Brigette lifted a hand to press it against her temple. The creature was giving her a headache.

"That doesn't make any sense."

Another condescending sigh. "The fact that she still had the stone with her meant she'd used it just before she became stuck in that void."

Brigette stilled, suddenly realizing what the creature was trying to say. "Oh. You think she made a wish and it put her in that...void or whatever that place was?"

"*Oui*." He held her gaze. "Wishes are dangerous things."

A chill wiggled down her spine. Then she glanced around the desolate village. She'd made a terrible mistake. Now she had the potential to make amends.

"I'm willing to risk it," she muttered.

Levet clicked his tongue at her stubborn refusal to heed his warnings. "What is your wish?"

"To change the past."

* * * *

Basq silently cursed as he studied Greta's covetous expression. He'd already realized that they'd been lured to this specific spot by this specific woman. And that she wanted something from Chaaya. But he hadn't once considered that it might be connected to her magical weapon.

Chaaya looked equally bemused. "My spear?"

Greta licked her lips, taking a step closer to Chaaya. "It's a powerful artifact."

Chaaya wrapped a protective hand on the hilt of the spear. "Why do you want it?"

Greta hesitated. Basq could sense she was eager to simply grab the weapon. So why didn't she? Did she fear a physical confrontation? Or was there something about the magic of the spear that made her wary?

"It can take me home," the older woman finally admitted.

Chaaya shook her head. "It doesn't create portals."

"I can create the portal," Greta insisted. "I just need you to use the magic of the spear to pull us through it."

Basq stepped to the side, pressing against Chaaya in warning. "This is a trap."

Greta hissed in his direction like an angry cat. "Stay out of this, leech."

He ignored the woman, concentrating on Chaaya. "She deliberately used Brigette to get you here."

Chaaya sent him a puzzled frown. "How?"

"She somehow realized that once Brigette escaped the dungeons, you would be the one chosen to track her down," he said. "You're the only one who can sense the darkness."

"Why not just try to call to me?"

"Would you have answered a strange voice whispering sweet nothings in your ear?" he asked.

Chaaya shook her head. "No. I would have assumed it was a trick by the beast."

"Exactly." Basq sent a narrow-eyed glare toward Greta. "Your aunt knows you well enough to find another way to lure you to this place."

"This is nonsense," Greta snarled, clearly sensing that her opportunity to escape was slipping away. "I told you what happened."

"Basq is right." Chaaya took a deliberate step backward. "It's too much of a coincidence that you would choose Brigette."

Greta balled her hands into fists, her eyes flaring with an ugly combination of emotions. Greed. Lust. Fury.

"I wanted to do this the easy way." She lifted a fist, as if intending to smash it into Chaaya's face.

Basq instinctively leaped to intercept the blow, grabbing the woman's arm and using it to throw her against a nearby hut. She hit with a satisfying thud, but with a speed that caught him off guard, she was on her feet and striding toward him with a furious expression.

"You are starting to piss me off, vampire," she snarled.

Basq moved to block the woman from reaching Chaaya. "Just starting?"

"This is my world," Greta warned. "I control everything."

Basq shrugged. "Not me."

Greta smiled, then she waved her arm in a dramatic motion. Instantly the ground disappeared beneath Basq's feet. With a curse he hastily leaped to the side.

"Everything." She smirked, giving another wave of her hand. This time a spray of white-hot coals from the fire zoomed toward him.

"Basq," Chaaya cried out.

He leaped over the lethal projectiles, his fangs fully extended. "I've got this," he assured her.

Greta instinctively backed away as he raced toward her. "You can't kill me," she protested.

"I'm willing to make you wish you were dead."

Basq grabbed her by the shoulders, already prepared when the ground disappeared. Still holding her tight, he jumped on top of one of the huts and slashed his fangs through her throat.

Blood spurted even as she used her powers to create a hole in the thatching. He tumbled to the ground, but with blinding speed he was out of the hut to confront the woman standing just a few feet away.

He growled in disgust. The blood stained her gown, but her neck had already healed. She hadn't been lying when she claimed she couldn't die. So now what?

As if capable of reading his mind, Greta smiled. "I did warn you."

Basq charged. He had to do something or Chaaya was going to leap into the battle. And he didn't doubt for a second that Greta would destroy her niece to get her hands on that spear.

Expecting her to do the whole ground opening thing again, Basq leaped toward her in a zigzag pattern. This time, however, she gave a peculiar twist with her hand and the air tightened around his throat.

Basq frowned. He wasn't human. He didn't need air to breathe. And a broken neck would do nothing but piss him off.

Then the invisible noose began to tighten and Basq was lifted off his feet. For several seconds he simply dangled off the ground, and Basq wondered if she intended to leave him hanging. Literally. He heard movement behind him and assumed that Chaaya was rushing to his rescue.

Before she could reach him, however, he floated through the air until he was swinging precariously over the dancing flames.

Shit. Basq struggled against the unseen rope. A broken neck wouldn't kill him. But the fire most certainly would.

"You will take me home, Chaaya," he heard Greta drawl. "Or I'll drop the vampire."

Chapter 22

Inga sat on her throne, her stupid crown digging into her scalp and the Tryshu tightly clutched in her fingers.

Beside her, Troy was standing with negligent ease, his red hair shimmering down his back and his lean body covered in a green velvet jumpsuit with sequins at the hem. In contrast, Inga wore a tie-dye muumuu in brilliant shades of purple and pink. The shocking contrast in colors had caused Rimm to wince, but his grim expression never changed as he led in the two heavily shackled guards.

Jord and Riza looked different from the last time she'd seen them. Both had their long hair hanging loose around their pale faces. Their tight braids had been yanked free to check for hidden weapons. And while they had on their armor, they'd both been stripped of their tridents.

They'd also been stripped of their arrogance, although Inga suspected it lurked just beneath their pretense of confused innocence.

"Your Majesty." Jord took the lead. No surprise. Troy had already warned her that he was the leader of the disloyal duo. "I don't understand what is happening."

"You kneel when you speak to your queen." Rimm whipped his trident through the air, hitting the two males on the backs of their legs to send them to their knees.

"Very tidy," Troy drawled. "I might need one of those."

"Tridents are the weapon of the mer-folk, not the common fey," Jord snapped.

"Watch your tongue, Jord, before I cut it out."

With a careless grace, Troy produced a dagger with a long, wicked blade. Inga arched a brow. Where had that come from? The jumpsuit the imp was wearing was so tight she would have sworn he couldn't have so much as a toothpick under it.

Deciding it was best not to ask, Inga regretfully shook her head. "Not yet, Troy." She turned her gaze back to the kneeling mermen. "Not until I have the truth from these traitors."

"Traitors? Never," Jord protested in an overly loud voice, glaring at Troy. "Whatever the imp has told you is lies."

Troy used the tip of his dagger to clean beneath his nails. The silver blade flashed with a lethal glint in the light from the overhead chandelier.

"So you weren't in the dungeons together discussing your plot to release Brigette and gain control of the Tryshu?" Troy asked.

Jord forced a humorless laugh. "How could we possibly gain control of the Tryshu? Its magic is too strong to be broken."

"Riven proved that there are ways to manipulate the magic if you're without morals," Inga reminded the fool.

Anger darkened Jord's blue eyes. He obviously didn't like being reminded Riven had never been the true king, but he was smart enough to keep his prejudiced opinion to himself. Instead he lifted his hand and pressed it against his chest.

"I swear I have no means to manipulate the Tryshu," he said, grimacing at the loud rattle from the chains that were attached to his wrists. "Besides, you saw me in this throne room when the prisoner burst in. How could I possibly have been involved? The imp is trying to turn you against your own people with his impossible stories of betrayal."

The doors to the throne room opened and a mermaid entered. She was wearing the armor of the royal guards with her golden hair pulled into a tight braid. Her pale eyes sought out Troy, a silent message passing between them before she halted next to Rimm.

"Your Majesty, this is Koral, one of the guards who was on duty the same time the prisoner escaped," the captain introduced the female.

Inga frowned. "I thought the two outer guards were knocked unconscious?"

"We were, Your Majesty, but Troy asked me to investigate the hidden tunnel he witnessed Jord using to enter the dungeons," she explained.

Inga sent the imp a questioning glance. He shrugged, his expression unreadable.

"Hidden tunnels? That's absurd," Jord protested. "I know nothing about hidden tunnels."

Inga ignored the idiot. "Did you investigate?"

Koral nodded. "Yes, I followed it to a rarely used corridor."

Inga leaned forward, sensing the tension that vibrated around the female. "Is there more?"

"Yes. It was just a short distance from the passage used by the Were to enter this throne room."

"You see, it couldn't have been me," Jord burst out in triumphant tones. "I was already here when she entered."

Koral surprisingly sent her fellow guard a glare of pure disgust as she lifted her hand to reveal a thin piece of metal that she held in her fingers.

"I also found this."

Rimm gasped. Confused by his reaction, Inga studied the metal, belatedly noticing the faint shimmer of the scale-shaped object.

"It's from the armor of a royal guard," she muttered.

"It could belong to anyone," Jord insisted. "It's probably been there for decades. Maybe centuries."

He had a point, but before Inga could demand to inspect it more closely, Troy gave a wave of his hand.

Instantly Koral moved until she stood directly behind the kneeling Riza. Then, with a solemn expression, she leaned down to place the scale on an empty place in the male's armor.

A shocked silence filled the throne room. Obviously Riza hadn't realized that he'd lost a scale during his travels through the hidden tunnels. But Troy had noticed. And he'd sent the mermaid in search of it.

Very clever, Inga silently acknowledged.

If either Troy or Inga had found the scale, the guards would have simply accused them of planting it to pin the crimes on them. No one could doubt Koral's loyalty to the mer-folk.

"A perfect fit," Inga said in cold tones. "How do you explain that, Riza?"

The younger male paled to a strange shade of gray. "It wasn't me. I was in the dungeon on guard duty." He turned his head, sending Koral a pleading glance. "You saw me."

She folded her arms over her chest. "I saw you before we were knocked out, but when we woke up you were gone."

"Because I was looking for the prisoner," Riza said, his voice raising several octaves as he tried to convince them of his innocence.

Rimm shook his head. "I've interviewed over a hundred mer-folk who were in the hallways at the time of the prisoner's escape," he told his guard. "Not one of them saw the Were, or you."

Riza's face turned a grayer shade of gray. The weird color emphasized the fear in his eyes.

"It's a mistake. I..." He stammered to a halt, glancing to the side in desperation. "Jord. Tell them it's a mistake."

The leader of the dunce squad refused to glance at his partner in crime. Instead, a cunning expression settled on his narrow face.

"I don't know what he's talking about," he assured Inga. "He told me he was unconscious in the dungeons when the prisoner escaped. If he lied, it has nothing to do with me."

"You bastard." With a choked curse, Riza surged upright, pointing toward Jord. "It was him. It was all his idea to release the prisoner."

At Inga's side, Troy flipped the dagger end over end, chuckling as the two guards exchanged malevolent glares.

"What did I tell you?" he murmured. "No honor among thieves. Or traitors."

* * * *

While Basq battled her aunt, Chaaya had stayed in the background, waiting for her opportunity to strike. She didn't know how to hurt Greta, but she suspected the magic of the spear would wound her. First, however, she needed to get close enough to sink the thing into her back.

Cautiously circling, she watched as Basq used his fangs to slice open Greta's throat. She assumed that was her opening. But even as she rushed forward, her aunt moved with that shocking speed. Worse, her wound knitted together as if it was nothing more than a scratch.

What the hell was she?

And how did they kill her?

She hesitated a second too long and a dark form surged past her. Basq. She started to race after him, but Greta waved her arm and suddenly the vampire was floating off the ground heading directly for the fire.

"You will take me home, Chaaya. Or I drop the vampire," Greta warned.

Terror blasted through her. Basq had always seemed invincible. Like a mountain. Solid and utterly indestructible. Now the stark realization that he was a breath from being destroyed ripped through her with a jagged fear.

"Basq."

Chaaya started forward only to be snapped to a halt as the same bonds that held Basq wrapped around her. A frustrated scream ripped from her throat as she glared at her aunt.

Wait.

She frowned as she realized that Greta wasn't moving. It wasn't like she was simply concentrating on holding Basq with her magic. Or smirking at her ability to hold Chaaya captive.

No. It was like she'd been frozen in place. Along with Basq. Even the flames were static.

What fresh hell was this? Chaaya furiously struggled to break free, but it was impossible. She was stuck.

"Easy, Chaaya," a soft female voice pleaded.

"Who…" Chaaya tumbled forward as the bonds around her suddenly loosened. Swiftly regaining her balance, she spun around, her spear in her hand as she studied the intruder who was stepping out of one of the huts. Shock jolted through her as she caught sight of the features that were eerily similar to her own. For a crazed second she thought Greta had somehow managed to duplicate herself, like a doppelganger. Then she noticed the narrow golden crown on top of the woman's long, glossy black hair and the simple white gown that fell to her bare feet. "Mother?"

The woman nodded, moving forward. "Yes."

Shaken to her very soul, Chaaya backed away. "No. This is just another trick."

"Not this time," her mother assured her, her eyes dark with a wistful yearning.

Chaaya stubbornly shook her head. "You're not here."

Keyrah spread her arms. "Only in spirit. My body was returned to the earth centuries ago."

Chaaya paused, forcing herself to study the woman. Her memories were vague, but the intruder looked like her mother. More importantly, she *smelled* like her mother.

The faint hints of rosemary and ginger laced the air, bringing unexpected tears to Chaaya's eyes.

"What's going on?" Her words came out as a soft plea.

Her mother cautiously stepped toward Chaaya, her features twisted into a haunted expression.

"Oh, daughter, how my heart has longed to see you again."

Chaaya squared her shoulders, shaking off her weird sense of unreality. If this truly was Keyrah, then she'd deliberately allowed the witches to take Chaaya from her bed, haul her to the burrow, and slit her throat. Not the sort of thing that created a warm and fuzzy mother/daughter reunion.

"Yeah, right," she muttered.

The woman faltered, her hand pressing against the center of her chest. "It's true, although I know it must be hard for you to believe me."

"Try impossible."

Keyrah glanced away, but not before Chaaya caught the immense sadness in her eyes.

"I'm afraid my time here is limited, so I can't convince you of my sincerity," she said, her voice not entirely steady. "I can only reveal why I made the decisions that caused us both such pain."

Chaaya snorted. "Both?"

She held up a slender hand. "Please, just listen, Chaaya. You are in great danger."

Chaaya wanted to argue. Hell, she wanted to throw herself on the ground and pound her fists like a child having a temper tantrum. Instead, she forced herself to glance over her shoulder to where Basq hung over the frozen flames.

This wasn't the time to try and punish her mother for the decisions she'd made centuries ago. She had to find out what was happening. And more importantly, find out how she could free Basq and get the hell out of there.

"Fine. I'm listening."

Keyrah waited until Chaaya glanced back at her before she began to speak.

"I was very young when our high priestess became ill. Barely eighteen. At the time it was expected Greta would take her place."

Chaaya squashed her flare of impatience. After endless decades of pretending not to care why her mother would choose to offer her as the sacrifice, she had the opportunity to discover the truth.

She had to know.

"What happened?" she asked.

"Adryn called me to her hut," her mother said, presumably referring to the previous leader. "I thought she needed me to help with her dinner. Or perhaps read to her as she rested. Instead she told me..."

"Told you what?"

Keyrah grimaced. "That she suspected she'd been poisoned."

"Couldn't she heal herself?" Chaaya asked in confusion. "I thought druid priestesses were impervious to poisons?"

"She should have been able to," Keyrah agreed. "The fact she couldn't meant that the poison had been laced with magic that made it lethal to a druid."

"A demon?"

Keyrah's gaze drifted toward the firepit where Greta stood as still as a statue, presumably wrapped in Keyrah's magic.

"She told me that she suspected Greta."

Chaaya wasn't surprised. Her aunt seemed like the sort of woman who would happily poison people for fun, but she assumed her aunt had a specific reason.

"Why would Greta murder the head priestess?"

"To take her place." Keyrah deliberately turned so she could no longer see her sister. "Greta was the obvious successor. Instead Adryn placed the crown on my head."

"I doubt that made Greta happy," Chaaya said dryly.

"She was furious."

Chaaya smiled wryly. When Greta had been telling her tragic tale of fleeing her home, she'd left out the detail that she happened to be a murderous bitch.

"Is that when you forced her out of the village?"

"No. I didn't want to believe my own sister could have such evil in her heart." There was no missing the self-disgust in Keyrah's voice. "I allowed her to remain, although I'll confess I wasn't unhappy when she chose to isolate herself from the rest of us. Her...unhappiness was a blight on the village."

"She said she took care of me."

"Never." The older woman shook her head in horror. "I allowed her to remain, but my trust had been shattered. You were too precious for me to risk."

Precious? Chaaya released a sharp laugh. "Is that a joke?"

Chapter 23

Keyrah flinched, as if Chaaya had reached out to slap her across the face. Then, sucking in a deep breath, the woman pressed her hands together. To keep them from shaking?

"Do you know what happens when one becomes head priestess?" she asked Chaaya.

Chaaya shrugged, trying to ignore her faint pang of guilt. What the hell did she have to feel guilty about? She wasn't the one who went around sacrificing daughters.

"You get a crown and people start bowing to you?" she asked in flippant tones.

"There is that, but during the passing of the crown, the priestess is given a vision," Keyrah told her.

"What sort of vision?"

"It's different for each priestess," she admitted. "Some are warned of natural disasters or of plagues that are destined to spread through the land."

Bleak. If Chaaya had a vision, she'd want it to be filled with upcoming lotto numbers. Or Keanu Reeves in the shower.

"What was yours?" she asked.

"Utter destruction."

"Of the village?"

"Of the world."

"Bummer," she muttered.

"It was...overwhelming." Keyrah wrapped her arms around her waist as if there was a sudden chill in the air. "I could see the evil spreading through the land. I could even smell the death and destruction."

"Was it the beast?"

"Yes."

Chaaya considered her mother's revelations. It hadn't occurred to her that there'd been an early warning system to send out alarms about the incoming tide of evil.

"Was the destruction connected to the druids?"

"No, it was a threat to the entire world." Her mother shivered. "Humans, demons, witches, and druids. We would all have been devoured by the deluge of evil."

A similar shiver raced through Chaaya. She didn't have to have visions or try to imagine what it would be like to be exposed to the beast's evil. She'd actually been trapped in the hell dimension with the creature.

She shook away the memory, concentrating on her mother. "You were eighteen when you had the vision?"

"I was."

Chaaya grimaced. She didn't want to feel sorry for this woman. Still, it couldn't be fun to be a teenager with visions of Armageddon dancing in your head.

"Did the vision show you how to halt the beast?"

"I was shown you. My daughter. And then…" Her words died on her lips as she stared at Chaaya in helpless regret.

Chaaya lifted her hand to draw her finger across her throat. "This?"

Tears shimmered her Keyrah's dark eyes. "I wanted to scrub the image from my mind. How could any mother sacrifice her own daughter?"

"But you did."

Keyrah lifted her hands, almost as if she intended to reach out and touch Chaaya. Then, seeing Chaaya flinch back, she let them drop to her sides.

"The vision was seared into my soul," she said, a stark horror in each word. "I dreamed of it each night. I knew I would condemn the world to destruction if I didn't fulfill my destiny."

Chaaya turned away, staring at the empty huts. She could almost see the images of white-robed women moving through the village, the sound of their light laughter echoing through the air.

The women who depended on her mother for their protection.

"So you went to town and got yourself pregnant?" She tried to make the words teasing. Instead they came out like a croak.

"Not exactly. I left the village determined to discover a man who could give me something very specific—"

"Ew." Chaaya shook her head. "TMI."

Keyrah ignored the interruption. "Eternal life for my daughter."

The low words caught Chaaya by surprise. Whirling back, she stared at her mother in confusion.

"Eternal life?"

Her mother sent her a gaze filled with an emotion Chaaya wasn't ready to accept.

"I couldn't change destiny, but I could do everything in my power to offer you an opportunity to survive."

Chaaya hesitated before asking the question she'd tried to ignore her entire life. "Who was my father?"

Keyrah's expression softened, as if the memory of Chaaya's father stirred the same sort of melty emotions that Chaaya felt when she thought of Basq.

The sight was...unnerving.

"I thought he was just a mist sprite."

"But he wasn't?"

"He was much more." Keyrah smiled. A small, secret smile. "Aer happened to enter a glade where I was resting. It was only later that I realized he had been brought to the precise spot by his own fate."

An ugly sensation twisted Chaaya's heart. "A pretty story for a one-night stand," she sneered, then she slapped her hand over her mouth. Okay. She was bitter. And it hurt that she'd never heard her father's name on her mother's lips when she'd been young. But for the first time, she was beginning to accept that Keyrah hadn't handed her over to the witches without regret. It was becoming increasingly obvious that her mother had tortured herself with the decision she'd been forced to make. "I'm sorry," she muttered.

Her mother waved aside her apology. "You're angry. And I understand if you hate me."

Chaaya swallowed the annoying lump in her throat and concentrated on what her mother had just revealed.

"Why do you think it was fate that brought you and my father together?"

"We spent several weeks in a small cottage." An unexpected blush touched the older woman's cheeks. "He was extraordinary. So kind and gentle. When I knew I had to return home, he handed me the spear and said I was to make sure you had it with you at all times."

Chaaya discovered exactly what Basq must have felt like when her aunt had removed the ground from beneath his feet. Her stomach lurched toward her throat before it crashed down to her toes. And she didn't know if it was because she'd discovered her mother had actually had feelings for her father or because the spear had been given to her by the mysterious male.

She glanced down at the weapon, her brow furrowed. "My father?"

"Yes."

Her fingers stroked the ebony shaft. "But the glyphs are druid."

"They are," her mother assured her. "Aer used magic to create them. He promised they would help to protect you. He also promised that the magic would disguise the fact you were not entirely human."

Stunned, Chaaya lifted her hand to touch the matching glyphs that ran down the side of her neck.

"Is that why you tattooed the same marks on me?"

"Yes. It strengthened the spell he placed on you."

Something shifted inside her. Something huge. Not just because she was beginning to understand who she was and why she'd become a martyr to the cause. But she also understood her place in history.

She hadn't been randomly sacrificed because no one cared whether she lived or died. Fate had chosen her.

"I sensed I was different, but..." She shook her head in bemusement. "A mist sprite. Did you ever see my father again?"

"I went in search of Aer many times, but I could never find him. Even the cottage disappeared. No doubt it was for the best, but..." Her words trailed away in a sigh of loss.

They shared a silence, both grieving the past that had demanded so much pain.

"Why did you drive Greta from the village?" Chaaya at last asked.

Keyrah's face abruptly hardened. "She tried to kill you."

"Me?" Chaaya widened her eyes in surprise. "Why?"

"She'd tried to take your spear more than once, only to be thwarted when the magic scalded her hands. I assume she thought killing you would break the spell so she could claim it as her own."

Chaaya held up the spear. She'd assumed it was just a weapon. Sure, it had magic. And she looked badass when she was using it in a fight. But she'd never considered it might be worth killing for.

"What did she do?"

"She stole you from your bed and tried to drown you." The words were clipped, as if Keyrah was still furious after all these centuries. "If you had been a human you would have been dead before I could reach you."

Chaaya frowned. She didn't remember. Either she'd been too young or she'd blocked it from her mind. That would explain why she'd been so disturbed when she'd entered this strange dimension to find Greta waiting for her.

"What did you do?"

"I told Greta that she could leave or die. There was no other choice."

"She left, I assume?"

"Yes." Keyrah nodded, the gold of her crown glinting in the muted light. "I heard rumors that she'd joined with a human wizard who shared her fascination with forbidden magic."

Chaaya returned her attention to the spear. Why would her aunt be so desperate to get her hands on it?

"Maybe she hoped the spear could give her powers," she murmured her thoughts out loud. Then she gasped, turning her head to stare at the immobile woman. "Or she had her own vision."

"Why do you say that?" her mother asked.

"She claimed that she lured me here because she needed my spear to escape. She might have foreseen her entrapment and realized her only hope was to have the spear with her."

"You're right. It's quite possible." Keyrah stepped toward her. "You need to leave, Chaaya. Now."

Chaaya nodded. Her mother wasn't going to get any argument from her. The sooner she was away from this place, the better.

She pointed toward the firepit. "You have to release Basq first."

"I can't. Not without also releasing Greta." The older woman grimaced. "You must leave him behind."

Chaaya was shaking her head before her mother stopped speaking. "No way."

"Chaaya, no one understands the agony of sacrificing the one you love more than I do—"

"No."

Keyrah made a sound of frustration. "You can't allow Greta to return to the world."

"What does it matter?" Chaaya stubbornly demanded.

A pained expression rippled over Keyrah's face. As if Chaaya was forcing her to remember something she preferred to forget.

Chaaya knew the feeling.

"During her time with the wizards, she discovered the magic of raising the dead," she abruptly revealed.

"Zombies?"

"That's the human name for them." Keyrah's lips pressed together in intense disapproval. "Demons call them abominations."

Chaaya ground her teeth. She understood the dangerous magic of the dead. The mer-folk had endured a ruthless tyrant who'd used a zombie medallion to control the Tryshu. But she didn't care. Not if it meant leaving Basq behind.

"I won't sacrifice Basq."

"Then you condemn the world to Greta's madness," her mother said with blunt simplicity.

Chaaya winced. There was a bitter irony in the realization that she was faced with the same choice that had cursed her mother. She either sacrificed the person she loved, or she condemned the world to evil.

"There has to be a way," she rasped.

Her mother...faded. She could still see the shimmering outline, but she was no longer the solid form she'd been just a few seconds earlier.

"Chaaya, I can't stay any longer," she warned.

"You're leaving?"

Chaaya thought a sad smile touched Keyrah's lips. "Unlike you, I truly am dead."

A wrenching sense of loss cascaded through Chaaya. "I won't ever see you again?"

"No, but we will always be together. You are in my heart, daughter. My love will never waver, never end." There was a last flicker of movement, as if she was holding out her hand. "And I am so very proud of you."

"You might not be so proud if I release a horde of zombies on the world," Chaaya muttered.

"You will do what is right. Because that is who you are," her mother insisted.

"Who am I?"

"A hero."

Chaaya shook her head, watching her mother slowly disappear. "I wish people would stop saying that."

Chapter 24

It was the crackle of flames that warned Chaaya her mother's disappearance had shattered the spell that had frozen Greta. Whirling around, her gaze first landed on Basq, who was shaking his head as if he was disoriented. Could he sense that he'd been wrapped in magic?

"Well, Chaaya?" Greta snapped. "What's it going to be?"

Squaring her shoulders, Chaaya met her aunt's fevered gaze. Her emotions had been in turmoil since the second she'd stepped into the portal to chase after Brigette. She'd been angry, frustrated, terrified, and at the same time giddy with joy to be sharing her journey with Basq. And most unexpectedly of all, at peace with her past.

Now all those tumultuous feelings drained away. She wasn't numb. Just…determined.

She knew what she had to do.

"You win," she said.

Basq's eyes narrowed as he glared at her in disbelief. "No, Chaaya. You can't."

Greta used her magic to lower Basq toward the flames that curled and hissed just below his feet.

"Shut up, vamp. She's doing the right thing."

"Chaaya, no," Basq insisted, his gaze locked on her even as the fire threatened to consume him.

"I'm doing what I have to do."

"Of course you are." Greta smiled with a smug satisfaction. "You've already sacrificed enough in your life."

Chaaya snorted. She was so freaking tired of that word. Just once it would be nice if someone else had to do the sacrificing.

"You'd think," she muttered.

Greta's smile faded, her expression suddenly suspicious. "No tricks."

Chaaya brushed her finger over her chest. "I cross my heart and hope to die that I'm going to take us home."

"Chaaya, you can't trust her," Basq rasped.

"I have to do this." She held his gaze, using their bond to send him a sense of calm assurance. "*We* have to do it."

Basq stilled, his gaze sweeping over her stubborn expression. "Our duty?"

"Yeah."

Basq slowly nodded, accepting that she wasn't going to make a crazy decision just to keep him from going up in flames.

"Okay."

She smiled wryly. His confidence was heartwarming but potentially misplaced. There was a very good chance her plan was just as crazy as he'd first feared.

Shaking away her ridiculous thoughts, she held her aunt's gaze. "You can release him."

Greta narrowed her eyes. "You I trust." She glared at Basq. "Him I don't."

"He's not going to try and interfere, are you, Basq?"

"No." The word came out from between clenched fangs.

"Fine." Greta glanced back at Chaaya. "Try anything and he's going to discover how fun it is to be burned alive." A sick pleasure sparkled in her eyes. "Or in his case, dead."

Chaaya battled back the urge to stick the spear into the woman's heart. She didn't doubt for a second the bitch would drop Basq into the fire.

"There's no need for threats. I'm going to give you exactly what you asked for."

Greta remained wary. She wasn't stupid. But she was desperate. Something Chaaya was counting on.

"Bring the spear here," Greta commanded.

Chaaya strolled forward, flipping the weapon from hand to hand. "Do you want to hold it?"

An age-old frustration twisted the older woman's narrow features. "You know I can't. But I do intend to hold on to you. You're not going to escape without me."

"Hold on as tight as you want," Chaaya taunted, clenching her teeth as her aunt grabbed her elbow in a grip that was strong enough to leave bruises. "Are you ready?"

"More than ready," Greta muttered. "What about you?"

Was she ready? Not really. She had no idea if her wild scheme was going to work or not.

Chaaya stiffened her spine. This was their only hope.

"Release Basq and form the portal," she said.

Greta's nails cut into Chaaya's arm. "No side trips. Just take me home." Chaaya nodded, and Greta slowly lowered her arm, setting Basq on the ground next to Chaaya. Then, with a last warning glare, she pointed toward a spot directly in front of them.

At first there was nothing. Then Greta spoke a soft word of power, and a dark hole formed in midair. It hung there for a few seconds, pulsing and expanding before a swirl of sparkling colors appeared, like diamond dust scattered on black velvet.

The hole continued to swirl and enlarge until Greta jerked on Chaaya's elbow. "Let's go."

Chaaya created a picture in her mind, making it as crystal clear as possible. She didn't want any mistakes. Not now.

Holding on to the image, she clutched the spear and stepped forward. Greta and Basq walked next to her, both holding on with death grips. Together they entered the portal, the sensation of weightlessness making it feel as if she was flying. Then, a second later, they were dumped out of the darkness and into a vast, empty landscape.

"At last," Greta exulted, releasing Chaaya as she spread her arms wide. Her happiness, however, was cut short as she suddenly noticed the strange light that filtered from the orange sky. "Wait." Whirling around, she glared at Chaaya. "What is this place?"

"You said to take you home. That's what I've done."

Chaaya waved her hand toward the barren scenery. In the distance there was a silhouette of dead trees and a parched riverbed, but there was no sign of living creatures. No buildings, no roads, nothing. Just dust and air so thick it was hard to breathe.

Oh, and evil.

A pulsing, crushing evil that weighed against Chaaya with a tangible force.

"This isn't my home," Greta screeched, her voice rising several octaves.

"No, but it's mine," Chaaya said, a cold smile curving her lips. "Along with the beast."

Greta swung her arm to strike Chaaya, only to recoil backward as Basq moved to stand in between them, his fangs fully extended. The older woman cursed, as if frustrated by being denied the pleasure of punishing Chaaya.

"Take us out of here or I'll—"

"I'd save my strength if I were you," Chaaya interrupted in a bored tone as she pointed toward the distant horizon. "That whirling tornado of fire is the beast. You don't want to burn again."

"No!" The woman sucked in a horrified gasp, her hands shaking as she waved them in a desperate pattern.

Was she trying to create a portal? A wasted effort. There was no way out of the dimension.

They were all stuck. For eternity.

* * * *

Basq had prepared himself for a surprise. Chaaya was nothing if not unpredictable. And while he'd initially been afraid she might give in to her aunt's demands in a misguided attempt to save him, it hadn't taken long to realize she had something planned.

But this…

He shuddered at the malevolent atmosphere that pressed against him. It was like a living force that crawled over his skin. And it was only getting worse as the tornado of dust and flames spun across the flat land.

"Can you get us out of here?" he demanded of Chaaya.

She shook her head. "No."

Instinctively, he reached out to grab her hand. At the same time, Greta turned toward them, as if intending to follow wherever they were going.

Yeah, that wasn't going to happen.

With a taunting smile, he called on his powers. Instantly they were shrouded in a blinding darkness.

"We need to run," Chaaya said, her voice brittle with tension.

"Okay." Keeping them hidden in shadows, Basq easily kept pace as Chaaya bolted away from the oncoming beast. "Where are we going?"

"There used to be a cottage that the beast couldn't enter," she said, her breath coming in harsh pants. Being back in this place was obviously already taking its toll on her. "I don't know if it's still here or not, but it's our only hope."

"Which direction?"

"If it still exists, it will find us," she told him. "Right now I just want to put as much space between us and the beast as possible."

"You got it."

Without missing a step, Basq wrapped his arms around her and swept her off her feet. Astonishingly, she didn't argue. Whether it was the knowledge he was faster or because she wanted to conserve her energy, it didn't matter.

"I feel like I missed something," he said, needing to keep his thoughts distracted. He refused to consider the possibility that Chaaya's cottage might be gone. They couldn't have come this far only to die. "What happened while that bitch was dangling me over the fire?"

"My mother made an unexpected appearance and did some sort of spell that froze you and Greta," she said, leaning her head against his shoulder.

"Your mother?" Surprise jolted through Basq. He'd sensed that he'd lost time, but he assumed it had been Greta's magic. "I thought she was dead. Is she a ghost?"

"Just a temporary one."

Basq couldn't see Chaaya's expression, but he could hear the hint of sadness in her voice.

"Why was she there?"

"To warn me not to trust Greta."

Basq grimaced. Her mother finally showed up and that's what she wanted to tell Chaaya? As if anyone with a brain wouldn't realize Greta was a treacherous bitch.

"Better late than never, I suppose," he said dryly.

"She..." Chaaya stopped, clearing her throat. Was it the thick dust that choked her up, or the thought of her meeting with her mother? Basq felt a blast of fury toward the woman who'd sacrificed her own daughter. "She also explained how she was given a vision that revealed the beast destroying the world. And that her daughter would be the only means of stopping Armageddon."

"Did you believe her?"

"Yes," Chaaya said without hesitation. "For my entire life I assumed my mother handed me to the witches because I was disposable. Now I understand."

"Understand what?"

"That sometimes duty has to come before love."

Basq frowned. His anger remained. A churning, soul-deep fury that anyone would dare to harm the female cradled in his arms. But at the same time, he sensed a newfound peace deep inside Chaaya. As if an ancient, nagging wound had been healed during the time that he'd been unconscious.

And there was something else...

"What are you trying to hide?" he muttered, using their bond to absorb her various emotions. He couldn't read her mind, but he could tell that she was trying to hold something back. Then he came to an abrupt halt. "Shit. You could have escaped."

Her arms reached up to wrap around his neck. "Not without you."

"Dammit, Chaaya."

She squeezed tighter, the tip of the spear she still held in one hand pressing into his back. He barely noticed. The mere thought that Chaaya had an opportunity for freedom, but she'd chosen to stay. For him...

"Did you know that Tarak and Waverly were trapped in the prison he'd just escaped after five centuries?" Chaaya demanded, interrupting his troubled thoughts.

Basq grunted. Tarak hadn't been willing to discuss his years being held captive by the King of the Mer-folk. The powerful vampire had been determined to put the past behind him and focus on his new mate. But he had described in detail how he'd savagely destroyed the male responsible for the endless centuries of torment.

"Yes, it was only one of the many reasons he took such pleasure in ripping out Riven's throat," Basq said.

"When Waverly told me what had happened to them, I swore I would rather die than be trapped again," Chaaya continued.

Basq's gut clenched. Enveloped in the darkness, it was impossible to see the bleak landscape or the approaching beast. But no darkness could keep out the evil that beat through the air like a predator hovering over them, ready to swoop down and consume them. Chaaya had known what was waiting for her, but she'd still chosen to come here.

"Then why?" he demanded.

"Waverly said that it wasn't a prison as long as she was there with her mate. I thought she was crazy. But when it came time to choose a life of freedom without you or being stuck in this place forever," her head nestled in the hallow of his shoulder, her sweet scent driving away the noxious odor of the beast, "being with you wins every time."

Her soft words sent shock waves of intense joy through Basq. The sort of joy that overcame the clinging evil and the horrifying fear that they were trapped in this place forever.

"And you claimed that I was the one with terrible timing," he chastised in teasing tones.

His head started to lower at the same time a piercing scream split the air. Greta.

Obviously the druid priestess was becoming personally acquainted with the beast.

"Actually, my timing seems to be perfect," Chaaya said, her voice hard with satisfaction as the screams faded to whimpers, and at last to a dreadful silence. "Now all we need is my cottage."

Chapter 25

Levet grasped his tail, anxiously polishing the tip. The clinging dirt felt polluted even after the beast had been driven out. Plus, he always rubbed his tail when he was nervous.

"*Non*," he said in pleading tones. "You cannot do this."

Brigette flattened her lips, her fingers closing possessively around the brooch. "You just told me the stone will give me any wish I want."

"But never in the way you desire." Levet clicked his tongue. It was discouraging how many creatures were willing to believe that a silly stone could offer them happiness. Life, especially eternal life, was a series of choices. Some good, some bad, most of them somewhere in between. "There is always a cost to the magic. Usually an awful cost."

Brigette released a short laugh, pointing toward the devastated village. "What could be more awful than this?"

Levet shuddered. "We do not want to find out."

She bit her bottom lip, as if considering his words, then a stubborn expression settled on her face.

"I have to bring them back."

"And if you do and they are destroyed in a devastating plague?" Levet pointed out. "Or another roving band of goblins appears to kill them?"

"At least it won't be my fault," she hissed.

Ah. Now Levet began to understand this female's fierce determination. This was why she'd been willing to follow a strange voice whispering in her head and to ignore her opportunity for freedom.

"Not all the wishes in the world can truly change the past," he said in a sad voice. "Not in your heart."

She made a choked sound as if battling back an emotion too large to stay contained.

"If I could just see them again..." Her gaze lingered on the broken foundation of her old cottage. Was she imagining they were standing there? Perhaps waiting for her to join them. "I have to tell them how sorry I am."

Levet reached to gently touch her hand. "They know."

"They don't," she insisted.

Levet cleared his throat. "It occurs to me..."

She turned her head to glare at him as he allowed his words to drift away. "What?"

"That your wish is rather selfish."

Her brows snapped together. "What the hell are you talking about? I'm not wishing for riches or fame. I'm doing this for my family." She waved her hand toward the empty village. "For my pack."

Levet shook his head. "You are doing it to ease your guilt."

She flinched as if his words had struck a nerve. "So what do you expect me to do? Walk away from the chance to rewrite history?"

"You cannot change the past," Levet insisted. "But you can change the future."

"What future?"

"As we were leaving the druid whackanoodle—"

"Whackadoodle," Brigette absently corrected.

"*Oui, oui.*" Levet waved a dismissive hand. "I could smell Chaaya entering just as we were so rudely shoved out."

"Good," she said in hard tones.

Levet clicked his tongue. "I thought you were attempting the whole new leaf thing."

"She wants to kill me."

"Not if you are no longer evil."

Brigette glanced down at him, disbelief etched on her face. "You want me to waste my wish on a female who means nothing to me?"

When she put it that way, Levet had to admit that it was asking rather a lot. Still, he had to do something to try and save Chaaya.

"Do you want to prove to your pack that you have become a better wolf?" he insisted.

"I..." She grimaced.

"A good demon puts others before themselves," Levet told her. "Wish for Chaaya and her vampire to be safely returned to their home."

"I thought the wishes were always twisted," she tartly reminded him.

"Not if they come from a pure heart."

"Pure heart." She snorted at his words. "That's a joke."

"*Non*, that is the only way to achieve what you truly want."

She frowned. "And what's that?"

"A new start."

Brigette faltered, glancing down at her hand. Slowly she opened her fingers to reveal the brooch. Time ticked past as the Were considered Levet's words.

"I suppose there would be one benefit if I do as you ask," she at last said in gruff tones.

"What is that?"

"I would never have to listen to your babbling again."

Levet parted his lips in outrage. "I do not babble."

A sad smile touched Brigette's lips; then, without warning, she leaned down to place a soft kiss on his cheek.

"Say hello to Inga for me."

Levet furrowed his brow in confusion. "Inga?"

Brigette stepped back and held up her hand, then closing her eyes, she made her wish.

* * * *

Troy leaped off the dais and grabbed the treacherous Riza by the neck. Enough. He was done playing with these fools. He wanted the truth and he wanted it now. Tightening his fingers, he lifted the merman until his feet dangled off the marble floor.

"Start talking," he commanded.

"Keep your mouth shut," Jord snarled.

Troy pointed his dagger toward the guard who was still on his knees. "One more word and I'll slice out your tongue, got it?" The male glared at Troy, but he was smart enough to snap his lips together. Troy returned his attention to Riza. "Well?"

Riza licked his lips, his eyes bulging with fear. Or maybe it was because Troy was crushing his throat. Hard to say.

"Jord came to me—"

"When?" Troy interrupted.

"A couple weeks ago. I don't know the exact date. He told me that he'd been contacted by a friend of Riven's."

Troy heard Inga suck in a harsh breath. Most of the mer-folk had celebrated the death of the former king, but there were a few who thought Inga was a usurper.

"What friend?" Troy demanded.

"That's all he would tell me."

Troy turned his head toward Jord. "Who was the friend?"

"I don't know."

Rimm used the butt of his trident to smack the traitor on the back of the head. "You were asked a question."

"She said her name was Greta," Jord groused. "She told me that she'd given Riven the medallion that allowed him to control the Tryshu. She promised me the same medallion."

Troy exchanged a glance with Inga. Who the hell would have a wizard's medallion? Or had it just been a lie to get the merman to do what the mystery Greta wanted?

Muttering a frustrated curse, Troy turned his attention back to Riza. So far, he had more questions than answers.

"You released Brigette and led her through the tunnels to the throne room?"

The male nodded. "Jord said that he had to be seen so no one would know that we were working together."

"Why?" Inga asked.

"To make Chaaya return to the castle."

Troy blinked in surprise. "Chaaya?"

"The voice told Jord that the price of the medallion was making sure that the ghost girl was here when the Were escaped."

Well, well, well. That was a twist that Troy hadn't been expecting. "So it was a trap."

"But not for me," Inga muttered.

Troy shook his head. "Why did—"

His words were cut short as a powerful magic blasted through the air. On instant alert, Troy tossed Riza aside and held his dagger toward the portal that was forming in the middle of the room.

"Protect the queen!" Rimm commanded, motioning the guards to stand in front of the dais.

As they scrambled forward, Jord took advantage of the confusion. Surging upright, he snatched the trident from Koral's hand as she passed by. Then, with a triumphant shout, he lunged toward the portal. At the same time something tumbled through the opening.

A small, gray object with sparkly wings and a squeal like a pig.

Levet.

Belatedly realizing the prisoner was about to make his escape, Rimm ran forward. Jord leaned down, grabbing Levet by the horn to dangle the creature in front of him.

"Stay back or I'll kill the gargoyle," Jord warned, pressing his trident against the side of Levet's head.

"No," Inga cried out, rising to her feet.

Levet, however, was clearly in a mood, sending a sour glare toward the merman holding him hostage.

"Not again," Levet muttered, waving his hand over his head.

Troy grimaced, crouching low as he placed his arms protectively over his head. He was too accustomed to Levet's magical mayhem not to prepare for the worst. Jord, however, was obviously ignorant of Levet's ability to cause utter chaos. The idiot ignored the fireball that flew from Levet's fingers and over his head as he continued to back toward the portal.

Instead, he smiled with anticipation. He truly thought he was about to escape. Instead, he only inched his way closer to the concussion zone as the fireball smacked against the closing portal.

There was a loud sizzle, then a tremor shook the throne room. Next... all hell broke loose.

Jord screamed as he was tossed like a rag doll through the air, hitting the high ceiling with enough impact to break several bones before dropping like a stone. A second later Rimm had him pinned to the floor with his trident.

Levet escaped the worst of the explosion, skidding over the slick marble to land at Inga's feet.

The large ogress gazed down at the tiny pest, her face soft with adoration. "My hero."

Troy tumbled backward, his laughter echoing through the throne room.

Epilogue

Chaaya was ready when Basq returned to their rooms in the basement of Dreamscape Resort.

It'd been over two weeks since they'd been mysteriously returned to Vegas. Levet claimed it was Brigette who'd used some strange wishing stone to release them from the hell dimension, which was the only reason she hadn't gone on the hunt for the missing female Were. But while they'd settled into a comfortable routine, Chaaya was still celebrating their escape. Each night was a gift. And she had no intention of taking them for granted.

Tonight was no exception.

Turning the lights on low, she arranged the round table in the center of the living room. It was a huge room with smoky gray furnishings and a black carpet. It was perfect for her and Basq, and even when Chiron had offered to build a larger apartment for them, she'd politely refused. This place had somehow become home to her. And as long as Basq was at her side, she never intended to leave.

Leaning against the table, she smiled as Basq stepped through the door. She was wearing her usual leather pants, but her top was a lacy halter that showed more skin than usual, and instead of her heavy boots she wore a pair of red heels.

A sharp chill swirled through the air, a certain sign that Basq liked what he was seeing.

"Very nice." He carefully closed the door, staring at her with avid appreciation. "Where are we going?"

Chaaya spread her arms wide. "Right here."

Basq arched his brows as he strolled forward. "I thought you wanted to spend your evenings gambling away my fortune and causing bar fights," he reminded her. "So far we've barely left these rooms."

She flashed a wicked smile, her gaze skimming over his lean body that was hard and perfect beneath the black sweater and slacks.

What woman in her right mind would prefer to be in a crowded, noisy bar when she could be spending time alone with this delectable vampire?

"There will be time for that," she assured him. "But first I made a promise."

He continued forward, his eyes glowing with a white shimmer. "What promise is that?"

Chaaya stepped aside, revealing the stack of cards and chips she'd placed on the table.

"Teaching you how to play poker."

His fangs lengthened in anticipation. "Strip poker?"

Chaaya chuckled, savoring the frigid power that brushed over her exposed skin. She was well and truly addicted.

"Is there any other kind?"

He lifted his hand to cup her cheek in his palm. "I warn you, I'm a quick learner."

"I warn you, I cheat." She ran her fingers over the soft cashmere of his sweater. "Get prepared to lose those clothes."

"The sooner the better." Without warning, he kicked off his shoes.

"Hey," she protested. "I haven't taught you how to play yet."

He smiled, revealing his long, sharp fangs. The memory of having them plunged in her neck while Basq thrust deep inside her made Chaaya shiver with an aching need. It didn't matter how many times she had this male in her bed, in her body, it was never enough.

"We can discuss the rules as we go along," he assured her, grabbing her lacy halter and jerking it off.

She should probably have been mad. It was a new top. Instead, anticipation sizzled through her.

"I like how you play, vampire." Wrapping her arms around his neck, she wiggled her hands beneath his sweater to explore his bare skin.

Mmm. Smooth and cool as satin.

He bent his head, scraping his fangs along the curve of her neck. "I like how you taste, mist sprite."

Chaaya smiled. Mist sprite. Someday she would go in search of any relatives she might have among the fey creatures. Until then, she was content with the peace she'd made with her mother.

"And half druid priestess," she reminded him.

Without warning, Basq scooped her off her feet, heading toward the back of the apartment.

"And all unique," he growled.

"That's something we can agree on."

They entered the shadowed darkness of the bedroom. "I think we can find something else to agree on."

Chaaya smiled as he lowered her onto the soft mattress and stripped away her clothes.

He really was a quick learner...

Printed in the United States
by Baker & Taylor Publisher Services